The PHOTOGRAPHER

E. S. BLAKE

Marotte

www.marottebooks.com

First published in 2022
by Marotte Books Ltd
51 York Avenue, London SW14 7LQ

www.marottebooks.com
Text © E. S. Blake 2022

A CIP catalogue record of this book is available from the British Library.

ISBN 978-1-7399851-0-3

Typeset by Elaine Sharples
Printed and bound by PULSIO SARL

Cover design by Liam Relph

For Alba

'Then for the first time the cheeks of the Furies were wet with tears ... Orpheus was permitted to take her on one condition, that he should not turn around to look at her till they had reached the upper air...'

Bullfinch's Mythology

PROLOGUE

Creating a negative is a precise and exacting process.

First, the glass must be cut, then the edges deburred. This creates ridges that allow the plate to hold the emulsion. It also prevents cuts, which would leave the photographer vulnerable to poisoning from the fixing solution.

Next, the plate is cleaned, first with rottenstone – sifted onto the glass through a muslin – and then with a fine brush. This readies the glass for the application of the collodion liquid, whereafter the photographer must 'flow the plate', tilting it gently from side to side, coating it evenly to create a fine emulsion. Any imperfections will greatly damage the quality of the end result.

The photographer then has a short window in which to capture life, a moment too long and the plate will dry out and be ruined. Within this time, the plate must be sensitised with a silver nitrate solution, a process taking approximately four minutes; the models arranged in their final positions, and then the plate loaded and exposed.

Finally, the negative is developed with a preparation of pyrogallic acid, rinsed with water to halt the process, and fixed in a solution of potassium cyanide. It is then ready to be used to create a print on paper.

Ten minutes from beginning to end. These few precious moments are all
we have. After which, the opportunity is lost. This strange concoction of chemicals that creates magic is left empty of its powers; soon to be nothing but dust. But, if we act quickly, and with purpose, we can create something permanent.

Something that will last forever.

1863

CHAPTER I

In which I am admonished by a pound cake

'Please, Mrs Dean. You need to hold your baby still.'

'I'm trying, Lord knows I am, but it's baking under here.' Mrs Dean's head emerges from beneath the black sheet hiding her form, projecting an expression in my direction that looks like it could melt tar.

'I'm sorry for your discomfort, Mrs Dean,' I reply, 'I truly am; but the baby cannot move.'

'It's a baby, Mr Franklin,' her husband interjects, 'babies always moves.' Ironically, he can barely move himself, squeezed into a Sunday best suit he outgrew not long after passing the baby's age.

'Well, the baby either keeps still,' I explain, 'or there won't be a photograph. It's as simple as that.' I try to hide the warmth I feel towards these people behind my petulance, but, as I retreat towards the camera, a smile spreads over my lips in the knowledge that the friction between us is nothing but sham, a skit on the stage at Wilton's.

'I'm just saying,' Mr Dean continues, raising himself to full height, a button on his collar threatening to detach itself and hurtle in my direction, 'babies don't keeps still, so Mrs Dean ain't doin' nothin' wrong.'

He makes eye contact with the aforementioned Mrs Dean, and she nods him a small but perceptible thank you, full of fragile dignity; the swarthy knight coming to protect his lady's honour.

But the issue, as always, is time, and, aware that our window is coming to a close, I plaster on my most gracious smile and address them both with all the charm I can muster.

'I'm not implying she's doing anything wrong, Mr Dean. In fact,' I add with blatant flattery, 'your wife is one of the best baby-handlers I've seen in recent months. Perhaps my whole career. However, if we fail to take the photograph within the next three minutes, we'll have to begin the process all over again. And that's to nobody's benefit.'

The blame shifted from the family matriarch to the eccentricities of the photographic method, the Deans seem placated, and (my compliment taken very much at face value) Mrs Dean discovers a newfound confidence in her abilities, deigning to retake her place under the blanket.

'All right, I'm doing it,' she tells me, withdrawing, 'but remember – if I end up a pound cake by the end of this, I'll be none too happy.'

'I assure you,' I reply, laughing, 'none of my clients has ever ended up a pound cake.' Although, it strikes me a pound cake has never given anyone the kind of glare Mrs Dean sends my way before disappearing.

I look towards the heavens in a plea for serenity, only to find myself suddenly mesmerised, their expanses visible through the glazing that makes up the southerly wall and ceiling of my studio. A cloud moves across the blue, subtly shifting the balance of light in the room, and, as I alter the configuration of blinds that dot the glass above me, for a moment, I feel that my plea has been granted. Despite the frustrations of the moment, of the failings that make up my life, I am content, and I know deep within that, as Solomon said (by way of Fitzgerald), *this too shall pass*.

'Right, let's try again.'

I return to the camera, poised to expose the rapidly drying plate, but nothing is ever simple, and, as I take my place, I find young Master Dean is now looking off towards the side. I click my fingers to draw his gaze, but to no effect, tracing the boy's eyeline to his father, who has now wandered off to examine a porcelain horse on the studio dresser.

'Mr Dean,' I say, trying not to sound like I am addressing a child, 'we discussed this. I need you to stand next to the camera. Stand there and make the baby look at you.'

'What? Again?' he exclaims, his surprise entirely genuine, 'I thought we were done.'

'No, we are not done.'

'So should I just stand over here then?' he says, pointing to the spot I indicated barely moments before.

'That would be good, thank you.'

Mr Dean huffily relocates himself, but not before Mrs Dean's muffled voice has also joined the fray.

'Are we done? Like I said, I'm baking!'

'Almost, Mrs Dean,' I call out, 'but you need to actually *hold* the baby's head – put a hand either side, like a vice.'

'Like this?'

'No, you're covering his face…' I say. 'It's important we can actually see him.' She adjusts her hands, and the child appears once more. 'Yes, like that.'

And suddenly, everything is right. The baby is still, he's looking in the appropriate direction, and then, as if on cue, the clouds shift, flattening the light to perfection.

'Excellent. Don't move!'

I crouch down for one last moment to check nothing is amiss, then reach round, and remove the lens cap from the camera.

***

'They're unusable.'

I hold the plate back up to the window, the fading summer light bringing the inverted image to life like stained glass from

7

the land of Fae. The child's face is blurred, I'm sure of it, even with his face blackened like a sweep's boy. It strikes me I should perhaps one day photograph a child who has just emerged from the chimney; at least then I'd be able to tell if the bloody negative was in focus.

'You always say that before you print them.'

Behind me, Percy is busying herself at the fire, boiling a dinner of meat and potatoes, her hair tied up, a few ringlets of red falling from the fold. She's no cook, having grown up in a household coddled by servants, but we wouldn't have it any other way. Percy constantly rejects my suggestions of hiring a maid, and, as far as I'm concerned, I'd rather eat gruel looking at her face than the finest banquet bereft of her presence. Still, her words do little to reassure me, and I look back at my coal-stained child. Each imperfection feels like a pointing finger accusing me of insufficiency.

'It will turn out better than you think,' she continues.

I shake my head, as a sigh breaks out from deep within me. 'I don't know why I do this. I'm a terrible photographer. I can't get the blasted things to stay still.'

'You're very talented. Babies just aren't meant to stay still.'

She comes over and joins me at the window, edging over my shoulder to look at the plate, and, as I feel the soft warmth of her cheek against mine, her presence is like ether to my insecurity.

'I'll have to give them their money back.'

'Wait and see how the print turns out,' reasons Percy. 'They'll be overjoyed to see their child on paper. You do this every day. To them it's a miracle.'

I make a show of scepticism, but Percy brushes it away.

'You can think about returning their money when there's definitely a problem. You can't see properly now, anyway.'

I know she's right. The sun is almost set, the light gone –

enough to stop me from making out details anyway, but I wriggle away from her, wasting one of the matches Warwick brought me from Sweden to light a candle and hold up the picture to its flame. I try to will the truth out of it, careful not to set light to any possibility of getting paid, but no answers are forthcoming.

'You can't do anything till morning, so try to relax a little.'

'Sounds unbearable,' I reply, my will beginning to falter.

'I'm sure we can think of something to make the time pass quicker,' she whispers, approaching me from behind and nuzzling into my neck.

'Percy – I still have work to do.'

'Not that can't wait till morning.'

She raises her eyes to meet mine, and I realise all hope of resistance is gone. I kiss her, the lips that have met my own a thousand times unexpectedly soft. And once again I cannot believe she is mine. My *wife*. This woman I longed for from the moment I laid eyes upon her, by my side for a lifetime. Even though it has been three years, this is what truly seems a miracle; a young couple dressed in wedding finery appearing from nowhere as if brought into this world from the negative of my thoughts.

But she is far less mine than I am hers, and, as I take her delicate hands, I'm aware that they hold my fragile heart. I would give up everything for her. Everything. And, as we peel away from one another, I look into her eyes and it feels like she can see into my very soul. See the man who is forever grateful to be able to kiss her, touch her, have her presence fill his waking hours.

'What would I do without you?'

She smiles up at me, extinguishing my fears with a single glance.

'I'll never let you find out.'

CHAPTER II

In which I return to town

We awake in the early morning hours, the light assaulting us through a gap in the curtains.

The light. Always the light. Bringing life, wakefulness. It has been a hot June, and, once again, the night has been fitful. Our little cottage seems to amplify the weather; cold in the winter and blistering in the summer, its threadbare thatch providing scant protection from the elements.

Percy shuts her eyes again and pushes her head deeper into the pillow, her body covered by nothing but a thin sheet. I know it's indecent, but the weather doesn't bow to custom, and I can't help but wonder at the knowledge of her nakedness underneath. Images of the Ingres and Delacroix nudes I saw in Paris drift through my consciousness. She is one woman but all women.

I heard it said that Delacroix paints from photographs – that he commissioned a series of nudes as inspiration. Nude *photographs*. Only in France! (Although probably taken by the damned Swede). It's funny that my medium is subject to so many more impositions than that of the painters. A nude on canvas can decorate the walls of a palace, but on photographic paper? The notion seems absurd. It's too accurate. Too real. The idea comes to me that I should photograph her like this, drifting in and out of wakefulness, the curves of her body sensual beneath the cotton. Then again, perhaps I should photograph all my models unconscious. Their eyes would be closed, but at least they'd be in focus.

I take one last look at my sleeping beauty, and go downstairs to make breakfast. Though empty, this little room seems full. Percy's presence upstairs seeps into every last corner of this house and fills it with life. I open the front door to let in the morning air, then light the fire so I can fry some eggs and leftover potatoes from the night before. A fire is the last thing we need on a morning like this, but the bread we have has gone stale and I need tea and breakfast before I can countenance the train ride into town.

The smell begins to permeate the room, and, moments later, the creaking stairs announce Percy's descent. She's still in a fog of sleep, woken by the scents of cooking, but the nightdress she so quickly discarded last night has reappeared.

'Why didn't you wake me?'

'You were awake – you went back to sleep.'

She mumbles a response and we sit down at the table to eat. After we finish, I still have to make some prints, before I embark on the journey to Warwick's. I'd rather spend the day with my dishevelled bride, but a man must work to earn his crust. Especially a man whose guardian managed to embezzle his whole inheritance. That's by the by. Leaving will be all right. The knowledge that she'll be here on my return will be company enough.

***

I arrive at Warwick's just before midday. The town is even hotter than the country, the heat intensified by the crowds that line the streets of the Square Mile and sealed in by the smog that hangs above this city even on a cloudless day. The smell of the horses' evacuations fill the stagnant air, but the meek shade of my hansom cab is still better than the noise and bustle of the train that brought me to Waterloo Bridge. To think I could spend a journey

11

longing for the open-topped third-class carriages of my youth, but long for them I did, my copy of *The Whale* sitting unread on my lap.

I head towards a sign advertising 'Warwick's Photographic Emporium' that hangs above the steps down to his basement office. The sign reminds me of Warwick himself; boisterous and aggrandising, but with rougher edges than he'd like to admit. If only they could learn to make signs substantially more rotund, he'd have found his perfect representative. It's a short hop across Fetter Lane from my carriage to the door, so I carry the frock coat that is draped across my knees. A gentleman walking the street in a waistcoat and shirt sleeves – the decadence of the artist!

The bell rings as I open the door to the shop. Warwick is with a customer, so I get nothing but a disapproving glance by way of a greeting. It prompts me to put my jacket back on to preserve his sense of decorum, and I wander around the 'showroom' as Warwick finishes his business. Its walls are lined with work from his photographers, a skewed pastiche of the display that lines the walls of my home, the prints here more stilted, formal, as if the sitters have just been caught unawares by minor royalty.

Barnes's pictures form the majority of the hodgepodge. They're utterly without merit, each subject's pose identical to that of the next, from the humble clerk to the country gentleman. Nothing changes between photographs but the faces, the personalities behind them somehow absent, each image a projection of Barnes and his attitude to the world; pride masking inflexibility, rules he's not even aware of following fixing his victims into poses like clasps.

I am strolling around the display when another picture draws my eye and makes me smile. It's a moment before I realise it's mine. The Eglingtons. The image brings back memories of the sitting. He was tricky from the start, but his wife loved the camera. She's not smiling (on his request), but she's emanating joy. And it's all there. It's all in the photograph. A fear of hubris pricks my mood, but I cannot help feeling proud. Perhaps Percy was right. Perhaps I'm not completely without talent.

'Charles!' Warwick declares. It's a summoning rather than a greeting, but cordial nonetheless. I make my way to the counter from behind which he loves to hold court. He smiles at me, his expression tainted by a cluster of spittle at each corner of his mouth, a sharp contrast to the immaculately groomed moustache and Piccadilly Weepers that adorn his face. He's a preposterous man, but he's been good to me. Underneath the absurd exterior of an ageing dandy, he has a heart of gold, if not of the highest carat.

'Good day to you!' he exclaims. 'And what delights do you bring me on this fine morning?'

'A mother wrestling her baby into submission,' I reply.

Handing him the folder that holds the prints, he flashes me a playful expression of curiosity, despite knowing exactly what it contains, and pulls the photographs out into the world with the flourish of a showman.

His tongue shoots out, cleaning up the mess around his mouth as he contemplates the picture, before releasing a grin. 'Excellent as always, Charles. Excellent as always…'

'There's a second print, should you want it… For your wall,' I explain, attempting to imbue the words with a modicum of humility.

'Thank you, Charles. Thank you.'

He places the print for the Deans in an envelope, and his own on the counter, hopefully for framing rather than filing. I want to leave things at that, but my impatience is beginning to get the better of me, and the question that's been nagging at me since I walked in forces its way to the surface.

'Mr Warwick – I'm sorry to bother you with this again, but has there been any news?' I continue as if what I'm referring to isn't blindingly obvious, 'on the Disraeli commission.'

'They have your portfolio, Charles,' he tells me, consolingly. 'All we can do now is wait.'

The words set something off in me. Another of the same brush-offs I've received for the past two years. I can't hold my tongue any longer. Or perhaps I just don't want to.

'I seem to spend my whole life waiting.' The words come out more aggressively than I had intended. For a brief second, I see myself through his eyes, the impatient young man who wants nothing of the present. A child lacking wisdom, appreciation. But what does he know? How quickly the old forget the struggles that come with youth, the strivings, the insufficiencies.

'Then *don't*, my dear boy,' he bellows, his words confirming my diagnosis. 'Go out and enjoy yourself. Life is for living, for living! Things will change, my boy, they will change. So be happy. No man steps in the same river twice. You'll have the success you want soon enough.'

My brow furrows with cynicism. I've heard enough of his stoic platitudes to last several lifetimes, his embellishments of Marcus Aurelius or whichever Pre-Socratic's tome currently sits on his counter, attempting to inculcate his customers with a sense of his intelligence and erudition.

'I know you think I disregard your strivings, Charles, but I'm trying to help you. The future will come soon enough, trust me. And with it, its own problems.' He gestures round at his shop. 'Look at what I have – this shop, a fine town house, a thriving business. I'd give it all up for your youth, your hope. Believe me, that beautiful wife of yours is worth a thousand Disraeli commissions.'

His smile, which a stranger might read as predatory, is laced with a sadness that neuters any enmity, but his words skate across the surface of my worries, unaware of the depths below. And yet, he is right about Percy. She is something to hold onto. A rudder that can guide me through anything.

I re-emerge into the sweltering streets, still fuming. Warwick's bell rings behind me like a crier's call to attention, but my despondency is too great for it to register, and I trudge onwards, becoming lost in the crowd.

CHAPTER III

In which I dress two people

A light breeze flows through the open window of our bedroom as I help Percy dress. The weather broke a few days ago, but the cool air still feels welcome, refreshing.

My wife stands in front of me in her chemise and stockings, and I can't help but pause, taking her in like this.

'You shouldn't stare at a married woman that way,' she mocks, rebuking me for the openness of my gaze.

'Would it be better if you were unmarried?' I reply.

Her head tilts back in a laugh. 'Come on – help me with this.' She wraps the corset she was holding around her body, and buttons up the busk at the front, before turning to present me with my duties. I thread the slackened laces through the top few holes, one by one, using each as an excuse to draw myself in closer.

'You know we could get a maid to do this,' I tell her, burrowing in at her neck as I go to tie the strands. 'We have the money.'

Percy pushes back into my lips, and I feel the heat of that magical curve where her shoulder meets her neck. 'I like you dressing me. Besides, if a maid dressed me like this, I'd have to fire her. Tighter.'

She pulls away, and I tug on the strings, prompting a wince as the corset constricts around her waist. She takes a moment's pause, before letting out a strained laugh at the exertion. Then instructs me to pull once again.

I go to object, but stop myself, knowing what she'll say. That I think she looks perfect anyway, so who am I to judge? And she's right. As far as I'm concerned she could drape herself in sackcloth,

16

and be a worthy subject for Michelangelo, so I bite my tongue and tug upon the strings once more.

'Good,' she pants, in relief. I pass the laces around the front for her to tie, but instead she guides my arms into position and I knot them in place. 'In any case,' she continues, 'maids are for old, rich people who sleep in separate bedrooms. I like that it's just us here.' She turns to me, a hand on her newly exaggerated hip, 'Unless you're saying you don't like dressing me?'

'No,' I stumble, fixed in place by her coquettish smile, 'I... It's just a little unconventional, that's all.'

'Since when have you worried about being unconventional?'

I think back to when I met her, a woman betrothed to another man. Percy's mother shooting me wary glances as I positioned her in the family portrait, showing a little too much care, a little too much attention; Percy responding with smiles and looks that made me act like a schoolboy, giggling along with her. Hardly the way to declare one's professionalism. I offered to drop the prints off myself, and her mother declined. But I came anyway, not hoping, not expecting anything. Just one last chance to see the woman who already had my heart.

Percy threads herself up into her crinoline, drawing it down her body until the frame finds its place on her hips, its crisscrossed structure flaring out behind her like the web of a mechanical spider. I've tried to dissuade her from wearing it – the amount of stories we've heard about women setting themselves on fire because of these damned things – but to no avail. She is a slave to fashion.

'Don't look at me like that,' she jokes. 'This one's extremely practical. *The Lady's Newspaper* specifically said the waved hoops would allow me to ascend a steep stair or pass into my stall at the opera.'

I laugh. 'Why were you looking at that nonsense?' It's a far cry

17

from her usual insistence on *The Times,* and her diatribes about the American war, and the nobility of the North's hopeless cause.

'Hattie had it when I visited her in town.'

'Ah, Hattie! And you complain that you're not getting enough intellectual stimulation out here.'

She shakes her head at me. 'Perhaps I *should* get a maid. They're far less judgemental.'

'It would certainly free up my mornings. And think of the fun you could have ascending steep stairs together.'

She smooths her petticoats down over the frame, then puts on her camisole, feigning indifference as she continues to talk.

'That said, it may be better to put the money aside for a nanny.'

'Of course,' I say, not registering her implication, 'when the time comes…'

She looks at me, smiling, her meaning so clear that even a fool like me can read the signals. I feel the breath catch in my throat.

'Really?'

She nods. The revelation hits me with the force of a boxer who shuns Broughton's gloves. But, like Heenan and Sayers, somehow we're both still standing.

I spring in her direction, and she wraps her arms around my shoulders. A moment later, she has left the floor, as I twirl her in a circle, covering her face with kisses. A child. We're having a child.

I suddenly stop, wary, my hand moving to her stomach and touching it, hesitant.

'Sorry – was that too much?'

'It's fine,' she replies, her hand cradling mine. 'Nothing compared to this damn corset.'

'Oh God, we shouldn't have—'

'It's *fine.*'

My mind snaps into action, a ledger of practicalities and logistics.

18

'We need to get a crib … blankets… What else do you need for a baby?' I grab paper and pencil from the dresser, and start to compile a list.

Percy laughs at my mania, as I whir around the room to little effect like a broken automaton.

'You understand it's a long time before we actually have a baby?' she questions, making no attempt to hide her mockery. 'Nine months is traditional.'

'You're right,' I acknowledge. 'We can do the list later.' A new idea strikes me. 'We should take a photograph to celebrate.' I grab her hand, and start to drag her towards the stairs. She resists, giggling.

'I've not finished dressing. And I'm teaching the children at ten.'

'The dressing, I'll give you. The children can wait. It's not like they'll be checking their watches. I'll go and set up the camera.'

'I thought you were working today.'

'I'll send word to postpone. It's not every day a man finds out he's starting a family.'

***

The dress she wears is my favourite, wide necked and edged with a white lace that contrasts with the blue of the pattern. The difference won't show up on the plate, the peculiarities of collodion transforming it all to a uniform colour, clothing her from head to toe in white. It strikes me the reason I like this dress so much is not because of the thing itself, but because it allows me to see more of Percy; her skin, the lines of her neck, so delicate, so exquisite. It's a far cry from the high-collared blouse she'll don for the school later, but even in that my wife is a wonder to behold.

19

I set the chair up in front of our apple trees, the half-formed fruit unseen beneath the dense leaves that will provide the textured background of the photograph. The sun is still low enough in the sky that the branches of the willow behind me won't dapple the light, and the softness of the morning sun will provide a visual warmth that mirrors its feeling upon my skin. Everything is as it should be.

'Here?' Percy asks.

I nod, and she takes her place on the seat, lowering herself onto the chair. The wooden legs disappear beneath the fabric of her dress, and I bend down next to the camera to check the composition. It's perfect. I remove the lens cap, allowing the light to flood into the plate, transforming it from a concoction of chemicals into an object of beauty. My love, perfectly captured on glass. The cap replaced, I feel a new warmth, this time from within, generated by the knowledge that I have somehow preserved her beauty, this moment. And yet, I want more.

I go inside to prepare another plate, running back to the camera with unrepressed excitement. A moment later, it is on my shoulder, the weight of the wooden tripod heavy upon me, and I move in towards her. In this new position, the frame is filled with Percy's head and shoulders, only the lace edging of her dress revealing that she is clothed at all. It is even better.

'You're closer than normal,' she mentions, curious.

'I want to see as much of my beautiful pregnant wife as possible,' I tell her, drawing myself up to full height, then walking over to kiss her.

As our lips part, she speaks. 'I hope you don't use this technique on all your sitters,' she whispers, my mouth still inches from hers.

'Only on babies and elderly gentlemen. The occasional young woman if she's particularly attractive.'

I go inside to retrieve the plate from the sensitising box, and return to load it into the camera, finally set to remove the lens cap once more.

'Are you ready?' I ask.

'Yes.'

I reach around to the front of the camera, but a half-second before I expose the plate, she breaks into a smile as wide as her face.

'Percy!' I reprimand.

She shakes herself, attempting to regain her composure, failing time after time, before eventually forcing her expression back into the stillness of repose.

'I'm sorry,' she says, taking a deep breath, 'I'm ready now.'

I nod. But, as my hand reaches towards the cap, another grin erupts from beneath her affected tranquillity.

'Darling,' I say, 'I'm sorry, but you can't smile.'

'I'm trying.'

'I know, I know…' I pause, watching her repeatedly attempt to suppress her elation, only for it to bubble to the surface again and again. And I understand. She looks the way I feel inside. For once in my life I don't even feel a hint of professional annoyance, just utter adoration. But I want to capture this forever. To bottle it like a Djinn. I go over and kneel at her feet.

'Percy, my love, as beautiful as you look, you can't smile. You won't be able to keep it up for the whole exposure.'

A sudden look of seriousness comes over her, as if she is addressing the mob of children she'll be facing in an hour or so, one of them having uttered a particularly egregious falsehood.

'I hate to contradict you, my dear husband,' she replies, 'but I believe I will.'

I take off the lens cap.

And she does.

CHAPTER IV

A man of his time

The photographs are the best I've ever taken. I can even tell from the plate. The finish is faultless, the pour even, the focus perfect. She stares back at me from the glass, her face coated with darkness, her red hair a translucent white on the plate, a being from the underworld tempting me to follow her into the twilight below, but through it all, her beauty shines like a beacon.

The print is even better, like somehow her lost soul has been rescued, reclaimed by life. She is there on the paper, a moment turned to stone, but better; more subtle, more real. It's exactly what I've been dreaming of. It's not a photograph; it's art.

Percy gasps when I show her the print. A genuine noise of shock.

'Is that me? Do I look like that?'

I nod, smiling. 'What do you think?'

'I don't know what to say.'

'You don't like it?'

'No, I just… It's amazing. Not my face – the photograph. It's … lovely. I hope I don't sound conceited. It's me, but it's not me. I think it's beautiful.'

'You're beautiful.'

'No, it's you as well. You're in there. I can see you. It's not like when I look in the mirror. It's like I'm seeing myself through someone else's eyes. Yours.'

***

The bell on Warwick's door feels like an announcement; the butler at Cinderella's ball declaring her entrance, the wishing tree having worked its magic. Warwick can sense it too: the confidence that exudes from me, the assurance that I have found something, all fuelled by the prints in the carpet bag I carry in my hand.

'You're in the Park Lane Studio at ten. Mr and Mrs... Walker. And child.'

He passes me the handwritten address, business as usual, and I place my bag on the counter, nervous yet excited. I unclasp the metal fixings that have lost their shine after years of use, and pull out the prints.

'I have something to show you.'

He stops me with a gesture, a peeler halting a hansom cab.

'Before you do, I have to tell you something. It's about the Disraeli commission...'

His tone says everything, there's no need for him to finish, but the words still make it real.

'It went another way.'

I stand there, confused, unaccepting. In my head, it was already mine. I hadn't admitted it to myself, but this was what was going to change everything.

'...Which other way?'

'That's not important.'

'Barnes?'

He hesitates, his eyes searching for another method of deflection, but finding nothing.

'He's very experienced. People like a safe pair of hands...'

'A safe pair of hands that squeeze the life out of everything.'

'Come now, Charles—'

'He's talentless, Warwick. You know that. Doesn't ability count for anything in this damned business?'

Warwick pauses. I can see him try to temper his reaction, and when he finally utters his response, the words are clothed with a cloying serenity. 'Photographing the rich and famous is not something that comes to those with talent, Charles. Surely, you must know that? It's always been that way and it always shall be. Airs, graces and persistence are what allow you to rise above the throng in this business, my dear boy. But do not worry, I shall help you work on yours.'

I go to reply, but disappointment traps the words in my throat, and Warwick takes the opportunity to continue.

'Next time, Charles… Next time.'

'I just feel if they were to see my work…'

My hands reach towards the bag without thought, a falling man desperately grabbing for a handhold.

'They've seen your portfolio, Charles. They were very complimentary.'

'What I've been working on recently…'

I pass him the photo of Percy, my heart full of hope, as if somehow Disraeli's people will get word, rush in and demand I take over the commission immediately.

Warwick perches a pair of fashionable pince-nez on his bulbous nose, and looks down at the print. I can feel the smile forming on my face as he considers the photograph, as I see it again through new eyes, its energy, its rawness, its *reality*.

My smile is short-lived.

'This is shameful, Charles.'

I hesitate, unable to process what he is saying, struggling to make sense of his reaction.

'I beg your pardon?'

'Sharing your wife like this. It's indecent.'

Anger begins to rise within me. And, for the first time, I see him for what he is. An old man, stuck in the past. As much as he adorns himself with the accoutrements of the moment – a

24

flowered necktie too wide for a man his age, the ridiculous new eyeglasses he picked up in Paris – it's his attitudes that reveal the man beneath. He's a fraud, an imposter, playing at life, an absurd Mr Pickwick, a Phiz cartoon in a world of men. But I hold my tongue. I need him, so I hold my tongue.

'I would've thought you'd have had more affection towards her than that,' he continues.

'It's a photograph,' I say, attempting to shut the door on his judgements.

'And the fewer people who see it, the better.' His tone has taken on the smug surety of an old maid, condescension dripping off him like perspiration. 'We have responsibilities to our art, Charles. But we also have responsibilities to those we love.'

'I think it's beautiful,' I reply, managing to restrain myself.

His eyes dart down towards the picture once more, and then he removes his eyeglasses. As if leaving them on, he might again be assaulted by the impropriety of the image. Its '*indecency*'.

'I'm sure many think the pinchcocks of Whitechapel *beautiful*, Charles,' he tells me, speaking with the confidence of a man who has amassed a fortune, but knows nothing. 'A family man should have greater concerns than that of beauty. When one has a wife, Charles, one needs to protect her dignity, not display her to the world in the service of his "photography".'

I meet his gaze, defiant, then grab the print from the counter, so I can get out of this mausoleum before I say something I'll regret. I can feel my breathing becoming shallower, the walls closer.

I haul my bag from its perch, and start towards the door, but the fuse of my ire has been lit, and, before I reach the exit, words explode unbidden from within me.

'You're stuck in the past, Warwick. Peddling all these images of people looking like they're dead. You don't know anything about photography. About art.'

I see him tense up, but the look of anger he flashes is immediately replaced by a dignified composure, as if he means to demonstrate the self-control so lacking in me.

'You're upset, Charles,' he says, attempting to force calm into his words. 'And, as such, I'll forget those comments were ever made. I suggest you think twice before speaking to me in that way again.'

I stare at him with a barely concealed look of hatred, but inside, I'm trying to talk myself down. He doesn't know any better, he's a man of his time. If everyone understood art, there'd be no need for artists. Besides, I need him; him and his mindless workmanlike employment. I need them to live, to provide. I can't sabotage that. I have to control myself. For Percy. For our *child*. But reason has no affect on my humour, and the expression on my face can't be removed with the ease of a pair of pince-nez.

And yet… I curb my tongue. And that means everything. A picture may be worth a thousand words, but until those words are said, we can lie to ourselves about all that we have seen.

I turn around and leave the shop, the chirpy jangling of the bell jarring with my mood. The cool air of the street attempts to slap me to my senses, but to no avail, and I round the corner to avoid the gaze of the passing gentlefolk. In the alley beyond, I calm myself, my breath anchoring me to the world once again, lest I float off untethered into the heights of my mood, all sandbags gone.

CHAPTER V

When all is fair

'Barnes. *Again.*'

'His work is all he has. You said the poor man smells of cheese!'

'Underneath the more general smell of wine…'

Percy laughs, but I'm in no mood to join in. The joke tastes bitter in my mouth, like poison in the punch, and I curse myself for the detachment I feel. The evening is perfect, the sun still warm, the sky a calm blue, but tumult clouds the lens of my vision and I walk on, struggling with the cufflink on my right wrist, the perfection of the world eluding me.

Percy takes my hand.

'You shouldn't worry about him. You've got your whole life ahead of you,' she says. 'He's sixty years old. Without meaning to be morbid, I doubt he'll be blocking your path to fame and fortune for much longer.'

Percy smiles at me, and, for the first time the warmth of the evening starts to penetrate my heart. 'I can't ever see him dying,' I grumble, my lamentations beginning to lose their bite. 'Not that I'd wish it on the man… Perhaps if it were humane. If he suffocated on a pound of Double Gloucester… At least the old fool would die happy.'

'Forget about him. The night is young. And we're still reasonably young.'

'You are. I'm pushing thirty,' I reply.

'Charles,' she says, stopping, and taking my other hand as well, 'please be with me for one night, my love.'

'It's just so frustrating.'

Her hands rise to my face, the fingertips soft on my cheeks. 'Just be here with me now. Please.'

Looking into her eyes, I know she's right. How many of these perfect summer's evenings will there be until we're as old and decrepit as Barnes himself? A few hundred? Not many more. That's if we even last that long... But, being here now, I can't believe it. Looking at Percy, it seems like she can never grow old, as if she is eternal, fixed in time like one of my photographs, and within moments the concerns of my ambition disappear like the contents of an opium dream, until all that is left are half-remembered fragments, my own Kubla Khan.

***

As we approach the village, the bustle that always accompanies a fair begins to fill the streets. Though a smaller incarnation, the atmosphere brings to mind the Greenwich fairs of my youth. The bakery is still open, Mabel is there in her smartest apron selling buns, comfits and sweetmeats. Other residents have turned their cottage fronts into makeshift tea shops, and the streets echo with celebratory cheers and the sound of wooden rattles, as young men and women draw the cacophonous rollers up and down each other's backs in noisy courtship.

Carriages and carts from far and wide line the uncobbled streets, pouring out new attendees desperate for the thrills they've been craving since Greenwich was shut down all those years ago. But there are no hills here for women to roll down, 'accidentally' flashing their undergarments in view of onlooking 'gentlemen', no drunkards firing pistols, no bachelors slipping into the Crown and Anchor dancing booth for whatever in tarnation went on in there. It makes me smile to think on it – at how little I understood back then. To me, the hill-rolling was harmless fun, sledding for adults in fine weather. But it makes me sad that Percy never experienced it – her family were as unlikely to take her there as to St Giles' Rookery – but at least we have this.

Percy's eyes are alight with excitement as we move towards the Green where the fair proper begins. I watch them drinking in the gypsies, the gin and ale pedlars, the monkey perched atop an organ, all of them reflected in her pupils, enriched by her joy. She's blind to the unsavoury characters who weave their way among the crowds, the pickpockets and cutpurses – their eyes on passing targets rather than the attractions that line the street – but they vanish as we enter the fairground itself, perhaps scared off by Reverend Arnett, the young vicar who stands there, greeting newcomers; his eyes the eyes of God.

We pass the gingerbread stands and toy stalls, our hands entwined, and Percy's untempered enthusiasm begins to spread to me. The light is fading now, and torches take over the sun's workload, the candle lamps on the stalls offering meagre support. The whole place feels magical, as if we have walked into a faery kingdom, full of wonders and mystery. The hawkers that line the path attempt to draw us in to their tents, one man claiming to have 'such wonders as no one ever saw a-fore!', his stall advertising 'a sheep with four legs and half a fifth 'un'. Another boasts of a 'fat child' within, while his neighbour's tent displays a poster that attempts to draw in passing trade with the promise of a 'learned pig'.

'Come see the swine that has been taught to read,' the man barks as we pass.

'I think I may have had him in the classroom earlier,' Percy replies.

We move along giddily, proceeding past a theatrical venture offering a 'journey into the underworld!', a self-penned recreation of the Greek myth. Its actors are dressed in dirty robes, as if the heroes of the ancient world were down on their luck. Hades himself looks the most ridiculous. The paint on his sceptre is peeling, and his attempts to strike fear into passers-by are undermined by his entourage, a small dog with two papier-mâché heads mounted on its neck. I edge away, mock-terrified, while Percy smacks me playfully on the arm, and we are carried along by our laughter. A passing child's screams are not so playful, and it brings to mind the time my father paid for me to look through a sailor's telescope as a boy. As I put my face to the eye piece, I found myself inches away from an empty gibbet on the other side of the river, and, as the old sea-dog described the horrors that once lay within, I could have sworn I saw the pirate's body, his mouth open and eyes pecked out, staring blankly in my direction. The dead brought to life once again.

The thoroughfare opens out to a central space that the pathways of stalls branch off from like the spokes of a wheel. Ahead of us we see a circuit set up for donkey rides. The rogue's gallery sitting upon the poor animals is something to behold. One has a matronly woman on its back so hefty it looks like the unfortunate creature might snap in two.

'We should report her to the Society for the Prevention of Cruelty to Animals,' deadpans Percy, but I don't hear the words. The display on a stall to my right has caught my eye. I wander towards it, transfixed, not noticing the 'tut's Percy gives me from behind.

The stall is as dense with photographs as bodies on a London street. They are mainly novelty affairs – a man in a diving suit next to his formally dressed wife, a banker playing cards with a dog – but it's the others that enchant me. In one, a woman carries her own head, in another, a man has his head on backwards, a third shows a young girl about to be assaulted by a transparent skull-faced ghost. I pick up the print of the headless woman.

'How did you do this?' The words come out breathless; my attempts to appear collected steamrolled by my curiosity.

'Tricks o' the trade, mate, tricks o' the trade…' he replies.

'No, you don't understand, I'm a photographer…'

The stall owner smiles enigmatically, but Percy is upon me. 'No. *No,*' she says emphatically. 'You must not talk to my husband about photography this evening. His job is to accompany his wife, not to talk shop with you.' I try to protest, but she won't take no for an answer. 'You promised me you were going to win me coconuts when we left tonight, and you're not getting out of it!'

Reluctantly, I let her drag me away, determined to return to quiz the owner later in the evening, but as we move away, the method comes to me.

'You print from multiple negatives, don't you?' I call back at him.

The chink in his expression tells me I've got it.

'I'm right aren't I?' I grin. 'I'm right!'

'Coconuts,' insists Percy, pulling me away into the night.

***

I manage to miss with all three balls. Percy laughs at me as I pay a second penny for another go, my initial reluctance to participate usurped by a dogged resolve to succeed.

As my third ball flies past its target, colliding with the tarpaulin behind, its dull thud prompts Percy to hysterical laughter.

'You need to have more faith,' I tell her, defiant. 'This time I'll hit one, you'll see.' I count the coins into my palm before handing them over, finally making contact with the third ball. Only for the cursed nut to stay on its mount.

'Damn it.'

An uncharacteristic look of sympathy graces the stall owner's face.

'Don't worry, sir,' he tells me. 'If you fail three times we give you a free one.'

Percy raises her eyebrows at me, her eyes glinting with amused mockery.

'I do not take charity,' I reply, determinedly. 'Three more balls.'

I heave the wooden globes towards their target, and the second one makes good. Triumphant, I hand Percy the third ball, and she manages to knock one off first time (although I think the barker's foot might also have been involved). He hands me a coconut.

'We won one each,' I protest.

He points to a hand-painted sign. It reads, 'mAXImum wone coco nut per go.' So much for charity.

'Your prize, m'lady,' I say presenting Percy with the strange hairy ovoid.

'Why thank you, my good sir,' she replies, echoing the mock-formality of my tone.

We walk on for a moment.

'I hate to tell you this,' she confides, 'but I don't even like coconuts.'

'I know, my love. But I thought you might make an exception for what has turned out to be the most expensive coconut in England.'

'Not even for that one.'

'Then why did you…?'

'I like seeing your face when you win them.'

I laugh, exasperated. But I can't be annoyed at Percy for long.

'Mabel,' I call over, spotting the woman from the bakery walking past. 'Could I interest you in a coconut? Free of charge, of course.'

'Despite it being the most expensive coconut in the British Empire,' Percy interjects.

'She's joking,' I clarify, 'just the country.'

Mabel makes no attempt to hide her confusion, but the promise of a coconut allows her to put it to one side.

'Much obliged, Mr Franklin. Much obliged. You're a good 'un, Mr Franklin, a good 'un.'

Her daughter, Molly, flashes me a shy smile from her side. She's fifteen years old, but hasn't lost the sweetness of childhood. She seems fascinated by the exotic nut. I smile back, glad at least that she and her mother will enjoy the literal fruit of my labours.

'Now you're taking me dancing,' Percy insists.

'What about the baby?'

She scoffs. 'I'm pregnant, not dying!'

We pass deeper into the fair, past a game of 'the hole and the stick', and a nut seller shouting 'Buy a penny's worth! Not a bad one among the lot!' until we finally reach a temporary dance floor, edged with a small fence-like barrier and decorated with bunting and hanging lanterns.

Percy leads me towards the floor, where I'm stopped by the owner.

'Tuppence for you, sir. The lady's free.'

Percy shrugs, and heads past him, smirking. I furrow my brow, annoyed, then flail about in my pocket for coins.

By the time I have been admitted, Percy is dancing with a portly man in his fifties who looks like he never takes no for an answer, both on dance floors and when asking if he can have second helpings of pudding. I go to cut in.

'I'm sorry, sir,' I explain, 'I've paid tuppence and I mean to dance with this lady.'

'We've all paid tuppence, young man,' he replies.

'She's my wife.'

'Then you'll have plenty of time to dance with her in the future. I intend to use this brief moment to enjoy her company in the present.'

33

I wander off, defeated, Percy mouthing me an apology. Lingering by the side of the floor, I listen to the accordion and fiddle play their spritely jig, unable to take my eyes off my wife. She keeps looking over, powerless to escape, making exaggerated expressions of horror for my amusement. But I cannot begrudge the old fellow his dance; if I were old and lonely, what I wouldn't give to spend a few minutes in her company. Each moment would be worth a fortune. But she's mine. And I hers. And for once in my life, I feel completely at peace.

The song ends, and Percy manages to extract herself, coming over and offering me her hand.

'I thought he'd never let me go,' she laughs.

'Perhaps I have to worry about Barnes after all,' I reply.

She smiles and we make our way to the floor as a new song begins. The music is tender, romantic, the violin carrying the melody while the accordion swells, long and slow, beneath its mournful tune. The moment is perfect, and, as she pulls me towards her, she whispers into my ear.

'You never have to worry about anything with me.'

And I trust her with all my heart. I breathe in her scent like the perfume of a nosegay, and, as the music intensifies into a merry song, we launch ourselves into the dance, swirling in time with the beat. Before long, the floor is alive with bodies, laughing and bouncing around, slightly out of time. But at the centre of it all is us, the calm at the eye of the hurricane, and I know that I love her and she loves me and that it shall always be so. And I dance, basking in the light that glows from within her.

CHAPTER VI

A new life begins

The winter has been a hard one. My relationship with Warwick has thawed over the intervening months, but the harsh frosts of January have continued into March, holding the country in its grasp, and refusing to let us move on.

The baby is late. Like all of us, it seems to have been waiting for the spring to come before it makes its way into the world. Today, however, its patience has come to an end, and I wait downstairs, while my wife attempts to bring our child into existence. The scene outside the window is filled with a strange silence, which cuts through the noise from upstairs, like a rip in the paper the world is printed on.

'Don't fret yourself, sir.'

I turn to see Effie, the nurse, coming down the stairs behind me to fetch clean water.

'She'll be done before you know it. You'd be best to busy yourself with something while ya wait. It don't benefits a man to think about what's happening up there.'

I nod, knowing she's right, yet frustrated that the doctor has kept me from the bedroom. Percy and I have been at each other's sides through everything since the moment we were wed. Why should this be any different?

I watch as Effie grabs a jug and returns up the stairs to the bedroom, then pick up my copy of *Techniques of Trick Photography*. It's little more than a pamphlet really, twenty sheets illustrated with amateurish drawings that I ordered from the Birmingham Photographic Society, the whole thing shamelessly codged from the talks that Rejlander gave them. I've scoured its pages endlessly, but today the fascination they've always seemed to contain is absent, as if it too is on hiatus until the Franklin child is come.

I put the pages down on the small table by the fireside and walk to the window. The fog is thick and grey, blocking the view beyond our squat front wall, as if it has erased everything but our little cottage – the last place left on this earth.

I pace back and forth, constantly checking the grandfather clock on the far wall of the room, its tick-tock a beat to accompany my march of frustration. Time feels like my enemy – a blockade between me and my love, refusing to give way and allow us our reunion. It has been hours now. I have no idea how long a birth is meant to take, and once again I find myself envying those with parents, with a mother who can guide them through the mysteries of womanhood, a father whose stern resolve can provide strength by way of example. But that was not my lot. And yet, I have something better. I have Percy.

A scream from upstairs knocks me from the bough of my thoughts. There have been screams throughout the whole ordeal, but this one is different – as if it has been ripped from her gut without consent. I stand still, my eyes moving to the ceiling in an impotent attempt to see through the wood and plaster. The commotion that follows confirms my fears, feet stepping faster, the bustle of panic, and then I am sure. Something is wrong.

I move to the bottom of the stairs, the doctor appearing at the door that opens onto their upper flight.

'Charles, there's a problem,' he tells me, attempting to suppress the panic beneath his words. Fear slithers down my spine, leaving behind it a trail of nothingness. 'Your wife is haemorrhaging.'

I know what the words mean, and yet they seem devoid of content, an extract of Lear's nonsense. Try as I might, I cannot engage with what they contain, and I propel myself up the staircase. As if seeing my wife will somehow make it stop. The doctor's raised hand brings me to a halt, and he looks me in the eye.

'I can save her,' he explains, 'but you'll lose the baby.' He pauses before continuing. 'Or I can attempt to deliver the child. The risks to your wife will be considerable. I'm sorry, Charles, but you have to choose.'

Images of our unborn child fill my mind. The life that we have envisioned as it has grown within her womb; a life now on the precipice of being snuffed from existence: an infinite set of possibilities never to become real, our imaginings merely a placeholder for the love that will be transferred to the person they become for the rest of our lives.

And yet, there is no choice to be made.

'Save her. Save my wife.'

The doctor nods and heads back into the bedroom. I descend the staircase, my head bowed in shame. What else could I have done? Saved the child? A creature I don't know, that I have never met. Over *Percy*? The woman that has filled my life with joy, with light? There was no choice. There never was a choice.

And yet, I have condemned the child to death. The thought weighs on me, dragging me down. What do they say of an unbaptised child? Can I really have damned my son or daughter's soul? Doomed them to nothing but suffering? What kind of pernicious God would do that? But what kind of God would make a man choose between the fate of his unborn offspring and his wife?

The guilt begins to suffocate me. I sit back down in my armchair, my breathing shallow and snatched. I know I have been selfish, but I cannot bring myself to wish I had acted differently. Would Percy have chosen her own life over that of our child?

Never. But that's an easy choice to make for oneself. I would condemn myself a thousand times over for both of them, but I will not sacrifice her. Not her.

The creaking of stairs behind me alerts me to Effie's presence. She waddles past, carrying something small wrapped in a blanket. It takes a few moments before I realise what is inside. She keeps her head down as she heads towards the front door, avoiding my eyes.

'Effie! I need you!' the doctor bellows from upstairs. 'We need water!'

The nurse looks about her in panic, then locates another of the pots she filled earlier. Unthinking, she puts her macabre package down on a sideboard and grabs the receptacle with both hands before straining back up the stairs.

And I am alone once again.

Across the room, I look at the rolled cloth sitting amidst the paraphernalia of our day-to-day, thinking of what it contains. A few pounds of flesh that should have been a life. That should have filled *my* life. Its presence taunts me, daring me to look upon what I have done. The tan of the wool is darkened with the bloodied echoes of Effie's grip, but beyond that its appearance is innocuous. Innocent. A stranger would know nothing of its contents.

Tears threaten to overtake me, but I do not avert my gaze. Instead I force myself to my feet, almost stumbling, and walk towards the bundled cloth. Each step is a challenge, as if I am wading through tar, but soon I am at the sideboard. I reach my hand out to the cloth, feeling its roughness against my fingertips; my son or daughter hidden beneath. Dead.

I hesitate, but know I must face the consequences of my choice. My hand traces its way along to the edge of the cloth that is tucked beneath the package and I take it between my thumb and finger. Ready to encounter what I will never be able to unsee.

'Charles. You need to come now,' the doctor's voice calls to me from the foot of the staircase. I turn to look at him, his face solemn.

'Why? What's happening?'

'I couldn't stop the bleeding. You need to come.'

In an instant, what lies beneath my fingers is forgotten, and I start to move across the room.

'But you said…' I stutter.

'I'm sorry, Charles.'

I stumble up the staircase after him, supporting myself on the banister as I take three steps at a time, then push past the doctor and into the room.

For the first time, I see the extent of what has happened. The blood on the floor, pots strewn throughout, the blackened red of the sheets. Effie hastens to cover the scene with a clean blanket, but it is too late. Lying there within the chaos is Percy. My poor Percy.

She lies unmoving, and my hand comes to my mouth, fingers splayed, as if to suppress a silent scream.

'Charles…' The words come like a breeze over her cracked lips. She's still here. Thank God she's still here.

'My love.' I move to her bed, intertwining my fingers with hers. They're cold. So cold.

She looks at me, confused.

'Charles?'

'I'm here, my love. I'm here.'

'What's happening? I don't understand what's happening.' I grip her hand tighter, the warmth of tears lining my eyes. 'Where's the baby?'

'She's in the other room, sleeping,' I tell her, the lie stinging as it comes out. I don't have the heart to tell her the truth.

'Is she all right?'

I nod, not noticing the tears streaming down my cheeks. 'She's beautiful. Just like her mother.'

She smiles, weakly, a shadow of the joy so often within her.

'I want to…' she says, straining to sit up, but unable to lift her head from the pillow. I stroke her hair, letting her know it's all right.

'You need to rest. You're too weak.'

'It hurt so much, Charles. It hurt so much.'

My mouth begins to spasm into a wail, but I control myself, imposing a smile upon my lips. If she is taken from this world, I want her to know that she is loved. That she will always be loved.

'It doesn't hurt any more.'

'That's good, my love.'

Suddenly, she winces again, grabbing my hand with all the strength left in her, and I wish for nothing but that I could take her pain onto me. But then the moment subsides, and, her pain withdrawing, she looks me in the eye, trying to make sense of it all.

'Am I dying, Charles?'

I don't know what to say. But my hesitation says everything.

'Oh, God. I don't want to, Charles. I'm not ready. I'm not ready.'

'I know, my love.'

'I'm so scared.'

I try to stay strong, but I am weak, and I grip onto her, trying to save her from the current that is dragging her away, trying to save myself. I draw my head in, to be close to her. One last time.

'I love you,' I whisper.

'I love you so much,' she whispers back, an inch away from my mouth. 'I don't want to leave you.'

'You won't,' I tell her. 'I'll always be with you. I'll always be true to you. Nothing will keep us apart. Nothing. I'll love you forever, no matter what happens.'

She smiles, a look of calm coming over her.

'We had a good love, I think.'

I nod in reply.

She smiles again, and her eyes close slowly, and I watch the light inside her go out, forever.

'Percy,' I plead. 'Please Percy, don't go. Please don't go.'

I cover her head with kisses, her face, her hair. But something is gone, and I feel an emptiness inside that I know will never be filled.

And thus a new life begins.

A life without Percy.

CHAPTER VII

Crepe in two colours

I had wanted the funeral to be a quiet affair, but Percy was Percy, and all of the village are in attendance. My annoyance at the infraction is soon replaced by a quiet resignation. How could it be otherwise? She touched so many lives. How could someone know her and not love her?

And so I am forced to share my grief.

The churchyard is quiet, despite the many attendees. The grey of the church's stone is reflected in its surroundings, and even the bright colours of the spring flowers that adorn a nearby grave seem flat and muted. The women are present, the people of this village not standing on such foolish ceremony. They wear the traditional black, their dresses repurposed from losses of their own, while their husbands don their darkest work suits, their gloves black in a nod to formality, as if mourning had assaulted their extremities like frostbite. Children flit around our ankles, dressed in white. At first they irritate me, but with Percy so close by, I see them as she would; free, unaffected. A bittersweet smile plays on my lips, and, for a moment, I think I hear her breathy laugh in my ear, '…Babies aren't meant to keep still…'

We stand around the two graves, a stone for both mother and daughter; Persephone Margaret Franklin, and, next to her, Emma, our child that never was.

A mourning doll, supplied by Percy's parents, is propped, sitting, on our daughter's grave. A child from the village goes to pick it up only to be slapped on the wrist by her mother. I cannot help but wish her attempts at larceny had been more successful.

Seeing it there provokes a profound nausea within me – the sand-filled monstrosity staring vacantly ahead of itself, its eyes open to the world in a way that Emma's never were.

Across the grave stand the doll's benevolent donors, Mr and Mrs Wright. Though Percy's mother is hidden by a heavy veil, I can feel her gaze upon me, blaming me for their daughter's fate. But if anyone is to blame it's them. Disowning their child, disinheriting her for choosing me – a man who loved her, who would have given her his very soul – rather than the empty parody of a marriage they attempted to push on her. The idea of doing that to a child, turning them away in their hour of need, refusing to put their happiness before your 'principles'… it makes me hate them. But what do I know? I'm not a parent. And now I never shall be.

But deep down I know no one's to blame. Only the sheer meaninglessness of it all.

I stand at the graveside long after the multitudes have left. Their exit passes me unnoticed, but I am grateful for a few more moments in her thrall before she is lost to the earth. People talk of the veil between life and death, but there is no veil, just six feet of stone and earth. No River Styx between the living and the dead, just clay and loam; and soon she will lie there, covered, Michelangelo's David once again trapped in marble.

I am thankful for my solitude. Grief is not something to be shared. Those others didn't love her like I did. How could they? Their doleful costumes may have declared their loss to the world, but that is nothing but surface. And how can the surface ever capture what lies beneath? It is nothing but a fraud, a macer trying to pass off counterfeit goods. True grief walks alone. It is a hermit, where these shows are mere ornament. Our queen may paint all the railings in London black, but what has it done for her sickness? How much less blackness is left in her heart?

Walking the woodland path to our cottage feels final, as if I have turned my back on her, abandoned her memory. It's a route I have trodden many times, often unaccompanied, but this is the first time I have been truly alone. Spring is starting to show itself, taunting me with the promise of new life, the green of seedlings and ferns emerging from the ochre of the forest floor. It feels like a mockery of my grief, nature's narrative of renewal a lie to placate those who have yet to feel the sting of loss. And, though change will no doubt come to the world, my heart will still be deep in winter, the branches of my soul barren and angular, the life that once adorned them forever departed.

The sight of our front door brings me a moment of hope, before part of me remembers that home is now buried in the dirt of the churchyard two miles behind me. Black and white crepe adorns our knocker, a warning to callers to knock gently so as not to disturb those in mourning. My fingers roll the textured fabrics between them, the black for Percy, the white for Emma; an acknowledgment of her innocence. As if Percy lacked it. As if she were guilty just for being human.

I open the door to silence, the space inside somehow more empty than the world behind me. I close it and walk to the fireside, but there is no wood in the grate, no warmth in the room. The ticking of the clock is gone, its pendulum brought to a halt at the hour of her passing, the mirrors covered with cloth so Percy's soul should not be 'trapped' on its way to the other world. These base superstitions that haunt a million households seem foolish, but what need have I of a looking glass? Of time? My soul is already trapped on this plane, unable to escape and find solace by joining her in death.

But then I see the photographs. Always the photographs, their tendrils interweaving with my existence like bindweed. And I am glad. Custom expects me to cover them, turn them face down lest they be possessed by the dead. But as I stare into her eyes, living on paper, I know nothing would bring me more joy, more relief than knowing she was somehow in there. That part of her was still with me. She looks so innocent, so joyful, naive to the fact that she has just received a death sentence, that I put a killer inside of her.

'I'm sorry, I'm so sorry.'

The words sound like they have been spoken by someone else, but I know they are my own. I find myself going through the trunk of her belongings, searching for the flowered dress she wore that day. I hold it in my hands, bringing it to my face, searching for the last vestiges of her scent. But there is nothing, just the faint smell of fabric intermingled with memories of her perfume, a phantasm stuck between the worlds of reality and remembrance. And that is all there ever will be.

CHAPTER VIII

An alternative to life

Time has stood still, but the world has not. Its movement is now marked by the dwindling of my funds, the grains of the hourglass replaced by pounds and shillings, filtering through into the nothingness below. And thus I must return to life once more.

I push through the crush at Temple Bar, coming onto Fleet Street. Crowds of stovepipe hats stretch as far as the eye can see, like smoke stacks ready to carry away the smog of humanity. London seems so different to the last time I encountered it. Now, the seedy underbelly of the 'world's greatest city' looms garish and blatant, like the workings of a steam engine uncovered for all to see. Urchins sweep up dung from the streets, unnoticed; others dodge between cart wheels in search of opportunities to fulfil the whims of the bored and disinterested gentlemen whose cabs have drawn to a standstill.

I move deeper into the city, the streets that branch off the main thoroughfare offering glimpses into lives that lack the civility of these cultured promenades. Gone are the genteel, the cultured; in their place children in dirt-encrusted clothes, ruffians and painted women, ignored by the blinkered throngs around me marching to their next place of amusement or commerce. The knowledge of this city's workings sickens me, a sight of horror, like a body exposed by the anatomist's knife, but I force myself onwards to my destination.

As Warwick's comes into view, I feel a sense of relief, its familiarity offering safety in a world that suddenly seems so alien; but, as his jaunty bell once again announces my entrance, a feeling of resentment comes over me. Towards Warwick, but also towards myself. I should never have allowed him to drag me from my solitude; my savings could have sufficed for a few more weeks at least. But instead, I am here, exposing myself to his inanities and consolations. Uncharacteristically, Warwick comes forward to meet me on the shop floor, abdicating the authority of his position behind the counter. He greets me with a look of sympathy, as if encountering a wounded animal.

'Charles…' he commiserates, placing a hand on each of my shoulders.

'You wanted to see me?' I ask, coldly.

Warwick takes a breath, then begins to pace back and forth, determining how best to approach the poor broken soul that stands before him. Eventually he decides on the words that strike him as appropriate.

'How are you, Charles?'

'As might be expected.'

He nods as if taking in the profound depths that echo behind my words, offering up nothing in response.

'What can I do for you?' I ask, impatient.

'I thought that, perhaps,' he struggles, 'you might be interested in a return to work?'

'Are you in need of photographers?'

'Always, Charles, always,' he replies, the first semblance of a smile our conversation has prompted playing on his lips. 'But I thought, perhaps, it would be … beneficial. For you. A tonic.' He scans me head to toe. 'It's not healthy for a man to indulge his grief.'

The smile I offer him in return is far less amiable, my teeth bared like a dog about to bite. 'Is that what I'm doing? "Indulging"?' He pulls back from the aggression in my tone.

'I didn't mean anything by it, Charles. I was merely

suggesting…' he stumbles, 'if you'll allow me … that, from my own experience, the distractions of the trivial can sometimes be … beneficial.'

'And what experience is that, pray tell?'

Irony sits heavy on my words, but Warwick appears unphased as if he has finally found a subject on which he can speak with assurance.

'My wife passed a number of years ago,' he explains, 'before I knew you. We had spent twenty wonderful years together.'

'I'm sure your loss was very painful,' I reply, 'and I'm sorry, I truly am. But you had twenty years together – we had three. I'd have my soul burn for twenty years – for another *day*. So don't talk to me about your "experience".'

Warwick flinches again, but this time his hesitation is replaced by a pudgy bravado. 'Charles,' he says, with puff-chested dignity, 'I realise your outburst comes from a place of great difficulty, so I shall refrain from a response. But, I am trying to help you. As a friend. A friend whom I wish to aid.' He ignores the cynicism of my expression and continues regardless. 'I've seen men destroyed by their grief. You need something to keep you tethered to life. A continuity.'

'And what if I don't want to be tethered to life?'

'Then you might as well be done with it.'

Warwick regrets the implication immediately, but his words wake me up like the ice water at Bell Street's Ottoman baths. *Is that what I want?*

To leave this plane behind me. As much as I wish to be reunited with my wife, wherever she may be, I shall not reach there through death. Not if it is by my own hand.

I think of my situation, of what Percy would have wanted, of the coins and banknotes now sparse in my desk drawer. But the idea of going back to the life I knew disgusts me. Knowing what

I know. Seeing what I have seen. Of how little care life has for those that live it.

'If I return,' I reply, 'I'm not photographing any more babies. No more happy families. No more smiling children.'

As I say the words out loud I know that I truly mean them, and so does Warwick. He nods, serious, and then I see an idea forming within him. He pauses, filled with hesitation, his eyes scanning an invisible ledger as he tries to work out the implications of what he is about to offer me.

'Would you say you are a squeamish man, Charles?'

'No more so than the next.'

'Then perhaps there is something I can offer you. It's not for everyone, but there's a good living to be had. If you've got the stomach for it.'

He looks at me, trying to determine if he is making the right decision. I return his gaze, curious for an explanation, but none comes. Instead, he writes down an address, and hands it to me in a gesture filled with a confidence that belies the creases that scour his forehead.

'Be there tomorrow at eleven,' he tells me. 'Then you can decide whether you want to be tethered to our world or not.'

CHAPTER IX

Orpheus descends

I stand outside the Kensington town house, the drizzle falling upon me persistent in its assault. A few droplets find purchase on the brim of my hat, while others flow into a confluence, releasing intermittent drops into the shallow puddle at my feet, splashing my boots with rainwater. The house itself is a stone's throw from the site of the recent exhibition, but where once crowds lined the streets, their bustle has been replaced by a ghostly silence. I have never liked this part of Kensington – too much money, too much white – but today, infused with the melancholy of the weather, its blankness suits me. A sombre limbo that is neither one thing nor the other.

The nothingness in which I reside is interrupted by the sound of horses' hooves on the cobbled street. Their clip-clop, muted by the rain, announces the arrival of a carriage, its top piled with trunks that I have seen enough times to recognise as the tools of my trade. But here there are more. More boxes, more paraphernalia. Curiosity threatens to rouse me from my deadened state, but it knocks gently, as if in respect of my mourning, and, unstirred, I stand as blank as the houses around me, awaiting the carriage's arrival.

The carriage pulls up and a bedraggled man in his forties emerges, his hair thinning, his face soft around the edges and hard in the middle. Yesterday's shave now seems like a distant memory, and bristles litter his chin like the singed brush of a sweep.

'You Charlie?' he asks, his accent coarse, his tone over-familiar.

'Charles,' I correct him.

50

He bares teeth crammed in like paupers in a city slum. I'm sure it's what he considers a smile.

'Most humbly begging your pardon, my good sir,' he replies with mock respect, before continuing in a tone that suggests anything but. 'Grab some boxes and make yourself useful ... *Charles.*' He spits my name like an obscenity, before nodding in the direction of the trunk the driver offers from the roof. I take it and carry it towards the town house behind me, depositing it at the top of the small porch stairs before coming back for another.

'Warwick explain what we're doing?' he asks when we're done.

I shake my head.

'Fair enough. Just do what I do. And keep your mouth shut if you know what's good for ya.'

I nod, and he rises into a more formal pose before lifting the knocker on the front door. For the first time I notice it is tied with the same black crepe as my own. A maid answers and greets us with a whisper.

'I'm Bates, the photographer,' my new colleague replies, the roughness of his manner gone, as if the person I saw before was a trick of the light, 'and this is my assistant, *Charles.*' This time his mockery is more subtle and it goes unnoticed by the maid, who bows her head respectfully and invites us inside.

'If you'd like to follow me to the sitting room.'

I go to grab a case, but Bates stops me.

'Leave it,' he tells me, his urbanity evaporated once again. 'They'll bring it up.' A swarm of servants tiptoe past us at high speed and then start to haul the heavy trunks up the stairs with neither noise nor grace.

'Careful, or I'll break your fucking legs,' Bates growls at one of them in a whisper. The boy looks aghast at the threat, his busywork replaced by delicacy as he communicates the instructions to his colleagues and they rethink their approach.

51

From then on, they carry the trunks one at a time as if they contained the eggs of a rare bird.

The maid leads us deeper into the house, down a corridor to a place where daylight no longer penetrates. The gloom of the outside is replaced by an eerie half-light, that is neither day nor night, the atmosphere heightened by the paintings that line the walls, each one in deep oils, the colours seemingly infused with black. In one, Orpheus attempts to drag Eurydice from the darkness behind her, his lyre in his hand, its whiteness the picture's only sign of hope. Another is a still life where a skull sits amidst carefully arranged flowers and candles, yet strangely seems the only thing alive. But the one that strikes me most is that of a woman. She stands in a nightgown amidst a barren and empty landscape, its sky dark with storm clouds, her expression suggests she is sleeping and yet her eyes are open, wandering nowhere, without purpose, without direction.

'Pssst!' Bates hisses at me from down the corridor and I realise I have halted. Shaking off my bewitchment, I follow him down into the gloom, my glance lingering on the somnambulist's gaze once more as her form fades from view.

We take our places in the sitting room at the rear of the house. The curtains are drawn, the only light is that from a few candles and the dying embers in the untended fireplace.

'What are we…?' I start to ask, but Bates cuts me off.

'You'll see soon enough. Thinking about it beforehand ain't to anyone's benefit.'

I realise for the first time I'm nervous. I hadn't thought it possible in my grief, but I am wary, on edge. I attempt to sit back in my chair, forcing relaxation, but my body fights the posture and my head and shoulders remain detached from the upholstery.

The place is like a temple to death. Taxidermied animals grace the room, sculpted into poses that mimic the vigour of the life that was taken away from them, probably by the very rifle that sits atop the mantle. Snakes and doe-eyed kudu stare at me from every direction, the expression in their glass eyes in turn predatory and docile. I want to block them out, but they offer a strange fascination, looking at me as if they are challenging me to look back, to see past their surfaces to the morbid reality that lies beneath; to the moment of their passing, the unexpected pain, the flesh ripped apart, the lead penetrating their bodies, all cunningly disguised by the taxidermist's art.

'They're ready for you now.'

I turn to see the maid in the doorway. Bates nods sullenly, and stands up, walking out of the room without looking in my direction. I follow.

The stairs moan beneath our feet as we ascend, the smooth banister cold and clammy against my palm.

'Through here.'

The maid gestures in the direction of a curtained doorway as we reach the top flight. Bates leads us towards it, then draws back the scarlet fabric and enters. I follow close behind.

The room is dark save for the flickering halo of candlelight that rings the bed and outlines the figures that surround it in silhouette. What must be ten family members stand there in silent vigil. A creaking floorboard alerts one of them to our presence and the man peels off from the group, the others following suit like parting waves, opening up a passage for us to the bed. As we pass them, I can feel their furtive glances upon us, a mixture of respect and fear.

Beneath the blankets lies the body of an elderly man, his head ensconced in the valley of a pillow. His position suggests he is sleeping, but his real state is plain to see, and, despite his closed eyes, his expression of peace no longer convinces me, a muntjack minutes after the slaughter.

As we draw closer to the corpse, images of Percy start to suffocate me; her body lying in our bed, as still as the specimen before me, her bloodied sheets hidden by fresh blankets, the remains of our child wrapped in cloth in the room below. Panic starts to overtake me, crawling over my skin like tiny spiders, and I realise I have to get out. I look towards the exit, trying not to upset the dignity of the scene, trying not to show my distress, but, as I start to edge backwards, I feel these people's expectations upon me. They are looking to me for something. To perform a role, a service. And even though I begin to suspect what that service might be, the sense of duty calms me, and I find my breathing becoming slower, more measured.

Ahead, I see Bates talking to the dead man's widow. She looks strong; composed and formidable despite her loss. She nods assent to Bates's instructions and he walks over to me.

'Do you know how to flow a plate?'

I nod.

'Good. They'll clear the room, and then we can get to work.' His back to the room, he flashes me a wonky grin as if to let me know how little he cares about the scene unfolding behind him, and then returns to the widow, a picture of respectability once more.

***

We stand in silence as the mourners file out of the room, leaving the two of us with the body and the maid. As the last family member exits, Bates drops his decorum like a whore's gown.

'Let's get the fucker dressed then shall we?' he announces, upbeat, before turning to the maid. 'Sure you have more than a passing acquaintance with his drawers?'

She looks flustered but tries to hide it, going to the wardrobe to fulfil this strange man's request.

Bates rips open the curtains and light floods the room. He chews his lip as he scans his surroundings, trying to find the corner most suited to his purpose.

'Right,' he says, his eyes alighting on a suitable location. 'I'll set up over there. You help her with the body.' Bates throws a handkerchief in my direction. 'Tie this round his 'ead. Don't want him open-mouthed for the photographs,' he barks, before letting out a crude laugh. My expression of uncertainty prompts him to another crooked smile. 'Under the bottom, over the top,' he tells me, as if addressing an idiot. 'Think Jacob Marley.'

What we are about to do hits me with full force. I have heard of these people. The photographers of the dead. But they were a world away from my existence, from my reality. Bates, however, doesn't allow me a moment with my thoughts.

'Come on, hup to it. I was told you wanted to work, not stare off into the distance like William fucking Wordsworth. Sit him in the chair and she can go from there.'

The maid lays the dead man's clothes over a chaise, pretending not to have heard another of the obscenities that spray from Bates's mouth like spittle.

I go over to the bed, and peel back the blankets, trying to steel myself for the task. Reaching down, I hook my hands under the man's arms, bringing his face uncomfortably close to mine. I react instinctively, moving my head to one side to avoid his breath upon me. A moment later, I realise he has none. Pulling the body to sitting, the head lolls back at an impossible angle. I try not to give it notice, but its proximity allows me no escape, and as I wrench the body from the bed clothes, standing to full height, I fear the head itself may snap off.

The dead man is smaller than me, but his body has a surprising weight, as if dispossessed of the lightness that soul provides. I edge backwards towards the chair that Bates has set up, the dead man's gnarled toes dragging along the wooden floor behind him. Looking down at my load, I see the man's mouth has flopped open as Bates suggested it might. The sight distracts me, and I find myself tripping over a raised board flat onto my back.

A moment of shock is followed by the sudden awareness of the body above me, the cold skin of its face pressed against mine. Repulsion runs through me, and I attempt to squirm out from underneath, struggling with its mass, before finally pushing the corpse to the side where its face plants gracelessly onto the floor.

'Ain't you got no respect for the dead, Charlie?' Bates laughs. 'Could do without breaking his nose before we start setting 'im up, if that's all right with you? Come on.'

Bates grabs the man's legs and we lift the body to the chair together. He examines the abrasions on the dead man's cheek, but looks unphased, brushing his hands together, as if to clean them of non-existent dust. Impatiently, he snatches the handkerchief I still hold in my hand, and wraps it under the man's chin, tying it in a knot at the top before turning to the maid.

'Right, little missy,' he instructs her. 'Put some clothes on 'im.'

She busies herself as he turns to me, 'Not the best part of the job, but it's got to be done. You might need to help if she's struggling. If it's a nice bit of frock they usually insist on doing it on their own though. Shame,' he continues in a drawled whisper, 'only time you wouldn't mind lending a hand.' He flashes me a smile that makes me sick to my stomach.

Bates gestures towards the trunks in an offhand manner. 'Stuff's in there.'

I open the trunk to be presented with the trappings of my craft. The bottles and trays provide a comforting familiarity in this strange world in which I have found myself, the cold of the glass between my fingers a stabilising influence.

I begin to set up the lab, familiarising myself with the feel of the bottles, so I will be able to identify them when I withdraw to darkness in the upcoming minutes. Out of the corner of my eye, I see Bates arranging various stands and clamps around the chaise longue. The maid has now stripped the body of its nightshirt, and the cadaver sits slumped in the chair in its greying underwear. She wrestles his arms into a starched shirt, and I feel glad she has not requested my assistance, her proprietary instincts serving me well. The sheer practicality of the process sends a shiver through me, and I am glad to have the distraction of my own work to focus my attention on.

By the time the plate is ready to be flowed, the body has been dressed and arranged, in situ on the chaise in a position that mimics that of a sitter on any given day in a London photography studio. The effect is disturbingly lifelike. The man looks as if he is merely resting his eyes between exposures, preparing himself for the next photograph. But, as I walk around the diorama, the changing angles reveal a network of stands and fixings suspending the corpse in place. Bates touches up its face with powders to disguise the sallowness of the man's cheeks, then turns to me, revealing his tombstone grin once more.

'Time to fetch the missus then.'

***

When the woman of the house enters, the tableau she sees before her has a dramatic effect. The widow, who had previously seemed unflappable, stumbles and almost loses her balance, her maidservant rushing to her elbow to offer support. The woman raises a hand to cover her open mouth, before managing to reclaim her poise with a few snatched breaths. A moment later she is unceremoniously pushing the maid away, before walking over to Bates and her husband's sedentary corpse.

Bates takes her by the hand and touches her arm. 'This will be disconcerting for you, but it is unfortunately necessary to achieve the desired photographic effect.' She nods in understanding and he offers her a sympathetic smile before turning to me and rolling his eyes.

Bates takes her to the chaise, where she sits next to her husband while he explains the process, before returning to consider the composition through the camera. He gestures me over to examine what will be the frame. From the shooting angle, the effect is perfect, husband and wife sitting together, receiving visitors on a Sunday afternoon. The only giveaway, the man's unopened eyes.

'Thank you so much for doing this,' the widow enunciates to us from across the room. 'We never had a photograph together before.' She is almost in tears as she speaks. 'I sometimes think he was ashamed of me.'

'Well,' Bates whispers in my ear, 'he ain't got much of a fucking choice now, has he?'

Before I can react he is replacing the curtain over the window, sealing up any gaps where the light can peek through. Then, he picks up his pre-prepared candle, now the room's sole source of illumination and nods towards my work bench, where I take my place, ready to finish my preparations.

He licks his fingers, and extinguishes the flame with a flourish, plunging us into complete darkness; so the miracle can begin.

CHAPTER X

The Haymarket

We sit in a panelled coffee shop, dimly lit by a scattering of oil lamps. Opposite me, Bates seems distracted, his eyes constantly darting around the room. Perhaps in search of acquaintances, perhaps merely to size up the unsavoury characters that occupy the neighbouring booths. The place puts me on edge. Violence simmers below the surface of every conversation that drifts towards us, each table seemingly alive with impropriety and conspiracy.

A waitress approaches our table, sporting an asymmetric smile. It vanishes the moment she clocks Bates.

He gives her a sarcastic grin, then hands over what looks like a couple of chops wrapped in paper. 'Bread, butter and coffee. And put these on the grill, will ya? I'll have a brandy while I'm waiting. And one for my friend.'

The waitress looks at me strangely, and I feel a tingle of embarrassment at being associated with such an unmannerly creature. But Bates has already seemingly lost interest, and the woman takes the chops and heads back towards the kitchen. As she leaves the table, Bates turns his eyes to her once more, ogling her behind with undisguised lust.

'I enjoy her trips to the kitchen. When I can see her face, I get the impression she doesn't like me.'

I deny him the smile he expects in return, and he scoffs, before returning his stare to her backside.

'Perhaps if you were a little more courteous,' I suggest.

'Courtesy's for them that benefits from it, Charlie. When you

59

do what I do, people ain't that open to liking. Still, when you got cash, whether people like you or not, they tend to be obliging.'

'I think you'd be surprised by the benefits good manners can bring.'

'Would I, Charlie? Would I?' he mocks, lampooning my reasonableness. 'I could shower that dirty puzzle with pleases and thank-yous till judgement day; she'd still be wearing her bloody married face.'

I shake my head in exasperation. The man is beyond hope. But for a second he looks at me seriously, the simmering amusement of his normal conversation gone.

'You don't understand, Charlie,' he explains. 'People are scared of us. You spend enough time around dead bodies, it rubs off. People start treating you like one.'

The waitress returns and dumps two glasses of brandy on the table.

'Thank you, my dear,' says Bates in his best work voice. 'I am much obliged to you for your diligent service.'

The waitress sneers before turning her back on us, and I begin to suspect he might have a point. Then he lets out a laugh.

'Your plate work's good,' he tells me. 'Nice coverage. You got a knack. Last fella I worked with couldn't flow a plate to save his life. Shaking it like he was fetching the bloody mettle. Look at this.'

He pulls a print from his satchel, and my curiosity overcomes my recoil at his crudity. The photograph is of a middle-aged man. The print is good apart from the white splodges and black dots in the upper-right corner, and a speckled texture that powders the middle of the man's jacket where the plate wasn't cleaned properly.

'There's dust on the negative,' I observe. 'The pour's uneven.'

'And that was the best of the bunch,' Bates grins.

It suddenly strikes me. What the picture is of.

'Wait a minute, is he…?' I leave the word unspoken.

'I didn't take it for my health,' Bates replies. 'Certainly not for his.'

I look more closely at the picture – it had me fooled completely. The man looks … alive. A strange mixture of feeling runs through me, repulsion at what I am looking at, mixed with a complete fascination at the effect that has been so perfectly achieved. And then I realise why it is that I have been deceived so completely. The man's eyes. They're open.

'How did you…?'

'Tricks of the trade, Charlie. Tricks of the trade.'

I look again at the picture, then back to Bates. He can see the hunger in my eyes.

'Not saying I can't teach you. Just depends if you can cope with working alongside a ruffian like me,' he smiles. 'Question is: do you want them looking at you the way they look at me?'

I flick through a few more pictures. Each one is marred by technical imperfections, but the photographs themselves are miraculous.

'These are … incredible.'

'Good sitters, the dead. Don't start looking round halfway through the exposure,' he jokes, attempting to laugh off my compliment, but there is a note of pride in his voice at the recognition of a skill that has rarely seen praise, and I notice a softening in him. 'Look, I know my manners ain't all that, Charlie, but the people I keep company with don't seem to mind.'

He looks at me differently, as if taking the prospect of us working together seriously for the first time. 'There's worse out there to be spending your days with. The dead don't steal from you, lie to you; don't whisper sweet nothings in your ear and take your money while you're sleeping. No, they ain't so bad, the dead. It's the living you got to watch out for.'

His words float on the silence between us, and I realise that I too am beginning to consider the possibility of working together.

The waitress reappears, unceremoniously depositing his chops on the table, along with our bread and coffee. Her briskness hoists me out of my thoughts, and I thank her with a polite smile. She turns her back on me without so much as an acknowledgement, as if I am already tainted by the same malaise that surrounds Bates. A shiver runs through me at the rejection, just as a new figure appears at the table. The man is dressed in threadbare clothes, his hair sparse, his face elongated and malformed like hardened wax drippings on a well-used candle holder.

'All right, Bates?' he slurs, reeking of cheap gin. 'Decided to honour us mortals with yer presence again 'ave you?'

'Get lost, Farley.' Bates spits the words through a mouthful of pork, affecting to ignore the man, but I see his fingers gripping tighter around the knife in his right hand.

'Always the conversationalist,' Farley continues, refusing to take the hint. 'You could learn from him,' he says, turning to me. 'Can keep an audience enraptured for hours.'

Farley flashes me a blackened smile, and I feel myself physically inch away. I don't like this man. I thought I didn't like Bates, but seeing this weasel before me puts my previous feelings into relief. 'So how are you Batesy? I've known him since he was this high,' Farley tells me with an accompanying gesture. 'When Mr Bates was Master Ba—'

'And you was cracking the same jokes even then,' Bates interrupts, cutting him off mid-sentence and forcing him to regroup.

'Had your way with any bodies recently?' Farley slurs. 'My mother's on her last legs. I'm sure she'd appreciate you repositioning her limbs a little before she kicks the bucket.'

'Can't afford her fees, Farley.'

For the first time, Farley seems to react, his head jerking to one side as if pulled by a noose, but he returns to his swaying equilibrium almost instantly, the expression in his eyes wily and calculating behind the fog of drunkenness.

'I'll let that go on account of you being about to buy an old friend a drink,' he smiles.

Bates smiles back. 'Didn't I tell you to go?'

'Sorry – I was forgetting. Buying drinks ain't your style.'

'Never just one though is it, Farley; never just one… That scoundrel you call a brother still lurking round? You'll know if you see him, Charlie, ugly as this one and parts his hair with a towel.' Bates shows me the mask of a smile, and I turn to the room, looking for the aforementioned.

A snatch of motion on the edge of my vision pulls my gaze back to the table, and Bates's hand darts beneath the scarred oak of the table, emerging moments later with a skeletal arm in its grip. The arm's owner follows his limb's trajectory, as his baldpate appears above the tabletop like a whale surfacing from the ocean.

'Here he is now,' Bates announces, as casually as if the man had walked through the door from the street. 'Charlie – allow me to introduce Limmy – Farley 'ere's brother. As fine a cunt as you ever saw. On 'is knees beneath the table again – anyone would think we was at the Argyll.'

Limmy starts to pull his mouth into a grimace, only to find the point of Bates's chop knife an inch from his eyeball.

'I see your hand round my pocket again and you'll be telling people why you're wearing an eye patch in a high voice – you get that?' He pushes Limmy backwards, and the man's brittle body collapses inelegantly to the crusted wood of the floor.

Limmy dusts himself off as he raises himself to his feet in an attempt to regain the dignity he never had. 'Can't blame a fella for tryin', Bates,' he spits, by way of an apology.

The smug satisfaction of his reply irks me, and I find my ire rising to the surface. 'Leave us alone, scoundrel.'

'Oh heavens!' mocks Limmy, his accent a pastiche of gentility. 'He thinks I'm a scoundrel! 'Ow will my reputation ever recover?'

'*Leave*,' I continue, rising to my feet; but Limmy's fear has left him, and he steps forward towards the table, swollen up like a scarecrow on a windy day.

'I'd like to see you make me, you fucking Mary.'

He lurches forward suddenly, and I stumble backwards into my pew. Limmy looks at me, then laughs, amused by the effectiveness of his feint and I suddenly feel ashamed, embarrassed at my instinctive cowardice. But, as I look back at him, I realise it's more than that – the wariness, the repugnance I feel – it's not just to this man. It's to everything: this place, this world they inhabit, and, as I think towards escape, to the world outside, I find my feelings of repulsion infecting it too, consuming everything in their path like a cancer, until all is infected, unclean.

Farley grabs his brother by the arm and drags him away from the table.

'Let's leave them to their dinner. Don't want the "Mary" having an 'eart attack before he's finished 'is coffee.'

As they walk off, I feel the rush of confrontation flood through my body, my muscles tingling with alertness, the movement of my hand to my mouth coloured with the subtle shaking of conflict.

I turn back to Bates. He is staring at me, and I am surprised to find his expression free of the mockery of the brothers who now stand in a corner across the room.

'Who were those men?' I ask.

Bates stuffs a chunk of fatty pork into his mouth before answering, slowly chewing in rumination. He swallows, then picks a piece of gristle from his teeth with the point of the knife that a minute earlier was threatening to blind his fellow human being.

'The living, Charlie. The living.'

***

The fresh air is bracing after the stagnation of the coffee house, but the darkness that has fallen outside surprises me, despite the hour. The streets, as usual, are lit with gas lamps, but two in every three have been smashed, incapacitated. This place is wont for darkness, and those that walk the streets seem to revel in the cloak that it provides. Strangely, the lamps' meagre flames only seem to intensify the blackness – denying my eyes the adjustment they make every evening as I walk the unlit path to my cottage.

Bates takes a deep breath, drinking in the cold with a chaser of snuff – a thimbleful of the stuff snorted into his right nostril. He offers a pinch in my direction, but I shake my head, and he shrugs a 'suit yourself', shoving a second dose up his left. As we stroll down the ill-lit street, the place strikes me as a modern day Gomorrah – as alien a world as one could imagine, all just ten minutes from the studio in which I ply my trade. A group of the well-heeled stumble out from behind a rickety door, some raucous, others despondent and subdued, followed by a man dragging dogs on a lead, and holding the massacred corpse of a badger in his blood-drenched hand. A pack of women descend on the men in an instant, successfully peeling off members of the group and leading them into alleyways and boarding houses, until all that is left are a pair whose allowance has already been squandered. Other men are not so modest, engaging in encounters in darkened corners in the sight of any who choose to surreptitiously glance at them, of which there are many. Still more play cards and dice at folding tables beside makeshift fires, or bully passers-by, friend and strangers alike, the encounters occasionally descending into violence, each time attracting a crowd as eager for bloodshed as those that watch the animal baiting.

But it's the women who disconcert me the most. They are everywhere, their face paints heavy and absurd, entrancing me with feelings that stalk the boundary between attraction and repulsion. My wariness towards them is cut through with Percy's concern. She'd often talk of the plight of these women – denied the right to respectability, forced into the servitude of intimacy in order to put food on the table – but here they don't seem like that at all. Their veil of unquenchable desire for company is all too convincing to my male eyes, and I feel ashamed once again to be both foolish (and base) enough to be taken in.

I see a young man emerge from an alleyway with one of them, blond curls overflowing beneath his hat, his grin quickly replaced by a look of panic as he feels his jacket pocket, emptied through the knife slit at its base. He has lost his innocence in more ways than one tonight, but sympathy seems like an abstraction with which I cannot engage. Each of these people is merely dressing to my story (as I'm sure I am to theirs). It is only when Bates starts to talk, that I remember I am not alone.

'See anything you like?'

'I … no.'

'You're young, Charlie – you got needs. Ain't nothin' wrong with needs.'

As if an actress waiting on her cue, a young woman materialises from the corner she has been skulking in. She's younger than most out here, but a woman at least (unlike the poor child I see flit into a doorway with a man old enough to be her grandfather). Her face still has the freshness of youth, so she is free of the pastes and rouges of her older colleagues, the only nod to her profession the dark cherry of her lips. When she speaks, the coarseness of her tone is unexpected, jarring.

'Lookin' for a good time darlin'?'

'I'm always looking for a good time,' says Bates winking, 'but I ain't found it outside a stiff drink and a meat pie.' He keeps moving, the interaction doing nothing to break the rhythm of his step.

'What about you, honeybun?' she asks, trailing behind.

'No ... no, thank you.'

She mistakes the stumble in my voice for interest, and pursues us, walking alongside.

'If it's a sweetheart you're worrying about, gorgeous, she don't need to know,' she says, touching my arm. 'Or is it an absent lover, far across the seas?' She imbues the words with a degree of theatricality that makes it clear she doesn't care if her suggestion is true, and I shouldn't either. 'I could be her. I could be anyone you want.'

'He said *no*,' growls Bates, coming to a sudden halt for emphasis. 'Not in the mood for a bun that's already been buttered, love.' Her face contorts into disdain, displaying the lines that soon she will hide with French chalk like her older colleagues. A second later, she has turned her back on us to seek more forthcoming clientele, her departure accompanied by an elegant farewell.

'Go fuck yourselves.'

Bates laughs, but Percy's words must have had more effect on me than I thought. Rather than balk at her crudity, I feel a strange kind of sadness come over me; sadness that we live in a world where one as young as her can be brought so low, where a girl's virtue can have the life strangled out of it by the cruel hands of necessity.

'I don't know how they can do this,' I say, shaking my head.

'They're just offering a service, Charlie. Ain't nothing wrong

67

with that,' he replies, matter-of-fact. 'Not that different from us when you think about it.'

He mistakes my look of doubt for a question.

'It's a noble art, Charlie – taking something dead, and, just for a moment, making it live. There's magic in that. You got an education, who's that fella that made the people from mud – the Greek one?'

'Prometheus.'

'That's the one. Well – that's what we do – sculpt the clay, mould it into human form, and then the camera comes along, and…' he blows out theatrically, 'breathes in life.'

A woman in her forties, her frame leant against a ramshackle doorway, sees us approaching and reaches out both hands to Bates, a big smile on her face. She touches his face tenderly as he approaches. She's clearly a prostitute, but there's an affection between them that goes beyond what he's about to pay for. Bates turns back to me.

'People may scorn us Charlie, but we give 'em something. As much as they whisper behind our backs, throw us their little sidelong glances, we let 'em see their loved ones again. That's beautiful. Did your husband after he passed didn't I, Clarissa?'

The woman nods with a sad smile, and for the first time I notice a scar down one side of her face; a wound once deep, now 'healed', yet forever present, a raised line of pink tissue dividing her cheek in two, a story that can never be untold.

'If there's a need, Charlie, sooner or later, someone's gonna fill it. That's 'ow life is. And like I said – there ain't nothin' wrong with 'avin' needs.' As if to illustrate, he brings his face close to Clarissa's and their lips touch lasciviously. I turn away only to find myself face to face with the debauchery of the street – the same sordid interactions as before, only the faces and details changed.

'So Charlie – the question is: who you gonna choose? The living or the dead?'

I turn back to him, distaste running through every vein of my body. 'The living I can do without.'

'Your apprenticeship continues tomorrow,' he tells me, all traces of amusement gone from his voice. He disappears into the void of the doorway. 'Walk that way a couple of minutes and you'll hit Piccadilly. Hope you can find your way back out.'

CHAPTER XI

What goes around their neck…

I stand in the mid-morning cold, waiting for the steamer to arrive. Underfoot is the river's bed, uncovered by the low tide, sloping grey and gritty down towards the water's edge. The fog hangs heavy but lacks the murkiness of London's coal-coloured mists. Through it, I can make out my fellow travellers, silent and wrapped in black, staring out blankly towards the Thames. The pale faces of children poke out from under their mother's shawls, each one mirroring the expressions of the adults that stand behind them. In their parents I see my own desire to be done with things, to forget, but perhaps that is merely a trick of the mind; a wish that we were standing before the Lethe rather than the cloudy waters of the Thames.

The journey is slow and plodding, but that suits my mood, as does the price. I find a place on the edge of the deck, watching the current as it pushes against us, empowered by the tidal swells of the river. My fellow passengers are wrapped in blankets, huddled round the middle of the deck where the heat of the engine leaks its warmth. The stink of the river increases as we pass Putney and Hammersmith, but so does the crowd, and by the time we reach Westminster I feel relief at not being one of those cramped in at the boat's centre, an umbrella of black smoke spewed up by the high chimney above their heads.

As we approach Blackfriars Bridge Pier, I find myself transfixed by the bridge's absence. Just a few years ago it seemed an unassailable part of the capital, now I stare at the space where it once was, nothingness carved into its shape by my mind's eye.

Leaving the boat, I walk up the banked street towards my appointment, foolishly tossing a penny to a wretched woman pleading for her offspring. Within moments the vultures are upon me; men, women and children, their faces all sallow with hunger, hands outstretched in the hope that my generosity has not reached its limit. But were I to give them everything, their wants would not be sated, their needs would not be met, and I find myself quickening my step, the whip at my back impotence underscored with fear.

I lose them as the density of walkers increases, and by the time I reach Ludgate Hill, I find myself in a swell of people. The crowd pushes towards Newgate prison, and they drag me along in their current, the stench of bodies recalling the river itself. Unlike the steamer, I have no need to fight the crowd's flow, and I let myself be swept onwards in their mass, relieved to vanish for a moment in the mindless throng.

As the roads open up to Newgate, the source of their excitement becomes clear. Across the courtyard, before the prison, a raised platform that is to be the stage for a hanging towers twenty feet above the watching crowds. A small chain fence marks the platform's boundary, mere ornament compared to the wooden one below that keeps the hungry onlookers at bay. It seems like an acknowledgement by the powers that be that, should the condemned man attempt to escape and deny the crowds their entertainment, his fate would be worse than execution; the barriers there present for his protection rather than his imprisonment.

The prisoner steps forward, the hangman at his arm, and the crowd erupts into boos and jeers. Their enthusiasm sickens me, and I turn away, pushing against the crowd up towards Smithfields, desperate to distance myself from the noose before the event takes place.

I am a few streets away when I hear them cheer.

'This goes round their neck.'

Bates moves back from the stand he has just assembled; a vertical metal pole, with an arm like a two-pronged fork extending out from it at right angles. It's similar to the posing stands I've used for years to help sitters hold their poses during exposures, only this one is weighted at the bottom for structural support. It lacks the usual padded headrest of the posing stands. Although the dead may require comfort in their caskets, outside of their final resting place, their demands are lesser.

'Right – first question you ask a client: do they want them dead or alive? Don't think I need to tell you, but you may need to afternoonify the language a little.' He walks over to the woman's corpse on the chaise in the corner of the room, a crate wedged under her legs bending them at right angles at the knees and hips. Bates doesn't mention it, instead addressing the corpse with the overemphasised tones he uses to lampoon civility.

'Would the good lady prefer to recline in the eternal repose of sleep, or sit up as if she is about to drop one?' The lack of respect he normally shows for the dead is compounded this time by the absence of company, and my obvious distaste for his gallows humour.

'A lot of people want 'em sleeping nowerdays – takes all the fun out of it as far as I'm concerned. Like to imagine them at peace – particularly if it's their kid – convince themselves that they'll see them again when they "awake on the day of judgement".' He scoffs at the thought, but his mention of children blindsides me. It wasn't something I'd thought of.

'Children… I don't want to do children.'

'Suit yourself, Charlie. But a job's a job. Point is: *ask*. You don't want them expecting sleeping beauty, then walking in to find their loved one sitting up like they want a fucking cuppa.'

He looks at me, my thoughts still on the possibility of doing this to a child. To my child. 'Look, Charlie – no one's gonna make you do anything you don't wanna do – but you need to toughen up a bit – your skin's thinner than a whore's nightgown. Still – best to push 'em away from sleeping if you can. Can't charge as much if you ain't performed a miracle. Right – give me a hand with the lady of the manor.'

Together we lift the body towards the chair. She's stiff in a way yesterday's corpse wasn't, rigor mortis having taken hold of her form, and Bates lets me take the legs. Locked in their bend, the bulk of the weight is pushed towards me, but Bates still struggles with the lift, the tobacco that he's smoked and snorted over the years taking its toll. 'Not so light on her feet as she was a few weeks ago, I'll 'azard a guess,' he pants, laughing at his own joke in the absence of an appreciative audience. We put her in the chair, the bend of her legs fitting perfectly into a sitting position, and Bates holds her by the shoulders as he continues with his instruction.

'The chair is your friend, the backdrop's your friend. Anything you can use to hide the stands, or take their place,' he explains, 'but that don't mean you ain't gonna 'ave to improvise. Every single one you do is different, so you gotta find a way to make 'em work. Take this one for instance – she's a little what you'd call "top 'eavy" if you know what I mean.'

He lets go of her shoulders and she starts to tip forward before he grabs her again.

'Probably served 'er well in life, but right now her kettle drums is only gonna mess things up for us. Chuck us that bag.'

I hand him the portmanteau that he is referring to, and he gestures for me to take the weight of her shoulders. Bates pulls out some scissors, and starts to cut up the back of the woman's dress, making a small hole in it, before pulling out a rope and threading it under her clothing and around the front of her body.

73

'Beggin' your pardon, Missus!' He guides the end of the rope back round to the hole, before pulling it out and tying it to the chair. And then he tells me to let go.

I tentatively take my hands away and the woman's body remains vertical.

'And she's up! It's easier 'ere in the studio – and not just 'cos you got a proper lab – you probably ain't noticed, but the chair's nailed to the floor.'

He tips her head up and clamps it back into the neck stand. 'There's no rules to this – you do what you 'ave to. Tie 'em, prop 'em, stick a nail through their hand if that's what it needs. It was good enough for Jesus…' he says smiling. 'It's the end result that matters. If you can't see it, it ain't there. Not like they're going to be complaining anyway!'

He finishes tightening the clamp. 'This thing's always a problem,' he says offhandedly, indicating the prongs around her neck. 'It's why you ask 'em to send 'em with their hair down. Not that they always do.' He draws out a lock of her hair to the front of the head and uses it to cover the ends of the clamp. 'Done.'

We finish the rest of the arrangements, neatening up the woman's clothing and arranging her arms. The left goes snugly into her lap, whereas the other won't bend as we want it to. Bates sighs, then pulls it out to the side.

'You may want to turn away for this one, Charlie.'

I shrug, doubting that anything can phase me after our previous hour's work, and Bates raises his knee to her elbow. He jerks her hand back, and breaks the woman's arm at the joint in a single motion. The sound of it snapping rings through me and I spend the next five minutes at the window, trying to get air so as not to be sick. When I turn back, everything is prepared. Both hands are in her lap, and she sits in the two-dimensional library of Bates's set, relaxed and at ease, but something is still not right.

'The eyes?' I ask, tentatively.

'The eyes…' Bates echoes, 'the eyes, the eyes, the eyes…' He goes to the corpse and beckons me over. 'Try 'em.'

Reluctantly I join him, and hesitantly touch them. The cold of the skin makes me jerk my hand away, but Bates signals for me to try again, and I push through the repulsion I feel and try to open them.

'They're stuck.'

'Rigor mortis, ain't it? The eyelids is the first to go. So, if you got a subject that's as stiff as a John's whore-pipe, you know they ain't gonna open.'

'However – catch 'em early enough, you can usually force 'em up with a teaspoon. You take the 'andle, and push the bottom down and the top one up – bottom's easy, but the top 'uns a beggar. It'll flop down, so you really gotta force it till it sticks. Needle and thread's 'andy if it won't stay. 'Course, then you're left with a couple of eyes pointin' in different directions, which ain't to most people's tastes (although I think it lends them a certain confused charm), so you have to move them till they're lookin' at the camera. You can use the spoon if you want, but your finger's better. Not that you'll be takin' that route I imagine.'

His words conjure the images in my mind, and I find myself unable to contradict him.

'Luckily for you – most people don't want that. Particularly if they're gonna sit with 'em. Plus, like Pandora's Box, once they're open, they ain't easy to get closed – beggin' your pardon if your name's Pandora love – and most of your clientelle ain't so keen on seein' their loved ones staring at them for the four days until the funeral. So – in situations like this, you got to resort to other methods.'

He pulls a flat wooden box out of his bag, and a fine, dainty paintbrush.

''Ope you got a steady 'and.'

***

I stand back out of the light, while Bates paints upon the woman's eyelids. First, he applies a base of white, then, after cleaning his brush, he draws a black line at the top to mimic the lashes. I watch on with perverse fascination.

'If it's a sitting like we did the other day – someone with a pulse wants to sit in, I mean – you paint 'em on the print. Don't want them soiling themselves before the shoot – get enough of that with the corpses.'

He details the edge of the iris and then the pupil, large and open to the world.

'But in situations like this, the eyelids is far more practical. This way it's on the negative, so you can do multiple prints with minimal effort.'

I lean in more closely to examine his work – it's crude but does the job. He cleans his brush again to colour the iris. 'The temptation is to copy the eye colour, but not if its—'

'Blue.'

'Exactly – you do know somethin' after all. Safest to go with a brown – unless their eyes was really light, then you can push the boat out and use a green – the yellows give enough pigment to come through. There. Want to do the other one?'

I take the brush from him, and paint the white base on the other eyelid, then begin to work on the detail in black. My wariness around the corpse is quickly displaced by the concentration necessary for the work, and I find myself absorbed in the task, trying to keep the outlines smooth while the brush catches on the folds of the loose skin. On finishing the pupil, Bates looks at me and nods approvingly, handing me a rag and a palette with the brown paint.

The iris coloured, we stand back together from the corpse. The

76

eye I painted is obviously inferior to Bates's, but it's not completely without merit. Bates takes the brush from me and enlarges the pupil with black, until the sizes match, then joins me once more, and we nod at one another. It feels that somehow the gap between us has narrowed and, when he speaks again, although his words are as crude as ever, his tone is softer, as if he is no longer using them to keep me at a distance.

'Now, from where we're standing she's obviously a fucking monstrosity, but over here by the camera…' We walk away from the labyrinth of poles, stands and ropes supporting the body towards the place from where the photograph will be taken.

'Old Mother Hubbard has once again joined the ranks of the living…'

Here, the composition is as effective as yesterday's – more so with the corpse's eyes painted on and the controlled lighting and setting of Bates's studio. He turns to me with a grin. 'Want to get your plate done?'

I nod and head to the room he uses as a lab, returning a few minutes later with a plate to load into the camera. The preparations complete, Bates turns to me and smiles.

'If you'd like to do the honours,' he says, pulling out his pocket watch to time the exposure, while I move to the lens cap, waiting to remove it on his cue. 'The dead can live again.'

***

The atmosphere in the public house near the studio is raucous and unwieldy, but here, unlike at the coffee house, my self-appointed mentor seems part of the place, rather than an outsider. I stand at the bar, away from Bates and his cronies, leaning against the polished mahogany of the counter, a small part of the elegant parlour beyond that has somehow strayed into this space. Here it sits ill at ease, surrounded by the rough wood of the taproom, but it provides me something to hold onto as I drink. As much as I don't want to be here, I cannot stomach the trip back to my cottage, and alcohol seems my only hope of getting any sleep on the chaise at my old studio. With that in mind, I down my brandy and order a pint of porter. Perhaps a night away from the cottage will do me good, but I doubt it.

'Charlie!' Bates calls from across the room. 'Come over 'ere, I 'ave some personages desirous of your acquaintance.' He laughs, amused at his own wit, and I wander over – decency and good manners still holding me in their thrall, despite my desire to be left alone.

'Right,' announces Bates as I join the group, 'this is Charlie – a newcomer to our ranks. He's a proper gentleman and everything, but don't hold that against him. Underneath, 'e's not so bad.'

Bates makes the introductions. They're a ragtag bunch if ever I saw one – on the periphery are a few faces I recognise from the shadows at Warwick's, people who lurk in the corners while the world goes about its business, but the rest are strangers. 'Thread' is as long and thin as his name might suggest and sits ill in his clothes – his egg-like head seemingly balanced on his neck as if not truly attached. Joe is short and round – his skin unusually smooth and hairless, but jollier than you'd imagine a man in this profession could be. Lucas barely moves in his seat, a personification of lethargy, except when a crude joke takes his fancy, and he explodes with laughter, like a geyser unplugged. Andreas is Austrian and so old he looks like he probably still works in daguerreotype, but he has a pleasant air about him, if undercut with snideness. It's strange seeing Bates among them – I had imagined him without friends, without associates – but here, he seems part of some kind of … community. An archipelago of islands united in their rejection by the world, but, although I stand in their midst, I am immune to the joy their revels seem to bring them, the distance between the shores of our experience too wide to traverse.

I walk down Holborn with them after they leave the public house, refusing their invitation to a supper club, knowing the bawdy songs and enforced jollity would sit uneasy with me. At the edge of Covent Garden, I take my leave, heading towards Scott's for my supper where I dine at the counter on oysters and sprats with plenty of bread to soak up my inebriation, but in my current mood, the experience seems as dry as the day-old loaf they serve.

It is at the far edge of Leicester Square that I see her.

The same curls in vivid red that I have woken up next to time and time again, disappearing around a corner into a side street. I shake myself to my senses, knowing that it cannot be so, but it is as if I am in a dream, not questioning how or why she is here, only knowing one thing: that there, not far away, is Percy.

She vanishes into the alley and I find myself pushing through the crowds to follow. The women and swells that block my way vent their protestations as I barge past, but their indignation is soon forgotten, or perhaps I merely pay it no heed, for I have but one thought – to reach her.

Leaving the square behind me, I enter a back street, scanning my surroundings to find she is gone, releasing a breath I had no idea I had been holding. But then, she is there again, a streak of colour in the distance, manifesting from the darkness like a will-o'-the-wisp. She vanishes once more around a corner, and I sprint across the street towards her, narrowly missed by a passing carriage. Running along a footpath at the road's edge, I ignore the mocking solicitations and calls of 'she must be somethin'' from the wits around me, turning as I reach the junction, only to find a street devoid of life. In a pique of desperation, I continue onwards, the ground reverberating through my body with every stride. Then, at the next corner, she is there again, a moment later absent, our game of hide and seek continuing, but lacking the joy of childhood, in place of its lightness, the desperation of an escaped prisoner. Or lunatic.

Each glance of red taunts me with hope, and I push myself way past discomfort until my breath can no longer support me, and, finding myself in a dead-end alley, I collapse to my knees, breathless and confused in the near darkness, a single oil lamp fixed next to a doorway inset in the wall my only source of light.

A man and woman appear from the door a moment later, and I see beyond them what appears to be the backstage of a theatre. They edge away from me as they shuffle past, their faces ripe with distaste as they look upon this creature who has the audacity to be dressed in the garb of a gentleman.

It is through their eyes that the reality of my situation begins to dawn on me, and with it, a sense of horror. Percy is gone, not walking the salubrious streets of London's West End. And yet I am here, on my knees, breathless from chasing a phantasm, almost crushed beneath a horse's hooves in the process. But she was here – I am sure of it. Percy. The woman I love. Loved. Somehow.

The idea of madness runs through me – that my mind has snapped with the weight of her loss – but I push it from my thoughts, willing it forgotten in the circumlocution office of my memory. I dust myself off, returning to the main street, hoping that the light of the gas lamps will provide an illumination that shall make these nocturnal thoughts wary to reveal themselves once more.

Ten minutes later, I let myself into my studio with the key I should no longer possess, and make my bed upon the chaise, wrapping myself in a backdrop of a country garden that Percy painted two years before. I leave the blinds mounted upon the glazed ceiling open to force me awake when the dawn breaks, aware that the first hire may be early, and none too pleased to find me within. And then I lie there, clutching my makeshift blanket around me, hoping that through it, Percy will find a way to visit me in my dreams. But no sleep comes, and instead I spend the hours staring at the night sky until the sun rises, looking for stars, but finding none; merely an unending blackness that seems to go on forever.

CHAPTER XII

Home once more

Sitting before a dying fire, the only sound I can hear is that of the wind; echoing through the thatch and the empty space of the room above me. It swells and fades like the roll of a timpani, but never disappears entirely – as if it knows there is a gap that needs to be filled, attempting to do so in the only way it understands, its naive attempts almost childlike in their inadequacy. The clock across the room seems to challenge me with its stillness. The hour it marks, my gateway into this new world, this strange limbo I now inhabit – time having replaced space as the prison in which I am forever trapped.

My months with Bates have been an education. Not just in the techniques of his craft (now mine), but in the reality of death. The bodies which once seemed objects of horror, no longer hold their fear, having become mere props in composition, their arrangement a puzzle to be solved, a challenge to be taken up. Death is no longer a threatening spectre at the periphery of my existence, it is my constant companion, in body, as in spirit. Within the dead, I see myself, their flesh as cold and lifeless as my soul, their hopes and dreams as absent as my own, and I feel a kinship. A solidarity.

I have not seen Percy since that night. There is a red-haired prostitute that frequents the Haymarket who I now suspect to have been the source of the apparition. She has spoken to me on occasion, her predatory manner so different to Percy's that the idea of mistaking her for my love seems absurd. Besides, madness is no longer something I fear. For how can one become mad, who cares for nothing? Who wants for nothing? The blankness within me is a comfort, white paper without a print. The plate was too imperfect, too flawed. And thus it is better left alone.

The knocking at the door jars me from my thoughts, its presence as unwelcome as the uninvited guest that lies beyond. Strangely, the inclination to jump from my chair that once defined me is gone, the rivulet of politeness that ran through my character dried up and filled. But the knocks continue, each one grating like the wheels of an unoiled engine, and, as the fourth attempt echoes around the room, I reluctantly make my way to the door, with nothing but a desire to make it stop.

Standing on my threshold is Mabel, the baker. I haven't seen her at my house before, perhaps she visited Percy, but not to my knowledge. Although I have seen her many times in the bakery since my wife's passing, I have paid her no heed, handing over the coins, my thoughts elsewhere; but somehow, here she is – invading the sanctuary of my home.

'Mr Franklin! I thought you wasn't here!' My lack of response only encourages her to continue. 'I knocked three times but I didn't get no answer. I thought you was out.'

I nod an acknowledgment to halt her warblings, but she merely presents the basket she is holding towards me. 'I brought you something,' she explains, before pulling the basket back and raising the tea towel draped over it, revealing its contents. 'It's a loaf cake – I thought you might like it. It's good toasted with butter.'

'Thank you,' I say, trying to put an end on it. But apparently Mabel believes our interaction has only just begun.

'Why don't I make you some tea?' she says, pushing past me into the cottage. 'Why, Mr Franklin! Your fire's nearly out – it's cold today with the wind 'n' all – I'll get it goin' and put some water on.'

'That won't be necessary.'

'No bother, Mr Franklin, no bother at all.' She begins to busy herself at the hearth, and within moments has rekindled the flame, a kettle of water hanging from the frame above it. Her task complete, she is on her feet in an instant, 'Don't look like it's been cleaned round here for a while neither. I'll tidy up.'

'That really isn't necessary, Mrs Clark,' I protest as she shuffles past.

'No trouble, Mr Franklin, no trouble. Besides, I owe you a debt,' she tells me, deeply serious. 'After all, you gave me England's most expensive coconut.'

I smile, despite myself. The rising corners of my mouth threatening to dislodge the tears that are constantly behind my eyes, but I keep myself in check, sitting down in resignation, waiting for her to be done.

***

Mabel places a plate with a slice of the buttered loaf cake on the table beside me, and pours tea through the strainer into my cup. She does the same for herself, then stands there, hesitant, moving from foot to foot, like a lizard on a hot stone.

She looks towards the empty chair opposite. 'May I?'

'Of course,' I reply, my voice tinged with irony, 'you're my guest.'

She smiles and makes herself comfortable, and for the next few moments we sit opposite one another in silence.

'She was very pretty, your wife,' Mabel comments, invading the quiet like she has already invaded my home. I follow Mabel's gaze to the photograph of Percy on my desk, and once again I am there with her, my wife and I sat underneath the branches of an apple tree, her eyes fixed on mine, filled with optimism and hope, our future ahead of us, yet nothing real to us except that moment.

'We all liked her very much.'

Her comment snatches me out of my reverie, like the hand of Gulliver's giant, and I realise I do not want this woman here. I do not want to discuss Percy. To reminisce. To *think*. How dare this woman, whom I hardly know, push her way in here? How dare she claw off the scabs that were healing, or if not healing, scarring over, the wounds failing to regain their feeling?

'We're worried about you, Mr Franklin. It's been six months. Maybe it's time you started getting out of the house a little more. Summer's still here – not that you could tell that from the weather – but, being out in the world before the cold kicks in, it ain't such a bad idea. A little bit of sunshine'd cheer you up no end.'

'I've *been* out. I've been working.'

'Not in the village you ain't. We haven't seen you at church. You weren't at the fair.'

'I don't think fairs are for me any more,' I reply, sardonically, but Mabel appears deaf to variations in tone.

'Fairs is for everyone. Keeps your spirits up! You can't run away from life, Mr Franklin. There's a lot of people here who's very fond of you.'

I get the sense that she is leading to something, and for the first time my curiosity is piqued. I sit back in my chair.

'My daughter was asking after you only the other day. You remember Molly? She's been away for a while – staying with relatives. Only she's back now. Oo, and we had her picture taken. Sorry we didn't ask you – we thought you'd be busy.'

She opens a locket, and hands it to me. Inside is a picture of her little girl, Molly, only very much changed. She is in the first flush of womanhood, and beaming with life.

'She's seventeen now,' Mabel continues, 'turning into a right pretty young lady. A lot of suitors from the village, but she don't seem interested. Got her mind set on someone else probably.' She looks at me guilelessly, 'She always thought you was very handsome.'

I sit there, taking in her implication, confusion running through me at her apparent naivety, at her lack of understanding of who I am, of what I have lost. The tea I am holding, the delicate handle still warm around my finger, no longer feels like a gesture of friendship – merely a cog in her machinations.

'Thank you for the tea, Mabel. I think I need to be getting on with some work.'

It is now Mabel's turn to look confused, and she is suddenly overcome by a concern that she may have overstepped the mark, 'I don't mean no offence by it, sir.'

'None taken. There're things I have to do.'

My words do little to reassure her, and I feel a stab of guilt. She nods and heads towards the door, but, at the threshold, she pauses and turns to me.

'She's not coming back, y'know. We'd all like it if she did, but she ain't. Them's that dead ain't here no more. You need to accept that.'

She shuts the door and I launch the cup towards the wall. It shatters to pieces on impact, and I sit back down in my chair, alone once again, but for the sound of the wind echoing round the room above.

CHAPTER XIII

Two bodies

The stretcher that bears the corpse is purely for appearance. The dead have no need for such niceties, but here, our modus operandi of dragging the body unceremoniously to its destination, has been replaced by a more refined method of transportation. The man's middle-aged son walks alongside us, and other relatives are scattered around the manicured garden in their black suits, as if they are have worn the wrong outfit to a garden party.

In this case, the stretcher is a godsend. Even with two of us carrying, it's a struggle to move the dead man's corpulent form. I cannot imagine how we'd have got him across the garden without it, his feet dragging ridges into the wet ground, like the wheels of a cart on a well-used lane. As it is, it's all we can do to prevent tipping him off face-first onto the grass, a manoeuvre that I doubt would be appreciated by the po-faced onlookers.

'Over there would be best, I think,' says the son, gesturing towards the far end of garden. His manner is offhand and distant, but it does not seem to be a result of his father's passing, as much as a more general disconnection from life. Too much ease, too much protection. 'Do you see the place I mean? Over by the roses.'

'Where we've set up the chair?' Bates asks sarcastically from the front of the stretcher.

'Yes – exactly,' he continues, 'I feel that would be a fitting tribute. My father always loved his Celsianas.'

'Could have done us the courtesy of dying a bit fucking closer to 'em then,' Bates mutters under his breath, raising his voice to normal volume as the son stops to consider the wonder of his idea, and is left behind, out of earshot, 'Cunt.'

The two hundred feet to the end of the garden feel like a mile, and when we finally lower the stretcher to the ground, Bates winces as he bends.

'Agggh. For fuck's sake,' he says, straightening up and pressing above his right hip in an attempt to correct the sprain. He shrugs it off, but I can see his spine curving out to the side like the centre of a letter S. 'Sort it out will ya?' he spits in my direction, leaving me the body and turning away to walk off his injury.

I commandeer one of the servants who has been loitering to assist me in lifting the body onto the chair. His hesitance reminds me of my own only a few months ago, flinching at the cold of his master's skin, the proximity of death making him uncomfortable, nervous. I look upon him coldly, like a scientist examining a new species, his qualms now so difficult for me to understand.

The two men we hired for the day reappear after a convenient absence carrying our kit. I check the wind direction with my finger, and instruct them to set up a screen to block off the breeze. Corpses may be good sitters, but the challenges of taking a photograph outdoors remain. Many a rogue gust and the resulting blur has wrecked what would have otherwise been a fine plate.

I make them set up a second screen between myself and the rest of the garden, preferring to work without an audience of watching eyes, then finally send them off to fetch the mobile darkroom still attached to the horses at the front of the house. This photograph will be not be cheap, but, judging by the surroundings, this family are not for want of money, so I take my time, and begin to arrange the body.

The sheer mass of flesh makes the corpse difficult to manipulate, and Bates is still trying to walk off the crick in his back, so I am forced to work alone. I tie the body to the seat, wooden limbs extending from the rear legs of the posing chair held down with a heavy counterweight. Even with the mechanical advantage of the lever, it's barely enough, but it works. I rest the man's left hand on a cane that is held in place by the chair itself, an innovation I devised a few weeks ago. Bates thought it ingenious, and I have to admit I took some pride in it myself.

Annoyingly, some of the other limbs need 'cracking' to be put into place. It is the one thing to which I have yet to become immune, the sound so close to the breaking of bone that no matter what the reality entails (Bates claims it is the muscle that 'breaks'), I cannot shake the impression that that is what I am doing. It is only after I have 'broken' the man's other wrist, that I notice the son standing behind me.

'Sir!' I exclaim, as much from surprise as respect, a child who has been caught stealing treats from his mother's pantry. What he has seen hits me immediately; there is a reason we perform our métier behind closed doors. 'Perhaps you would prefer to rejoin your guests in the garden?' I stumble. 'The screen was designed to spare you the sight of this operation.'

'No … no,' he replies. 'I'll stay.'

He has a strange look in his eye, as if seeing his late father reduced to this is a catharsis of some kind. And suddenly I understand him differently, no longer as a spoilt and ineffectual dandy, but as a man who has lived long in his father's (not insubstantial) shadow; a man finally free from his shackles, his oppressor reduced to a piece of meat, manhandled and pushed around by a stranger. Perhaps I was unfair to judge him as I did. To soil him with the same conclusions that Bates's associates seem to cast on me. It is strange how often our own struggles dazzle us with so much intensity, we are all but blind to those of others.

I continue my work, aware of the man's almost predatory gaze upon me, drinking in his father's impotence and vulnerability. As

89

much as I empathise with his lot, there is a cruelty to his stare that makes me glad when I am finished. Bates draws closer, having finally worked out the kinks from his frame. He seems as uncomfortable as I am myself with the son's presence, but makes no comment, checking the work with a purely technical eye, before nodding at me in satisfaction, as we both stand back to take in the full frame.

'I would like to be in it,' the son blurts out, forcing our attention towards him. We turn to find him looking proud and assured. Watching our treatment of his father seems to have inspired something in him. 'I want to be standing with my hand on his shoulder, strong.' He hesitates, as if unsure whether to continue, but his normal boundaries seem to already have been breached by the transgression of the situation. 'I want him to look weak. I can give you more money.'

Bates looks him up and down, then shrugs, and starts to make the final preparations. The son strides away to gather himself, walking taller than before. We are in the process of removing the privacy screen and setting up the camera, when a boy arrives and hands Bates a note.

'Fucking Warwick,' he curses on reading. I look at him, questioningly, and Bates gives me an explanation for his outburst. 'Booked us in at the studio. For Christ's sake, he knows we're on this.' He seems annoyed, a potential job slipping through his fingers. 'Tell him we can't,' he says, handing the boy back the note along with a coin. 'He should know we're busy.'

'I can do it.'

Bates looks at me as if I'm as foolish as his employer.

'I need you on this.'

'We're set up, they've brought the darkroom,' I say, indicating towards the caravan the men have carried in. 'You can finish without me.'

Bates thinks for a second, then nods once more. 'All right. It don't pay much anyway. Be a good one for you to practise on.' I nod back, chasing after the boy who has already started to make his way back towards the road. Bates calls after me. 'Don't fuck it up.'

***

The tableau that greets me at the studio could not be more different from the one I have left behind. Sitting in the waiting room are the remains of a man, still living, his dead wife laid on the chaise across from him. The man is bent over double, in shirt sleeves, his hair and beard unkempt. He looks like a wild man or mad prophet, a wandering sage who has just realised how much life he has squandered away on nothing, dragged into modernity against his will.

'Sir…' I offer, by way of a greeting. For the first time, he seems to notice me. He looks up, his eyes red and raw, but nothing comes out of his mouth. 'I'm here to take the photograph,' I explain.

He looks at me as if the idea is an unexpected one, as if that were not the very reason for my presence. 'Do as you will.'

I turn towards his wife. She's young, not yet twenty-five, dressed in a nightgown, her body half-covered with a sheet, two coins on her eyes. She seems at peace, a vivid contrast to the tumult within her husband.

'People normally like their loved ones dressed in something particular,' I tell him. 'A favourite item of clothing perhaps?'

He points to a trunk up against the opposite wall. 'There are clothes in there.'

'Is there anything you would like her in? A dress she was fond of?'

'Anything's good,' he says, dismissively, then reconsiders. 'She liked the pink one. Put her in that.'

91

Taken out of context, his words could appear cold, but they are anything but. He wears his matter-of-factness like a shield, a dam holding back the torrent of emotion that is within.

'Perhaps you would like to dress her?' I suggest. 'I can help you with the body into the studio and then leave you with her?'

'No. I'm sorry, I can't. You'll have to do it.'

'Perhaps there is a maid or friend who could help?'

'There's no one. It was just us.'

I nod, feeling my own pain churning around inside me. This man has lost as I have, and his suffering grips me, like fingers into a wound, and I feel the front of my acceptance torn apart as if a corpse by carrion.

'It's all right,' I tell him, trying to sound as if I am in control. 'I can do it.' I know any attempt to comfort him would be a lie. A lie that death is natural, fair. That hated old men, who make life a hell for those around them live to see their twilight years, while those who are truly loved are ripped from this world without reason, without mercy.

'If you need me I'll be outside,' he says jolting me back to my senses. 'Be careful with the dress. I mean to keep it...' I see him trying to hold himself back from crying. 'Be careful with her.'

He heads out of the door and I lift the body through to the studio to begin the preparations.

I dress the woman while she is laid on the studio chaise. Being alone with the body feels improper, intimate. Her flesh is cold, but she has not yet gained the now-familiar stiffness of death, and, as I remove her nightdress, I feel the horror of my first acquaintance with a corpse return with a vengeance. She is so real, so close to *life*. Her skin is soft like my wife's but lacks the warmth, the humanity. And I want it. The warmth to return once more.

I lay her back on the chaise, ashamed of my thoughts, forcing myself away from her body and to the trunk that sits in the waiting room to fetch her corset and dress.

Returning, I wrap the corset around her midriff, then turn her onto her front, so I can thread the laces at the rear.

'I like you dressing me. Besides, if a maid dressed me like this, I'd have to fire her. Tighter.'

I pull the ends tight, and tie them, then prop her in the corner of the chaise so I can get her into her clothes. When she is dressed, I lift the body over to the posing chair, and, as I move her into the sitting position, her hair and neck draw near to my face, filling my nose with her scent, a mixture of her humanity, and perfume that once scented the fabric of her dress. The attraction it prompts in me makes me feel sick, and I almost drop her before reaching the chair, but I steady myself and lower her gently in place.

I clamp her into the stands and tease out two strands of hair to cover the place where metal grips her neck, before stepping back to check the composition. The effect is good, but her face looks pale and gaunt, as much an effect of a previous illness, I imagine, rather than death, but still, corrections must be made, so I pull out the case which contains Bates's rouges and powders, and begin the work.

Her skin is so soft it once again disconcerts me, her lips still somehow moist and full despite the fact that her breath no longer dances upon them. I find myself staring at them, the brush motionless in my hand, remembering how lips felt to kiss, the tender adhesion as they parted, the strange communion of souls made flesh by their union.

'I hope you don't use this technique on all your sitters.'

'Only on babies and elderly gentlemen. The occasional young woman if she's particularly attractive.'

I step back once again. The powders have worked their magic, and she is now womanhood in full bloom, as ready to drink in life as when she possessed it.

I clean the brush and set to work upon the final touch, her eyelids. My technique has improved over the months, and now my work can easily match Bates's, exceed it even, but still, the results irk me. Compared to everything else, they are crude, uncouth, a whore's make-up on a child. I wipe off the paint and redo them, twisting the wet hairs of the brush into a point with my fingers to make my lines more delicate, but the end result is the same, garish and lewd – a cartoon scribbled upon a masterpiece. A third time and my frustrations begin to make their way into the lines, the result even worse than before. I go to rub them off again, only stopping myself at the last moment, suddenly aware that the quality will only continue to diminish. My teeth bite against one another in annoyance. I edge backwards from the body, hoping distance will alleviate my failures, but the imperfections endure, and I fling the palette across the room in vexation. It connects with the wall, leaving reds and blacks scarring the bare plaster.

I walk across the studio and sit on my heels for a few moments, my stained fingers spread-eagled across my face, before moving to the camera. In the mirror across the studio I see myself, my hair as wild as the widower waiting downstairs, the smudged colours of the palette smeared across my features like mud.

I check the frame. It is no better.

But it will suffice.

After making my final preparations, I retire to the darkroom to flow the plate. Her husband is waiting and will need the dress returned. And a man cannot work miracles.

***

94

The next morning I sit in my cottage, Percy's dress in my hands. I bring it to my face, as if somehow her scent will have reappeared upon it, a mercy from on high to provide me comfort in my squalor.

I have not been able to bring myself to make the prints of yesterday's shoot. I know that seeing the images on paper would only pain me. Besides, I must make my way into town. For tonight I have other needs to fulfil.

***

The dress accompanies me into town, folded dedicatedly in the bottom of my travelling bag, and, as day turns to night, I make my way up from Waterloo Bridge towards the Haymarket.

It is an hour or so before I see her, standing in the doorway of a run-down hotel. I notice her before she does me, the familiar red of her hair beckoning across to me like a beacon, and she spots me almost instantly as if she has felt my gaze upon her. Although I am still across the street, she seems to understand why I am here, despite my previous rejections of her approaches, and walks into the building without so much as an acknowledgement, knowing I will follow.

As I step forward into the building, I find her paused on the stairs, waiting for my entrance, facing away from me. She does not look back, merely recommencing her climb as an acknowledgement of my presence. The room we enter together is basic and dingy, sparsely decorated except for a bed and dresser, scattered with creams, a trio of necklaces hanging from the triptych of mirrors that sit upon it. She finally turns to look at me.

'What you want then, love?' The harshness of her voice jars, but I try to put it to the back of my mind.

'I have something I want you to wear.'

A slight smile begins to form on her lips, disappearing before it truly emerges.

'Hand it over then.'

'No...' I reply, surprised into pausing by the force of my words. '...I want to dress you.'

She looks at me as if I was an acquaintance who had turned out to be a stranger, before releasing another smile. This time it is uninhibited, her amusement no longer constrained by a fear that she might lose my business, but then she nods and smiles again, this time as if the request has pleased her.

'All right.'

I open up my bag, removing the dress.

'How'd you want me? Down to my drawers?' she asks, going behind a screen to undress.

'Yes,' I reply, surprised not to feel any embarrassment at the unguardedness of my reply.

She emerges in her chemise and drawers, the cotton light upon the curves of her body, somehow revealing more than the exaggerated shape of the dress she was wearing a few moments ago.

'I can just take these off if you want to get started,' she explains.

I shake my head, laying Percy's dress on the bed, trying to ignore the feeling that I am soiling it, soiling her memory, but I can't stop myself. I want to feel life once again, to remember what it was like to be with her.

'Where's your corset?' I ask.

She smiles again and retrieves it from behind the screen, handing it to me with a hint of confrontation. I take it and she turns away, offering her back to me. I wrap it round her body and do up the busk at the front with my arms wrapped around her. She puts her hands on mine, the warmth of her skin thrilling me;

flesh – alive, pulsating. I draw away, threading the laces, intoxicated by the physical contact, my memories intermingling with the present: Percy, the dead woman from my studio, this stranger before me. I try to push everything away apart from Percy, imagining her laughing as I pull the cords in tighter.

'You can do it tighter if you want,' she says, looking at me coquettishly over her shoulder.

I pull the strings harder, but the lightness of Percy's reactions are gone, replaced by a tough noise in the woman's throat. 'You can hurt me a bit if you like,' she says. I look away from her face and she takes the cue and turns away herself. I tie the laces and withdraw to the bed for the dress, slipping it over the woman's head and body without the petticoats and crinolines Percy wore, as if any hesitation might risk the enchantment being broken. The dress slips down her body with ease, the train hanging long by her heels without a frame to support it, but for a second she is there, my wife. The dress, the red of her hair. I bury my head in the locks that hang down over her shoulders, feeling the warmth of her neck, the blood pulsating through her veins, enrapturing me like an animal approaching a kill. But it's wrong, the smell is wrong, the feeling is wrong.

'What's the matter?' she says sensing my hesitation.

'Nothing,' I tell her, backing away.

She turns to me, her smile wide and her eyes sultry.

'Then we should get down to it. After all, that's what you're here for, ain't it?'

She moves closer, her hand reaching for my crotch, her face drawing in, the garish red of her cheeks and lips making me flinch in their pantomime glory. All I can see is the face of the dead woman, the illusion of life, of health, her badly painted doll eyes staring at me as if in mockery.

'Your face,' I say. 'I want you to take your powders off.'

She pulls back, unsure.

'Well…' she says, for the first time truly wary of my requests, 'that'll cost you extra. It don't 'appen quick, putting my face on.'

'I'll pay.'

She smiles. 'You're a strange one, you.'

She goes over to her dresser, and uses a jug to fill up her wash bowl, soaping up a flannel within. Bringing it to her face, her eyes suddenly meet my own in the mirror. She turns to me, holding the moistened rag in my direction.

'You want to do it?'

Unthinking, I take the cloth from her, more as if I have been commanded to than acted in accordance with my will. I kneel next to her stool, then apply it to her face, wiping away the colours, the fakery. At first they smudge, the reds merging with the whites of the base layer, covering her whole face with a repulsive sickly pink hue, but I rinse the cloth and continue, and slowly the colours give way to the skin beneath. She's younger than I thought, and prettier. There are pock marks to the side of her left eye, the memories of a childhood illness, but the glimpse behind the veil calms me; she's not Percy, but she's a human being. A delicate, fragile human being.

'That better for you?' she asks, the exaggerated sexuality of her voice seeming even more absurd against the innocence of her unadorned skin.

I remain silent and she begins to undo my shirt and waistcoat, slipping her hands beneath my shirt, through the space between two still fastened buttons, one of which she pops open to allow her hand to continue. As she strokes downwards, the feeling of her between my skin and the thin cloth of my clothing reminds me of sheets upon Percy's naked body, and I close my eyes trying to focus, to drink in the sensation I thought I'd lost. She guides me to standing and her hand makes its way into my trousers. She's more aggressive than Percy had ever been, unfettered by the bounds of decency, and I feel her actions straining at the edges of my imagination. And yet, her aggression is seeping into me, my face hinting at the beginnings of a snarl, and, when I open my eyes, I see her watching my face, biting her lip as if she has found genuine pleasure in finally awakening something in me.

I go to close my eyes again, but she stops me.

'Open them. Look at me.'

She steps away, and walks towards the bed, staring at me seductively as she reaches beneath Percy's dress and takes down her drawers, dropping them to the floor. She hitches the low hem up to her knees and beyond, laughing as I try to contain my lust, my expression shot through with repulsion both at her and myself.

'Come on then – let's see what you've got under there.'

I walk towards her, then turn her away from me, pushing her down onto the bed face first to hide her alienness in the sheets. I start to unbutton my trousers, then pull up the dress to the small of her back, revealing her nakedness in all its glory.

'See – I knew you 'ad it in you,' she laughs from amidst the bedclothes.

I move on top of her, my actions those of a stranger, somewhere between passion and violence. I look down at the dress and the red hair, trying to remember my wife, but the tenderness of my moments with Percy are gone, replaced by a sickness of pure lust. I touch her hair, trying to reconnect with myself, my gentleness, to suppress the animal within, but to no avail, and my other hand starts to pull down my underwear.

But as I force her face down into the pillow, I feel something shift beneath my hand.

Almost imperceptibly, but it does.

'It's … it's a wig.'

She turns her face up towards me, shifting her hair back into place over the thread of bare skin that has been revealed. 'Course it is. It's a good one though – ain't no 'air from a dead woman.'

The revelation knocks me to my senses. I back away from the bed.

'I'm clean, if that's what you're thinking – the customers like it—'

'No, no, I … that's not it… I shouldn't be here. I'm sorry.'

I button up my trousers, shame sweeping over me with the force of a tropical heat, and pick up my bag from the floor, sealing the clasps together, before heaving it out behind me.

'You ain't getting' away without payin' if that's what you're thinking.'

'No, I…'

I throw the money onto the bed, probably more than I owe, my head bowed to avoid meeting her eyes, but the pattern of Percy's dress draws my gaze upward.

'I need the dress. I need you to take it off.'

I feel disgusted at myself for letting her wear it, as if I have handed something precious to feral children.

'I was right – you're a strange one,' she repeats. 'This your wife's or somethin'?'

I hesitate, not wanting to mention her name. 'Take it off.'

'Answer me question.'

'Yes.'

She nods, and slips the dress back over her head, before handing it to me.

'She dead?'

I look her in the eye. Although her powdered face has been off for minutes, for the first time I feel she is revealing her true face, the humanity within. Gone is the pastiche of attractiveness, her masquerade of lust replaced by empathy and vulnerability.

100

I go to speak, but my reply catches in my throat. A strange embarrassment overcomes me at my desire to unburden myself to this stranger that puts any discomfort I had in wanting to satiate my lust with her in sharp relief. Suddenly, nothing feels right, not just the situation; it is as if my very clothes do not fit.

I snatch the dress from her hand, and exit the room, feeling her gaze upon me as I enter the hallway, the feeling continuing as I descend the stairs and make my way along the street that leads to the Haymarket proper. As if within that final look the woman had given me, I had somehow succeeded in bringing Percy back.

And she had seen I was not the man she thought me to be.

***

The prints of the dead woman fill me with horror. Although the eyes might fool the casual glance of a disinterested viewer, to me they are nothing but paint on a corpse; lifeless, fake, absurd. I screw the print, unfixed, in my hand, and toss it across the room. There, it sits on the floor, a ball of angles, the picture continuing to develop within – each line seeping into the next, unseen by human eye, until eventually no details remain and all is blackness.

Frustrated, I open the door of the back room to the world outside. The door sticks as always, swollen by the damp in the air, until it comes open with a sudden movement. A gentle breeze fills the room with freshness almost instantly, and, as I step back, the dark of the room frames the pastoral scene beyond like a Constable landscape. The view seems to mock me with its perfection, its effortless beauty, my strained attempts to remake nature's creation inferior and sterile, an artistic blasphemy.

But then I see the apple tree under which Percy and I sat together so many times, and I think about how cold this artist is; this 'mother', treating her children with the disregard of a bitter

101

school ma'am, lacking in empathy or warmth. Underneath the fruit-peppered branches, the ground is strewn with windfalls. They lie there upon the grass, brown and decaying, slowing becoming one with the earth. Nature too has its imperfections, but when I think of my love, I can only sit in awe of what can be created. And what can be taken away.

Percy.

I rush to my bench, picking up the glass plate on which the negative of the dead woman resides. Holding it up to the afternoon light, a feeling overcomes me that I don't understand. I have failed this woman; failed her husband, but most of all I have failed myself; but perhaps ... perhaps...

I search round my bench for a tool, turning over botched prints and pushing aside rags still wet with chemicals, until I finally find the glass cutter. It has a flat edge near its tip on the block in which the diamond sits – it's not perfect, but will suffice.

And then I put the plate down on the bench.

And begin to scrape.

CHAPTER XIV

Celebrations and condemnations

We sit at a table by the window while Bates flips through the prints, the afternoon light that filters through the glass at odds with the twilight of the rest of the coffee shop, a mass of murky booths and corners to skulk in.

'Look at the smug bastard standing behind 'im,' he laughs. 'I tell you 'e offered to help carry the old man back to the house? I knew something was up as soon as he said. Spoilt shag-bag never carried a thing in 'is life.' He pauses for a moment and hands me one of the prints. 'This one.'

In it, the man's son looks particularly haughty, his father beginning to slump into the chair as if he lacked the strength to carry himself, while his child stands behind him. I know the son must have requested Bates to arrange it like this – to loosen a rope, lower a stand – it's the only way the effect could have been created. The father still looks alive, but ill, as if his gluttony were starting to get the better of him. Bates shakes his head.

'There's better – but he'll like it. Anyway, 'alf way to the 'ouse, he drops the handle of the stretcher, and the fat fucker rolls face first into the dirt. Next thing you know, the little bastard just pats 'is 'ands together and walks off without sayin' a word. If I'd been on the other end of the stretcher, I'd've been furious, but as it was, it was all I could do to stop from bloody laughin'.'

He looks up at me when I don't respond, confused by my failure to join him in his glee. But I cannot see any humour in the pettiness of the family dispute. Just sadness and pain.

Bates rolls his eyes. 'Your problem is you got no sense of

'umour, Charlie – send yourself to an early grave if you don't laugh once in a while.'

I shrug. He sighs in acceptance.

'Right – let's see the ones you did at the studio then.'

I hand him the prints, and he begins to scan through them.

'Good, very good. You're learning, Charlie. Could get the arm more natural, but they're quality. You might not be funny, but at least you ain't embarrassing to 'ave on the team.'

And then he reaches the close-up. Stopping in his tracks.

'How did you…?'

He puts the print down on the table, as if it is cursed, unholy. The dead woman's face, large in the frame, her eyes open and real, alive with hope.

I pause before answering, unsure as to what his reaction will be, but I realise I have no option but to tell him the truth.

'The eyes – they're my wife's.'

He continues to look at me, as if he is trying to understand my meaning, then picks up the print again; but this time with fascination rather than distaste. He examines it closely, standing and moving closer to the window to reveal any imperfections hidden by the gloom that may have encroached upon our space from the room beyond. But he finds none; and turns to me, the look in his eyes almost reverent.

'They're beautiful, Charlie. Fucking beautiful.'

***

I spend the next hour explaining how I did it. My use of Rejlander's techniques to print from multiple plates – scraping the eyes off the negative, then painting the spaces black to leave the image 'eyeless'; how I created a mask to isolate my wife's eyes on a plate I had taken of her. Scraping and painting would have been easier, but I couldn't bear to harm the negative – they're all I have left of her, their value beyond imagining, beyond life.

As I talk, the cynicism that forms Bates's usual mask becomes replaced by a childlike wonder at my description of the process. As I describe my construction of a sealed 'tunnel' to manipulate the size of the eyes to match – moving the plate of my wife's face away from the paper to subtly enlarge them – he seems to be taken by a kind of awe, and for the first time since my loss, I feel something approaching satisfaction. *Pride.*

When I meet the woman's widower a few hours later, his reaction is the same. Obviously, he has no interest in my technique or 'methods', but the tears that fill his eyes show a reverence of their own, his expression of loss scraped away, temporarily replaced with something that resembles peace, as, for a moment, he is reunited with the woman he loved.

'Thank you.' His words falter as they emerge, then he moves in closer, wrapping his arms around me in an embrace. I ignore my instinct to pull away, placing my hand gently upon the back of the head buried in my chest, as his tears begin to wet my shirt. The embarrassment I would have expected to feel is curiously absent, replaced by something that is almost … jealousy; a strange envy at his openness to grief, at his acceptance of loss, imagining the catharsis that must come with releasing your pain to the world.

But I also see weakness. For why should we accept, why should we let go of an anger that is righteous, appropriate? And yet… I can feel the draw of his emotions – the need to release, to grieve, to accept that this world is empty of one of its wonders. I push the feelings away, and with them the man through whom they have made their way into this world.

He looks at me, suddenly realising he is in the presence of a stranger, smoothing his hair to one side, and attempting to halt his tears.

'Just tell me which ones you would like,' I say, endeavouring to help him regain his poise, but he looks at me as if I am a fool.

'All of them…' he says, shaking his head. 'All of them.'

***

I make my usual journey to Warwick's later that afternoon, only to find him absent. His clerk tells me I am to go to him, giving me the address of a Turkish baths. I think Warwick means for me to join him within, but the idea of conversing wrapped in towels in a sub-tropical climate holds little appeal, so, on my arrival, I wait for him in the lobby.

The man at the door takes it upon himself to inform the great man of my presence, and it is not long before he comes to join me, hovering at the entrance to the baths proper, doing me the honour of donning a robe, as we remain in our respective locales, the boundary between us marked by the change of tile on the floor.

'And you're sure you won't join me?' Warwick asks, offering me a smile, but it is a crocodile's, intended to ingratiate. I wonder for a moment if it was ever such, my eyes blind to his fakery, the veil finally lifted as I come to see the world for what it is.

'I think not,' I reply.

'Hmmph,' he coughs, his grin replaced by an expression of seriousness. 'Yes. Well, down to business then.' He pauses, unsure as to how to proceed.

'Down to business,' I echo.

'Bates showed me the photographs you took.' I do not answer, standing there, waiting for him to continue. 'He also told me how you made them.'

I feel my mouth fall into a wry sneer. Part of me knew this was what he wanted. To scold me; to judge. And yet I came, as if responding to the call of a petulant father. I stand there, waiting for him to continue.

'I shouldn't have got you involved with him, Charles. It was a mistake.' He feels responsible, culpable. How touching.

'I make my own choices.'

'That doesn't mean they're the right ones.'

A member of staff gives Warwick a disapproving look as he squeezes past us, and Warwick squirms a little. For a man who shows so much disapproval, he seems to be able to tolerate very little himself – as if respectability were the highest good – and suddenly, he seems as keen to move the conversation forward as I am myself.

'I thought, perhaps, you might like to go away for a while…' he suggests. 'Margate's nice this time of year.'

He correctly interprets my silence as a rejection of the idea.

'What about France? You have the money, Charles. I doubt the food'll be up to much, but the climate's reputed to be excellent. I think it would be good for you; for your health.'

'If I want a diagnosis, I'll go to a doctor.'

'There'll be a job for you here when you return, if that's what you're worrying about.'

'And if I don't go, there won't be?'

Warwick seems almost offended by the implication. 'Not at all, Charles, not at all. I greatly appreciate your talents. I just hoped to urge you back towards work of a more gratifying kind… Your career was on an upward trajectory. I thought we should seek to continue that.'

'You saw the photographs. Whatever you think, they're good. Do you realise what I did? What no one else can do?'

'Charles, please. I'm not questioning your abilities. I'm merely concerned.'

'Your concern is appreciated. But unnecessary. Keep sending me the work. I'll keep making you money.'

107

I turn my back on him, leaving him standing on the boundary between our worlds. He calls after me. 'Don't waste your life on the dead, Charles.'

His words almost make me smile.

'The dead are all I've got,' I reply, before exiting into the street.

CHAPTER XV

With eyes that see

As the months pass by, I continue to refine my technique, composing my frames to match the plates I have of Percy, measuring every distance in precise detail so I can calculate how the eyes will appear on the plate, ensuring an exact match. Each iteration is a step toward perfection, a blending of past and present into one timeless whole. As much as I try, I cannot think of a method by which to resize the prints without a corresponding loss of quality, so I am forced to recreate the poses I have Percy in already, carefully arranging the bodies to match the prints that accompany me to the studio. At least that is what I tell myself.

I know I could pay a model to sit in to create new plates to use in composite, but I do not want that. I want Percy there, in the photographs. The need overwhelms me like a sickness, an obsession, but it is a compulsion I cannot shake, as if by doing so I have somehow beaten death; torn my wife away from his embrace and brought her back into this world. The bodies I am given become my canvases – their arrangement a challenge to overcome, and each success emboldens me – urging me forward to more.

For the men, I begin photographing myself in situ to use my own eyes on the prints. I feel a perverse satisfaction seeing myself staring back from their lifeless cadavers; wearing their dead faces like a mask; the feeling that I have somehow possessed them, taken hold of their bodies without their knowledge, become an interloper in the underworld, hidden, undetected.

The zenith of my art comes when I am tasked to photograph a couple killed in an accident, their cab having been turned over, both of them trampled to death by the horses. The moment of their being brought to the studio fills me with a delinquent thrill (the caving in of the back of their heads predictably easy to work with), and a day later, Percy and I are staring outwards from the paper, side by side, stately and poised, like a king and queen of the dead.

But my successes do little to lift my mood. As my prints climb onwards towards perfection, I find my soul trudging golem-like downwards, its descent steady and unfaltering; trudging into the depths of the abyss, my anger and hatred gradually being replaced by a kind of numbness, all humanity left behind me. And, as I sit, one afternoon, with a man whose face (along with most of his arm) has been taken half off by an industrial accident, arranging him in profile to disguise his injuries, I realise I am looking at myself. The truth turned away and hidden, part of him missing, while the world looks on, unaware.

Autumn becomes winter, becomes spring, becomes summer once more. Yet each day is the same. The same blank faces on the steamer I take to London, on the cramped carriage of the train that other times carries me to Waterloo Bridge. The same husks of humanity pass me on the street amidst the unrelenting din of London traffic; the dead in waiting, lumbering onwards toward their inescapable fate. I find emptiness where sorrow should be, absence in the place of compassion, as they walk by me, my potential subjects, unaware of their destination. And yet, one by one, their pictures fill my wall. Every time a score of nails seal their coffins, another is hammered into the brittle plaster of my parlour, and there they stand, dignified in their demise, resurrected within the frames, the cottage itself becoming a shrine to their memories. And within I sit. The man who has brought them back. Standing on the threshold between their world and our own.

***

The call comes as normal. An address, a time, a summoning.

As the carriage takes me down a country lane towards the house, I view my detachment with a stranger's eye. When I think back on my former self, it almost brings a smile to my face. The way in which I would have regaled Percy with tales of how nice it was to be working outside London, how *refreshing*; made suggestions that we take a picnic to a field I had passed next time the weather was fine; my talk of a bird I had spotted, a tree I had seen, a flower in bloom. Now those emotions, those conversations seem far behind me, worthy of mock and ridicule, and I feel almost comfortable in my acceptance of the pointlessness of it all.

'Mr Franklin?'

The maid who answers the door is slight and mousey, her face looking like a clay sculpture that has been pinched out of shape whilst still wet. Behind her the familiar miasma of grief seems to permeate the emptiness of the grand hallway. It has become as much a constant for me as the London smog. The moments of loss and pain that will haunt a family forever, now the ephemera of my day-to-day.

I nod my affirmation, and she gestures silently for me to enter. I tell the coachman to wait, and follow her into the panelled hallway. We can bring the trunks in when I've established the best place to work; there's no use in rushing when I'm so far from civilisation.

'Do you know the time of death?'

'About three in the morning, I think. The doctor was up there with them.'

I try to hide my annoyance. The body will be stiff and difficult to work.

'It's usually better to be here quicker than that,' I reply, allowing a subtle hint of reprimand to enter my voice, 'but we shall do what we can. If you could lead me to the deceased.'

'I'll take you through to the sitting room, sir. Someone else will take you up.'

I find myself rolling my eyes as she leads me into an ornate room off the central hallway. She takes her leave immediately, and I perch on the corner of a burgundy chesterfield, glancing towards the grandfather clock, attempting to determine whether it will be better to send the coachman off once the equipment has been unloaded, or have him wait while the photographs are taken. I am distracted by a display of prints on the wall to the left of the door, and wander over to examine them with a professional curiosity. They're surprisingly good. Although, given the opulence of their place of residence, perhaps there is nothing surprising about it. The couple in them are slightly younger than me, and judging by their clothing and the woman's hair being 'turned up' at the bottom, they're fairly recent. Part of me thinks they are foolish to have hired me, even I can't make a dead person look as good as these, but work is work. I'm used to keeping my thoughts to myself.

'Mr Franklin?' I turn to see a butler, who has entered from the hallway. 'If you'd like to follow me, I shall take you to the deceased…' He leads me back through the hallway and up the stairs to the first floor. I ascend them with an open mind, willing to assess the light in the bedrooms, but aware that I will probably have to persuade them to move the body downstairs to achieve the best result. Besides, I can't see the coachman being willing to bring the trunks upstairs, and I doubt the Lord and Lady of the manor (or their butler) will offer to help. We walk onwards down the landing, the deep oak of the panelling that lined the walls downstairs continuing to the first floor, only broken by the presence of lavish window seats that look out onto a manicured garden. As we approach the room that is our destination, the

112

butler breaches the silence to communicate his master's wishes. 'Mr Franklin? I do not know if you've been informed, but Mr Rowan has requested that the subject be sleeping in the photograph. She—'

I cut him off immediately, Bates's approach now so ingrained within me that my reply rolls off the tongue with the fluency of a coster's patter. 'I would advise against that. The few times I have agreed, the subject's relatives have been most disappointed. It's best for a man to remember his wife as she was when living, not as she is in death.'

We stop, having reached the door. Through it, I can see that the light inside is dim, the curtains no doubt partially drawn, but at least the room has a southerly aspect; perhaps if the windows are big enough the light will suffice to create a plate. The butler hesitates before entering, wary of the ominous mood that always surrounds someone's passing; but for me it is nothing, the tragic having finally been replaced by the inevitable, leaves falling from the tree as the seasons pass.

'I shall communicate that to my master, sir, but, to clarify, you misunderstand. It's not Mrs Rowan that has passed…'

We enter the room, and there, sitting by the bedside are the couple I saw in the photographs, their faces wan with grief, yet alive. There, before them, dwarfed in the sheets of the bed, lies their infant child, its eyes closed, its mother's hand stroking its downy hair; the baby's demeanour might be mistaken for that of peaceful sleep but for the mournfulness that frames the scene. Something breaks within me. My fortitude, which I thought as strong as a city wall, cracks, as fragile as the shell of an egg.

'I, excuse me…'

I exit the room, my breath struggling to find purchase as I back into the corridor. The floorboards beneath my feet undulate as if I am on the ocean, the patterns of the carpets morphing and

113

changing like creatures within their depths. I steady myself against the landing banisters.

'Sir? Mr and Mrs Rowan wish to know if you are all right? If you would join them in the bedroom—'

'I… I don't do children. I'm sorry. You'll have to excuse me.' I raise myself to full height, willing my composure to echo my posture. 'There must have been a mistake,' I explain. 'A mistake in the communications.'

'Please sir, Mr and Mrs Rowan are most distressed.'

'Be that as it may, I'm afraid I must leave.'

I stumble away down the corridor towards the stairs, when I hear another voice behind me.

'Mr Franklin.'

I turn to see the man from the bedside, he is taller than I thought, and although dressed in merely a waistcoat and shirt sleeves, has an air of solidity I was not expecting. 'I just wished to say we appreciate your coming here. This is a difficult time for us, and my wife and I are extremely grateful that you have come to support us.'

He has a softness to him despite his grief, a gentleman in the truest sense, and yet, I cannot countenance the task they wish me to perform.

'I'm sorry,' I reply, 'but as I was explaining to your man, I don't photograph children.'

I turn away, unable to look him in the eye.

'Please, sir,' the voice behind me is desperate, pleading. 'This is our only daughter. She's gone. We have nothing to remember her by. She was six weeks old.'

I feel tears wet my eyes for the first time since my own loss.

'Please, sir, make an exception…'

I wipe my eyes with my fingers, and continue to make my way towards the stairs.

'Sir, please…'

'I'm going to fetch my equipment.'

***

When the woman hands me the baby, I am surprised how light she is, almost weightless. The struggle and resistance of my usual subjects (as if they were fighting against being brought back), has been replaced by a tenderness, a vulnerability. The cherubs that decorate the walls of our chapels, suddenly make sense to me, their innocence never to be lost, eternal in their fragility.

'She was quite lovely.'

'Thank you,' Mrs Rowan replies.

'Perhaps you would like to pick something for her to wear.'

'We have her Christening gown.'

'That would be perfect.'

Mrs Rowan nods, and goes to fetch the dress, leaving me with the father and their man.

'Mr Franklin was saying he doesn't recommend that the baby be sleeping in the photograph,' the butler begins to inform his master, but I cut him off.

'No. Sleeping is fine. Sleeping will be perfect.'

I sit the parents in front of a fireplace in another drawing room. The light from the bay window is good, and the room is bright enough to provide an even coverage. I lift the girl's body from the crib in which she lies, and place her gently in her mother's arms. She looks so delicate, so peaceful, that I can almost believe she is sleeping myself, despite all I have seen.

'Perhaps, I could add some rouge to her cheeks. Would that be acceptable?'

Mrs Rowan nods her assent and I gather my powders, applying a subtle coating of red to the child's soft cheek.

115

Stepping back, the scene is almost perfect; a moment of domestic bliss, but for the sorrow that flows through every inch of its subjects' veins. But the perfection is what the camera will see; and I am determined that they shall too, every time they look upon the photograph.

'Please try to hold back your tears,' I say. 'Remember what was, not what is. Try to find the joy that the little time you spent with her gave you. We want to capture the happiness she brought you, not your loss.

The father composes himself for the camera, almost managing a hint of a smile, but the girl's mother still looks like her soul has been ripped from her.

'Be happy,' I say, trying to give them the words they need, not the ones I know to be true. 'For she is with God now. She has gone to a better place.'

The sentiment gives the woman a moment's respite from her pain, and I take the lens cap off the camera.

Looking at the child's face, I can almost believe it myself.

CHAPTER XVI

The end

Over the next few weeks, the words I spoke to the couple haunt me. My willingness to lie, to *deceive*. And for what? A photograph. A *picture*?

They express their happiness with the results (or as close to happiness as any in their position could), but I feel I finally know this work for what it is. A lie. A farce. A crude attempt to placate the grieving, a gag to suffocate a scream that should echo throughout this world, a neutering of the hatred they should feel towards all existence, towards the very being I invoked for their comfort.

Others do not seem to share my concern.

I sit with Bates on the stoop of his favoured knocking shop, watching the debauchery that enfolds around us, no longer shocked or horrified by the goings on, discomfort replaced by ennui. Bates has enlisted my company. His whore isn't at home.

'Once she's 'ere, we'll get supper. I just want to make sure she don't get booked up for later.'

I shrug, uninterested in the practicalities of his evening, examining the dirt beneath my feet.

'Jesus,' he continues, rolling his eyes at my unresponsiveness, 'I get more conversation out of the bloody bodies these days.' I don't reply, and his voice takes on a rare note of seriousness, concern. 'You all right, Charlie? Somethin' botherin' you?'

I look up at him blankly.

'Ain't picked up a dose of the clap 'ave you? There's a doctor I know who can give you something. Just don't want you usin' none

117

of the studio make-up to cover it up, if you know what I mean.'
I shake my head, annoyed with his constant descents into crudity, and return my gaze to the ground.

'Just trying to lighten the mood, Charlie,' he says, more calmly. 'You can talk to me if you want to.'

'What's the point?' I ask.

'What do you mean?'

'What's the point to any of this?'

'Christ. Not getting philosophical in your old age, are you?'

He looks at me, confused, as if he's surprised I don't already know the answer. 'It's a beautiful thing, Charlie. Giving people back their loved ones, even if it's just for a moment.'

'Not the sales pitch,' I snap. 'You know it's not true. We don't bring anyone back. We don't make anything better. How could we? When they're gone, they're gone. All we do is take one last photograph before the rot kicks in.'

Bates looks at me, sincerity lathered on with a shaving brush. 'All people 'ave is memories, Charlie. What we do gives them something to focus on. We recapture life, we…'

'For God's sake?!?' Bates straightens up, shocked by the ferocity of my response. 'We don't recapture life. We capture death. Half the things we photograph are probably decomposing already, so don't give me all that good Samaritan horseshit—'

'Evening, gents.'

I turn around to see the woman behind us whose room I ran from, who wore Percy's dress, but her eyes on Bates, not me. 'Can I interest you in a little stroll? Something more if it takes your fancy?'

She looks from Bates to me, and suddenly realises who I am. She flinches for a moment, before another remembrance flits across her consciousness, and a look of sympathy threatens to appear upon her face, her humanity at odds with the slut's mask she is wearing.

But I'm in no mood for compassion, my anger carrying me forward like the current of a feral river. I look towards her with disdain, any embarrassment I might have felt in normal circumstances submerged under its merciless waters.

'Leave us alone.'

The words fix her mask back upon her, and she flashes me a barely concealed look of contempt, muttering the word 'freak' before turning her back on us.

Bates watches as she leaves, then looks back at me.

'Come on – tell me,' I ask. 'What's in it for you? I know we tell lies for a living, but be honest for once.'

He pauses for a moment, chewing over his response like a cow on the cud, before he replies, his tone having lost its normal colour, replaced with a matter-of-factness that is almost cold.

'Same as anything, Charlie. Money. It's a job, ain't it? You eat this well when you was photographing babies? We make money. And we make more of it 'cos we're willin' to get our hands dirty.'

He looks across the street at the prostitute who just approached us. She's trying her luck with a man who could be her grandfather, a cane in each hand the only thing keeping him standing. Bates smiles before continuing.

'Most people ain't. So who gives a shit what the point is? Taking these photographs don't have to mean anything. Not to you. If it means something to them, that's enough. As long as they're willing to pay for it, it's enough.' He takes my look of horror as a prompt to continue. 'Come on, Charlie – we ain't a fucking charity.'

'I'm not a parasite. I don't want to prey on people when they're desperate, broken.'

'Everyone's a parasite. We're hungry, they sell us food; we're tired, they rent us a room. Every time you stick your cock up one of those dollymops, you think they're not taking advantage of you being desperate?'

119

'I don't—'

'I don't care what you do, Charlie. Just don't start judging me like some cunt.'

After a moment's pause, I get to my feet, brushing the dust off the seat of my coat.

'You can wait here if you want,' I tell him. 'I need a drink.'

We order our usual brandies at the bar. I down the glass and push it back towards the barman for another. The bottle still in his hand, he pours, and I take the glass from him and down it once more. The place is busy tonight – the same faces I see every day peppered with the occasional stranger who doesn't know what they're in for. At the door, there's some kind of commotion with a soldier throwing his weight around – the bright red of his coat standing out amongst his drab surroundings like fresh blood on a wound, but these tavern dramas hold no interest for me, and I ask the barman for another drink. Joe, the rotund hairless fellow who shares my trade, is across the bar, flirting with one of the waitresses. He raises a glass towards me, and we exchange a nod, before returning to our respective conversations. Bates is still cursing about Clarissa not being at her rooms, about how well he treats her, about how she better not have found a new husband if she doesn't want to end up as his next subject, but his words to me are just noise, more grist to the bustle that adds up to nothing but a deafening silence. All that matters is the bitterness of my porter, the fragile curve of my next brandy glass, each sip a step closer to the brief respite of sleep.

'Are you the death photographer?'

I turn to see the soldier behind me; probably looking to pick a fight, but I don't rise to the bait, turning back towards Bates and raising my eyebrows cynically.

'Are you?'

He grabs my arm above the elbow and jerks me round to face him.

'I asked you a question,' he growls. I look down at the grip he still has on my arm.

'Take your hand off me.' Reluctantly, he releases his grasp. He looks like he's been out of the country for a few years, an anger that he's been forced to kowtow to the civility of his homeland bubbling underneath his withdrawal. He continues to speak, but this time more cautiously.

'I have work. So I'm asking you – are you the death photographer?'

I look him up and down. Everything about this man puts me on edge: his waxed moustache, the impersonal formality of his uniform – a predator in the clothing of civilisation, treating people with the same disregard with which we arrange our bodies. I turn to Bates. He's drunk.

'I ain't gettin' involved. I'm waitin' ere till Clarissa gets back.'

I turn back. 'Do you have cash?'

'I do.'

'How far?'

'Ten minutes by foot.'

I don't like him; but I don't have to like him. I'll charge him extra for the inconvenience. It's money.

I nod. 'I'll send for my things.'

Ten minutes later, we are outside a small town house on a road that marks the boundary where respectability ends and the slums begin. Kirk (as the soldier has told me is his name) opens the door, fumbling with his keys and cursing when it doesn't open immediately, shoving until it eventually gives way. He leads me down the hallway to the stairs directly in front of us. The floorboards beneath my feet are bare, no rugs in sight, but small feminine touches suggest the aspiration of creating a home, if not the funds to achieve it. The place feels as if one of the houses in which I normally work has been miniaturised, shrunk sufficiently to take away its grandeur, but somehow having maintained its form.

'My sister's upstairs.'

I follow him upwards, and then around as the small landing loops back on itself, into the bedroom at the front that spans the width of the house.

'Through here.'

I walk into the room a moment after him, and instantly I am transfixed. In front of me is a woman, her flowing red hair running down the back of the chair like water on rocks. She looks towards the window and it is impossible to see whether she is alive or dead – the effect I try so hard to create, now achieved by the mere act of her facing away. I cautiously step forward, giving the chair on which she sits a wide berth. As the angles change, the vivid amber of her hair gives way to the delicacy of her skin, fair but not pallid, her face as still as the dead and yet living.

She does not look towards me as I enter her field of vision. Her eyes, framed with pink, stare relentlessly forwards as she looks into a future that no one else can see. Across the room, at a right angle to the direction of her gaze, a man lies dead on the bed, but I find myself unable to look towards him, my eyes fixed intently upon this woman, her delicacy almost having the translucent quality of china, her beauty as ungraspable as the present.

'Orpha, this is the photographer,' Kirk announces, talking as if he is addressing a deaf elderly relative, not the young woman in front of us. She turns in my direction, and for the first time, appears to notice me, although her gaze seems to penetrate my body, as if she can see the wall behind.

'Your husband?' I ask.

A single nod forms her response.

'I've sent for my things,' I tell her gently. 'If you'd like to leave the room, I can prepare him for the photograph.'

'I'll stay.'

I hesitate, unsure how to proceed, turning to Kirk but getting no reaction.

'You might prefer to return when the preparations are finished,' I explain, turning back to her.

'I'll stay,' she says, surprising me with the firmness of her tone.

I go to the doorway, where her brother still stands, anxious to take his leave.

'I really would urge her to leave while I do this.'

'She's her own woman,' he shrugs. 'She'll do as she will. I'll be in the bar when you're done. Come and find me, you'll get your money.'

He leaves down the stairs, and I move to the window to watch him make his way along the street, feeling a sense of relief at his exit. Then I turn to Orpha, who sits in her chair, as still as a statue, upright and unblinking.

'Then let us begin.'

***

After the trunks arrive, we discuss the practicalities of the photograph, and she remains seated as I arrange the body. Her husband is an older man, but I suppose many would consider him handsome. His corpse is still fresh, so easy to work with, and it's not long before I have him posed in a chair on the other side of the room, grateful that I have not had to 'crack' his limbs in front of his wife. Nevertheless, it feels strange working with her there, and I can feel her gaze upon me as I work, as if she is willing herself to look upon the truth of what has happened, defiant and unflinching.

'A strange life you lead.'

I look over to her. It's the first time either of us has spoken in half an hour, but no response comes to my lips. Instead, I squat next to her husband's chair to tighten the fixings, focusing on the task at hand, altering the counterweight to make the body more stable.

'Surrounding yourself with dead people,' she continues, 'with other people's misfortunes, their pain.' I pull the knot I was working on tight, and turn to face her, trying to understand the intention behind her words. Her tone, which I had taken as accusatory, now, coupled with her expression, becomes a genuine desire to understand; to comprehend why anyone would choose to do this.

'It's a good way not to think about your own,' I reply.

She doesn't respond. After a few moment's silence, I go over to fetch the camera from one of the trunks. As I arrange the stand, I find myself glancing towards her. She's looking at me too, as if I am a curiosity in a cheap circus sideshow. I turn back to her husband, neatening his clothing, as much in distraction as in preparation. When I turn back, she is still watching; me, the body to which she used to be wed. I start to talk as much from awkwardness as genuine enquiry.

'How long were you married?'

'Four years,' she answers.

'Did you love him?' I stop suddenly, the words having slipped out, circumnavigating my awareness.

'Very much.'

I nod. Strangely, I think her answer is the one I had somehow hoped for. Not that I should wish her pain in the moment, but that I wished her happiness in the past.

'It's done. If you'd like to join your husband.'

She stands up, and moves towards the body.

'You're married yourself?'

'I was.'

Her eyes widen slightly, the question unspoken.

'She died,' I reply.

'So you know how this feels?'

I nod. I not only know, I feel it every second of my waking hours. It permeates my very existence from the moment my eyes open until I go to sleep at night, and the gaps in between.

'Like you've had your heart ripped out. Like you're empty inside, and there's nothing you can ever do to feel whole again.'

I regret my answer immediately. The emotions she was feeling crystalise around my words and she starts to cry.

'I'm sorry—'

'No. No, don't be…' she replies. 'I shouldn't…' I offer her my handkerchief and she takes it, dabbing the tears from her eyes. 'I'm sorry,' she says, composing herself with a flick of the chin, but the tremor in her lip presages another collapse, and the tears come once again.

'He wanted a child, but I couldn't give it to him. My body just wouldn't…'

Her tears become sobs, and hesitantly, I step towards her, reaching out to touch her shoulder, a small gesture of comfort. Immediately, her head is in my chest, and I put my arms around her gently as she sobs.

'It wasn't your fault. There was nothing you could do.'

But her grief begins to infect me, the tears forming in my own eyes, a symptom of the malady.

'Part of him would still be with me. Part of him would still be here…'

'No, no…'

'It would. I failed him… I failed myself.'

When I reply, I think I intend the words to be a comfort, despite their content. And yet I speak them just the same.

'I lost my wife and child on the same day. The baby was stillborn.'

She looks up at me, as if she is looking to the abyss within herself.

'I'm sorry. I'm so sorry.'

I shrug a response, failing even to convince myself.

'Does it get any better?' she asks.

I shake my head. 'You just have to find a way to survive.'

Our foreheads come together, the contact between them providing a point of comfort in the emptiness all around. A flicker of relief in the cold expanse of pain. Slowly our faces come together, our cheeks meeting in a bitter communion of tears, the warm wetness of our crying at least *something*.

For a moment we just stand there, the contact enough. For the first time I can remember, it feels as if I am not alone. As if we are staring into the void together, our breath mingling and drawing us closer, two people desperately clinging to one another in an ocean of absence.

Her lips too are wet with crying, and as they meet mine, their softness is coloured with the salt of her tears. The kiss is hesitant, as if both of us are reaching out to see if what it offers is some kind of safety, of relief. And it seems to. Her touch feels like an opiate to my pain, the tears that breach my lips, water from the Styx. Our kisses become more intense, as we push towards the release that the physical seems to offer us.

We fall to the floor, lost in our embrace, as if losing contact would break the circuit of forgetting in which we are engaged. And, as we make love on the bare wood of the boards beneath us, our pain looms over us unseen, like the body that watches on from across the room as we give ourselves to one another.

The intensity of our passion is followed by a fragile silence. We both straighten our clothes, and get to our feet, unsure as to how

126

to proceed. I return to the camera, and Orpha checks her appearance in the mirror, before joining her husband in the photograph. No words are spoken, except my instructions on how to pose, and we perform the operation for which I was summoned. The task completed I pack my cases, and haul them out into the corridor.

Finally, we take our leave with a single nod of the head. She reaches out her hand to me, and I extend mine towards it, our eyes lingering for a moment as we touch, before she withdraws and turns her back to me.

And then I close the door. And we leave each other's lives forever.

***

I hail a cab to take the trunks back to Bates's studio, eschewing my usual care for the equipment in my need to be alone, and begin wandering the streets in a kind of delirium. My fingers press into my forehead and temples as I pace, in an attempt to contain the conflicting feelings within. Wishing that I could erase that which has happened, wishing that I could return to that moment and live it forever.

I walk for hours, then, looking around myself, I realise I am back on her street, as if the act we committed has tethered me to her location. My eyes dart from side to side, as if searching for escape, but there can be no escape from the past, a moment now forged in time, untouchable, irreparable. I find myself walking towards the small church that bounds the end of the street, moving forward like a man lost in the desert seeing the infamous water, having no care as to whether what is before me is real or mere illusion.

Inside, the chapel is empty, and I stagger forward towards the altar, falling to my knees upon the hard tiles of the floor. There, above me is a miniature Christ, splayed across the cross in suffering for all eternity, his paint chipped and worn like a sideshow act at the fair. The blood that trickles from his hands is dry, emotionless. And there is so little of it – the white cloth draped across the altar still pristine and unstained, not soaked in the black-red of death, its edges hardening with coagulation while the dying being upon the cross still lives.

I clasp my hands together before my face, the base of my thumb nestled at the point where my nose meets my brow, and I begin to beg. Beg to this being before me, this nonsense, for mercy. For isn't that what you are meant to grant, oh Saviour of Mankind? Forgiveness? Absolution? Grant us a new beginning, our sins, our regrets washed away never to return?

But where faith should be there is nothing but desperation; where belief should reside, nothing but a primal roar of challenge. Forgive me if you dare. If you truly have the power to do *anything*.

'Forgive me.'

The words leave my mouth like a chant upon a rosary, and I realise it is not him to whom I plead, not to this carved wooden idol mounted before me, nor the figure it represents. But to her. To the idol that looms large in every moment, her form carved from my memory; the woman whom I have failed, whom I want nothing more than to be with, she who I want to truly grant me forgiveness.

If any bore witness to these words, they would hear just another pilgrim searching for transcendence, another beggar looking for reward, but this God of theirs is gone to me. She is my Christ, the past is my heaven. Nothing the future could bring could save me, for she is gone: dead, buried, unresurrected. Life has gone from this world, its Promethean flame snuffed out, and all that is left are lies, parody and pain.

The sound of the church door opening behind me barely

registers; the footsteps that pound upon the brittle surface of the aisle an echo from another world.

The first thing I am aware of is the fist that pounds into the back of my head.

The force of the blow propels me forward, and my face folds onto the step of the altar, the corner crushing my cheek, my nose cracking against the harsh tile.

'What did you do to my sister?!?'

I push myself up, my vision blurred with pain, and see Kirk standing above me, his face rippling with fury and hatred.

'Answer me, coward! What did you do?'

I turn back to the altar in defiance, continuing my prayer, as if this violence were a mere inconvenience, a distraction from the task at hand, but Kirk grabs me by the shoulder and drags me round to face him.

'She kept her mouth shut, but I saw the look in her eyes, her skirt stretched, her petticoat ripped. Admit it. Admit what you did to her.'

I close my eyes, speaking the words under my breath. 'Percy, I love you, and shall for as long as I live and then beyond.'

His fist makes contact with my face, bloodying my nose, sending a tidal wave of agony through my body.

'Don't think you're safe here, in the house of some non-existent god.' He spits the words like a curse. 'I've slaughtered men as they prayed to their elephant-headed fictions, don't think yours is any different.'

I look towards the altar, the white now speckled with blood, as if the stigmata were finally weeping, and all I can think of is that night. Of losing her. Of the blood. Of her pain.

'My sister loses her husband and you take advantage of her like a common whore? Like some open-legged slut down a back alley. Admit it. Admit what you did.'

He hits me again. The pain almost making me feel alive.

'Please, forgive me,' I strain, hoping that the words will somehow reach her.

Kirk laughs joylessly, as if at a condemned man whose last words have been exposed as fraud.

'No one's forgiving you. No one's protecting you.'

He hits me again, and I feel a numbness come over me, as if this is finally ending. Finally over.

'Please…' I beg, for the first time in as long as I can remember, knowing what I want. What I truly desire.

'Mercy?' he mocks. 'You want mercy? You're asking the wrong person. I've taken too many lives to care about one like yours. I know people. I'll take your body and bury it in a pauper's grave. No one will even know you're dead.' His right hand wraps itself into a fist once more and he draws it back to deliver one last blow, and I plead with him for what would truly be mercy.

'Please … kill me.'

I close my eyes, waiting for the end, the end I realise I have been seeking all along. The only true freedom, the only true escape. The only reunion.

But the blow does not come.

I open my eyes, the anger in his expression replaced by repulsion and disgust. His fist is no longer raised, no longer clenched, and he drops me as if a leper, my sickness about to infect him.

'What … what in hell is wrong with you?'

'Please…'

He edges backwards, my condition now airborne, the act of merely being in my presence dangerous.

'Get away from here. Get away from here, you freak. I ever see you again, I'll cut the eyes out of your head. I won't kill you, but I'll make you feel more pain than you ever imagined possible. So stay away. Stay away from me and my sister.'

He turns his back on me, striding down the aisle of the church, a soldier after a massacre, wishing to leave the scene, to forget what has occurred. Around me, the chapel starts to spin, my awareness fading in and out as I lower myself down to the cold tiles. In the distance, I see the door opening, flooding the church with a divine illumination as if the afterlife were finally welcoming me to its embrace, and, for a moment, I think I see a woman standing over me, but I cannot see her face.

And then the world is nothingness once again.

1872

CHAPTER XVII

An unexpected visitor

I lay the flowers on Percy's grave as I have done for the last eight years, week in, week out, their form all that has marked the passing of seasons since she has been gone; the first daffodils of spring becoming tulips, roses, then dahlias, finally giving way to the snowdrops and hellebores of winter.

Although she still haunts my thoughts, it is only in these moments that I feel any connection with her any more. And though I know the gesture is empty, worthless, I allow myself this one brief respite of pretence, that something matters, that all is not futile.

The path through the village is muddy today. Puddles litter the thoroughfare, finding homes in cart tracks and the undulations of the road. A few villagers are out walking now the rain has cleared, pleased to be free of the confinement of their cottages, despite the inclement weather. They keep their heads down as they pass, knowing better than to talk to me. For a few years they would attempt to approach, bothering me with their small talk, asking after my health, offering their inane condolences, but soon they learnt. And it is better this way. For all of us. They knew I could see them for what they were. Wittering fools. Organ grinders with a broken barrel, spouting a soulless tune. And for a moment they would see themselves like that too – the truth of their meaningless existence. So now they keep their heads down as they pass.

'Sorry, sir!'

I look up, stopping suddenly as a child's hoop rolls past me, continuing its path onward, before teetering and falling sideways into a puddle. A child runs after it in pursuit, pausing as he reaches my feet, looking up and smiling, a stick dangling from his hand.

'I can't control it yet, sir. I ain't got the hang of it.'

His smile quickly fades, as he fails to find the approval he expected, his naive charms unappreciated by the stranger he has had the misfortune of coming across. He averts his eyes, then continues on his course, fetching his hoop from the puddle and cleaning the mud from the smooth wood. He shoots a glance back in my direction before returning to his play, now careful to not stray quite as far from his mother.

I pace onwards, passing the bakery where housewives have come to collect their Sunday roasts from its ovens. I will be glad when this place is behind me and I am walking in the woods that lead to my home. The people here are nothing but a plague upon this earth, merely thinking on their witless presence sends shivers through my body.

'Mr Franklin!'

I ignore the call from behind me, hoping its source will think better than to try again.

'Mr Franklin!'

I turn, making no attempt to hide my contempt, only to find myself face to face with Arnett, the local vicar, his smile unperturbed by my unwillingness to return it. He has not aged well over the years; his youthful features having now become lined and sunken, ill-set within a face that has become ruddy and jowled.

'Mr Franklin! Are you keeping well?'

I shake my head, at his inanity rather than as an answer to the question, and turn away from him once more, but he hops over a puddle, flouncing round and intercepting me from the front – his childlike movements lending him an air of indignity.

'I noticed you in the graveyard. Perhaps we might hope to see you in church again sometime soon?'

'I doubt it.'

'I'm sorry to hear that, but nevertheless, remember that God loves you. His arms are open, awaiting your return.'

I scoff, continuing on my way, as he walks beside me, attempting to prolong the conversation.

'Well, be that as it may, I want you to know that you would be most welcome should you choose to attend. Sometimes the company of others in God's presence can offer solace to those that suffer, Charles.'

'Solace?' I say, stopping for the first time. 'And why would I want that?'

'I…'

He hesitates, and I take the opportunity to push on, leaving him standing in my wake.

'There's a community here, Charles,' he calls after me. 'You'd do well to be part of it.' But I ignore his words, stomping onwards towards the forest path that beckons me.

***

The light is fading by the time I arrive at the cottage. I sit by the window and touch up a print of a dead child. There is some blurring by the girl's left hand, from the pour being bad, and I can't tolerate it. The boy I took on as my most recent assistant has no talent, and little capacity to learn. I'll have to let him go and find someone new; it's an inconvenience but I shall be glad to see the back of him. I only took him on so I could use his eyes for an older boy. There's little call for them, hence there was a gap within my library, but he has served his purpose now, and although his future will not involve a career in photography, he will live on in the work.

137

The years have been good to me, my work having become fashionable in society's upper circles. Though Cameron and Wynfield may be the names on the public's lips (with photographs that Warwick would have no doubt described as 'indecent' before they became a cause célèbre (for how could a progressive like he disapprove of them now?)), mine command the same sums. 'Almost worth dying for' as some third-rate wit said, a phrase which now seems to haunt me whenever I enter a house where some unloved relative has passed. Sometimes, I suspect them of having slipped the deceased something in their pursuit of the 'novelties' I offer. But I do not care. I'll take their money, and charge them twice as much as the others I work for. They've too much of it anyway.

Before long, it is too dark to work, and I restoke the fire, using it to warm the remains of a stew I had yesterday. They always say a stew is better on the second day, but I have never found it to be the case. People search for difference where there is none, as if change were the currency, but change is nothing but illusion – a way of maintaining hope, as we move from one dissatisfaction to another.

As I eat, I look at the photograph I took all those years ago, I don't know what has prompted me to take it out. My face broken and bruised, my nose bent, my eye swollen. It is one of the few photos of me I have, and, although the wounds that the soldier dealt me have faded (except the slight kink in the bridge of my nose), I believe it is the only one that captures my soul. The mirrors here, if uncovered, would lie, but that photograph reveals me as I truly am. Battered and beaten, skewed into unhappy angles, fixed in a moment that has long since passed.

The hammering on the door interrupts my melancholy.

'Franklin? Charles Franklin?'

I tear another piece of bread from the loaf beside my plate, dipping it in the gravy, unmoved by the urgency of the knocking, hoping that if I ignore the man, whoever he is, he will go away. A summons from Warwick no doubt – his desperation for coin enough to justify an intrusion so late in the evening.

But the knocking continues.

Reluctantly, I put down the bread, return the photograph to its drawer and walk to the door. Why the hell the man can't just slip something under it, I have no idea, but he sounds insistent.

'What?' I say, opening it. 'Be quick, you're letting the heat out.'

The man standing at the door isn't from the telegraph office. He's a coachman, from London by the sound of his accent, and he clearly lacks the poise of someone who delivers messages on a daily basis. At least to those above the lowest rungs of society.

'Mr Franklin?' he says hesitantly, fiddling with a grubby curl of hair at his temple.

'Yes,' I reply. 'Spit it out, man. I haven't got all night.'

'Yes, sir, 'course, sir. It's just…' He pauses, unsure how to continue.

'Just what?'

'A lady, sir. She died, sir.'

I release a snort of derision, waving him away with a gesture. 'Just give me the address. It's too late for tonight – there's no light. I'll be there in the morning.'

'No, sir, you don't understand. There's a child.'

I lost my fear of photographing dead children many years ago, but I can see he finds the whole idea very affecting.

'Be that as it may, it doesn't change the light. It will have to wait till the morning.'

'No, sir – she's here. On my cart. They said she's your daughter.'

He gestures towards the cart. On it I can see a young girl silhouetted in the eerie light of the half-moon, the sky now free of clouds after the day of rain, cold no longer held at bay by their blurred shroud.

'There's been a mistake,' I explain. 'I don't have a daughter. You've got the wrong house.'

I shake my head, annoyed at having my time wasted, waving him away and shutting the door. He puts a foot in it to stop me.

'No, sir – *Mr Charles Franklin*. I've got it written down 'ere. They was very specific.'

I look at the note he hands me. My name and address are indeed written upon it, but it doesn't change the fact that a mistake has been made.

'I don't know who gave you this, but they must have given you the wrong note. I'm a photographer.'

'Sir – I only know what I've been told. Her mother died. She left instruction to bring her to you. Her name was Watkins. Orpha Watkins.'

This time, the hesitation is mine. The name brings back a flurry of memories. But this doesn't make sense. I don't know why she would do this – I can only put it down to a moment of delirium on her deathbed. A blurring of events resulting in a chain of events that has led this man here.

'I assure you there's been a mistake,' I reiterate, but I am no longer confident in my appraisal.

'Like I said – all I know is what I've been told, sir.'

I step outside, my breathing becoming shallow and stilted. I look once again towards the figure upon the cart at the cottage gate.

'That's her?'

'Yes, sir.'

'Well, I can't… What do they expect me to do with her?'

'I don't know, sir. I've been paid to bring her here. That's all I know.'

'Well, take her back. This is absurd. Take her back to where she came from. There must be a relative or something.'

140

'There's no one, sir.'

The night in question comes back to me fully formed in my mind's eye: Orpha, our union, the church, Kirk.

'What about the brother? Why don't they take her to him?'

'No one can locate him. They think he's in India.'

'Sorry, no – she'll have to go back.'

'It's either here or the workhouse, they said.'

'For Christ's sake. What is wrong with this damned country?!? When did I become a bloody nursemaid?'

I stumble backwards into the cottage, raising my hands prayer-like to my face, each snatched breath echoing back to me from between my palms, as I attempt to parse the situation. A child. Mine. She had told me she was unable to bear them, but the fault could have easily have been with her husband. Men are so quick to shift the blame for their own failings…

'What do you want me to do, sir? Shall I bring her in or not?'

I nod. 'Yes. Bring her in.'

The coachman goes to fetch the child, and I stand there in my small downstairs room, unable to move, comprehension and reason lost to me. Suddenly, the bleak existence that I have been living feels warm and comforting, my dour home a sanctuary, about to be invaded by a stranger. She cannot be mine. She cannot be.

I turn to see the coachman, standing in the doorway, his hand on the shoulder of the child. She has her mother's hair – the same as my wife's – as well as the woman's features, as delicate as if they were cast from porcelain. Her clothes are simple, but decent, the threadbare cape, that of a genteel family fallen on hard times, but maintaining their dignity nonetheless. She keeps her eyes to the floor, unwilling to look at me, her hands clasped in front of her, a shield held but not raised for fear of offence.

'This is her, sir.'

'Yes. Thank you,' I reply. 'That will be all.'

The coachman stirs, but does not leave, moving impatiently from foot to foot, expectant. I go to the sideboard, and take out some coins, returning to press them into his hand. He looks down at them, seemingly satisfied, nods and leaves.

I shut the door behind him, and suddenly the child and I are alone. I look down at her, but her head remains bowed. The silence surrounding us that has been my constant companion for as long as I can remember, now seems awkward and oppressive. Moistening my lips with my tongue, I attempt to speak, but my throat is dry and the words come haltingly.

'Would you ... would you like to sit down?'

'If you'd like, sir.'

I indicate a chair, and her eyes flick up from the floor towards it for a moment, before returning downwards as she walks over to sit.

I pull out another chair from the table, turning it to face her, and sit down opposite.

'What is your name?'

'Aggie, sir.' Her voice is a whisper, barely audible even in the quiet. For the first time, I notice how thin she is, cheeks that should be full, taut on the bone, her arms bird-like in their fragility.

'Have you eaten?' I ask.

'No, sir.'

'What do you eat? I have bread, cheese. There's stew if you want it.'

'Yes please, sir.'

'Which one?'

'Anything.'

I nod and go to the fire, ladling out some of the remaining stew from the pot. It's still warm even away from the heat of the hearth.

142

It would have been good for tomorrow, but I can buy something from the village.

'They said I am to live with you.'

I turn to her, the bowl in my hand. She is looking at me now, attempting to make sense of things.

'I… I'm going to help you find your uncle. Then you can go and live with him,' I reply. 'Here.'

I put the bowl in front of her, and she starts to eat greedily, shovelling spoonful after spoonful into her mouth, the gravy staining her chin. Suddenly, she looks up at me, aware that she is being watched.

'I'm sorry, sir.' She sits up straighter and resumes her eating with a new sense of decorum, wiping her mouth, and taking each mouthful more slowly as her mother has no doubt taught her. I cut her a slice of bread and butter it. Again she eats it delicately, between mouthfuls of stew.

'How old are you?'

'Seven, sir.'

'And your uncle – he's in the army?'

'Yes, sir.'

'You don't need to call me, sir.'

'Sorry, sir.'

Her mistake causes no amusement, no mirth. I watch in silence as she finishes her food, no longer wishing to subject her to my interrogations. After she takes her last mouthful, she replaces the spoon on the table, continuing to sit quietly, her eyes downwards once more.

'Are you still hungry?'

'No, sir.'

'Tired?'

She nods her head.

'You can have my room. I'll sleep in here.'

I take her up to the bedroom. The stairs creak underfoot as I walk, but as I wait for her to join me at the top, they are silent beneath her steps, as if I am being followed by a ghost. She reaches the top and we go in. The bed is made, but has been slept in. I have no clean sheets, so she will have to make do.

'This is it,' I tell her bluntly. 'There's a pot under the bed. If you need to empty it, come and find me. Do you need a candle?'

'No, sir.'

She sits down on the edge of the bed. A sliver of moonlight from the shutters, slightly ajar, forms a crack on the darkness of the mattress. She does not speak again, so I nod her a goodnight and descend the stairs, shutting the door behind me.

The fire is low in the grate now, but still burns. I take a log from the basket, unsure as to whether to rekindle the flames. It's late and sleep beckons, but perhaps I am not yet ready for it. I squat down by the glowing embers, the log still in my hand, a bundle of indecision and numbness. As I look upon the fire, I think back on Orpha. Poor, lovely, Orpha; so lost in death at the moment of our meeting, but clearly so much more. A contented wife before, a mother after, but in that instant merely herself, hurt and broken. Her face is blurry, indistinct in my mind; more like Percy's than I'm sure it was, but Percy's face itself is only clear because it is no longer a memory, merely an amalgam of all the photographs I took of her. A thousand images reassembled into one.

I find it hard to mourn for her, this woman I knew for but a few hours, the prints I had of her destroyed in shame; harder still to believe that what I have been told is true. That she bore this girl, raised her, clothed her, fed her, alone, all without my knowledge; that this child has been in the world all these years past; my flesh, my blood, unbeknownst to me. But it is of no matter. She is not mine, not in any true sense. Tomorrow, I will find her uncle, find her somewhere to go, then things will be as they were before.

Above me, I hear crying. Small sobs muffled by the floorboards and plaster, but distinct nonetheless, for, apart from them and the intermittent crackling in the grate, the silence here is absolute. Slowly, they grow in volume, until they become mournful wails, loss filtered through the perception of a child. Unthinking, I toss the log into the fire, and walk towards the stairs to go to her.

As I mount the first step, the straining ache of the wood beneath gives me pause. And instead of going to her, I stand there, listening. She is not mine. Not my responsibility. I walk away from the stairs and sit down on the chaise in the corner. It is late; perhaps I shall try to sleep. I grab my coat from the side to use as a makeshift blanket, and lie back down upon the worn velvet of the upholstery, tucking a cushion beneath my head to use as pillow. Before long, the candle burns out, and I lie there in the semi-darkness, awake, listening to the sound of the fire. Trying to ignore Aggie's tears.

CHAPTER XVIII

In which Aggie accompanies me to the village

'Come on, this way.'

I emerge from the forest path out into the edge of the village. Aggie is lagging behind, unable to keep up the pace that I am used to. She doesn't complain, but constantly having to wait makes me irritable.

I stand there while she catches up, and we make our way into the village proper. I'll need more food now there's another mouth to feed, and I don't want to be dragging her into town while I am working because there's nothing to eat. We walk side by side down the road. The mud is still soft underfoot, but no longer wet enough to stick to our shoes. Aggie keeps up by breaking into the occasional trot, seemingly refreshed by the sight of sky above us, relieved to have put the oppression of the woodland canopy behind her.

As we walk, I can feel the villagers' eyes upon us, upon this girl who is at my side. Their looks are those of curiosity rather than judgement, but I am sure that would change were the truth to be known; a child born out of wedlock would be fodder for the wagging tongues of local housewives and gossips. I am surprised to find the thought bothers me, but it is as if I can already hear their imagined whispers, seeing another reason for them to involve themselves in my life, another imposition upon my peace.

Across the street, I see the boy with the hoop from yesterday, his mother absent now, as he diligently tries to perfect his purposeless skill. Again, he loses control of the wooden ring, sending it flailing into the centre of the road. He bounds towards it, but, on seeing me, stops, leaving the fallen hoop in its place, wary of approach. I carry on, regardless, but Aggie breaks away from our path to pick it up. I look round, annoyed, as she rescues it from the remains of a puddle, and holds it out towards him.

'Aggie, come on!'

The boy approaches, hesitantly, and takes it from her, offering Aggie a nervous smile in return.

'Hurry up,' I shout. 'We need to be quick. I have work to do.'

I start to walk, and she skips after me, her gait somehow unaffected by her mourning, the energy of childhood seeping through the weight of her loss. Another hundred yards, and we have reached the bakery. I see Mabel looking out through the window, her interest piqued by Aggie's presence, but by the time we are at the doorway, Mabel has vanished into the back kitchen, her daughter instead coming to the front door to greet us.

'Good morning, Charles,' Molly beams from the threshold.

'Molly,' I nod.

She walks ahead of us as we go inside, stepping behind the counter. I point coldly at the loaves. 'Two of those.'

'Certainly,' she says, offering Aggie a wink. It's irritating how people are around children. No doubt this is how it will be until I am rid of her. 'Would you like butter?'

I nod, and she wraps a slab in paper, then hands it over along with the bread, but I can feel that all of this is merely an extended prelude to her oncoming question.

'There we are,' she smiles. 'And who have we here?'

Aggie keeps her head down, shyly, as if engaging would be a breach of etiquette, so I cut in, answering the question myself, 'Aggie.'

Molly looks at me, attempting to hide her curiosity with a half-smile, but when she gets nothing more, she turns her attention back to the child. 'Is Mr Franklin looking after you today?'

147

'She's staying with me for a few weeks,' I tell her after Aggie's response fails to appear. 'Then she'll be moving on.'

Aggie looks up at me, as if my words have surprised her. They shouldn't have – I was quite clear when we discussed it yesterday – but children are a mystery to me. And yet, despite myself, I find myself offering an explanation to soften the sentiment behind my words.

'We're trying to locate her guardian.'

'He's not my guardian,' Aggie says, looking up at me cautiously. 'He's my uncle.'

Molly's face lights up at her words, as if a poor broken bird she was nursing back to health has uttered its first tweet.

'My mother died,' Aggie offers by way of explanation.

Molly's expression changes in an instant; hope dropping from her face like a ball from the hand of a child who just saw a man crushed by the wheel of a cart.

'Oh, you poor thing, you. Oh, darling, I'm so sorry. Mum!' she shouts through to the back room. 'Mum – come here, you need to meet Aggie.'

Mabel lumbers through, feigning curiosity about what is important enough to keep her from her work, even though she's clearly been waiting to come through since she spotted us at the window. Her apron is patterned with stray bits of dough beneath a dusting of flour, her face red from the heat of the oven. Molly leans over and whispers into her mother's ear, the change in Mabel's expression mimicking that of her own a few moments earlier.

'Oh, my poor dear. Bless you. Bless your heart.' She puts a hand to Aggie's cheek, leaving a streak of flour upon her, for a moment hiding the pink of Aggie's skin. Mabel spots it and wipes her hands on her apron, so she can go in to dust it off. 'We'll get you something nice, shall we? Would you like that? An Eccles cake?' she questions. 'A bun, maybe?'

Aggie flashes the first hint of a smile that there has been since she came to me. It lasts for barely a moment, never becoming fully realised, and yet it offers me a glimpse of who she was, probably but a few spare weeks before; a happy child, a bundle of joy and hope.

'A bun, please.'

Mabel leaps into action, transforming compassion into movement. 'We'll get you a nice bun, then. I've just glazed some fresh out of the oven. I'll bring them over and you can pick one. How does that sound?'

Aggie nods, and Mabel hurries off into the kitchen, Molly offering me a bittersweet smile. I avoid her eyes and look towards Mabel who is already reappearing from the oppressive heat of the back room, a tray packed tight with rolled pastries in her hands. The two women huddle around the tray while Aggie picks one out. It's strange seeing Molly and Mabel together – so alike in manner, so different in appearance. Mabel is short and squat, each passing year seeming to draw her closer to the ground, whereas her daughter is tall and slender, a strong nose doing nothing to diminish her prettiness. You would barely think them related but for the overbearing 'warmth' that they share, a river running through the generations. My eyes linger on Molly for a moment. I'm sure in my younger days I would have said her beautiful, but the time for such thoughts is behind me. I shake off the idea, sighing impatiently, repulsed by the sentimentality that has started to encroach upon my thoughts. Mabel registers the noise, but mistakes it for a call for attention, taking it as a cue to come over and talk to me.

'She's so pretty, ain't she?' she says, her eyes fixed on Aggie. 'Beautiful. You must be very proud. I didn't know you had a niece.'

'She's not…' I'm cut off by Aggie sidling towards us, her hand wrapped around the biggest bun from the tray, a mouth-shaped indentation in its side revealing a cliff of holey dough.

'Now you eat that before it gets cold,' Mabel continues. 'Don't let your uncle tell you to save some – they're never as good as when they're warm.' It takes me a second to understand who she's referring to, but I let her mistake lie. Better the village to think Aggie is my niece, than have her presence mired in scandal. Aggie doesn't say anything either, having taken Mabel's instruction with the seriousness of a sermon, filling her mouth repeatedly should she risk the temperature dropping below the level required for perfection.

'Come and see us whenever you like,' Mabel continues. 'We'll be your friends while you're staying. There're some toys you could play with if you stop by. You can come tomorrow if you like.'

'We're going into town tomorrow,' I interrupt.

'The next day then,' she replies, not missing a beat. 'They was Molly's when she was a girl. One day we'll pass them on to her little 'un, but that don't look like it's gonna be happening any time soon.'

She raises her eyebrows and Molly's face flushes with embarrassment. '*Mum.*'

'You'll regret it if you don't 'ave 'em. Trust me on that one.'

Molly looks over at me awkwardly, embarrassed that a stranger should be witness to this conversation. I take it as an excuse to leave.

'We'd best be going.'

I grab the bread, pushing it into my sack, and usher Aggie back out to the street.

'We'll see you soon though, yes?' says Mabel.

I ignore her question, only to find her hand grabbing at my sleeve before I reach the doorway. I turn to face her, looking down on her triangular form, the concern she had suppressed in front

150

of Aggie now, with the child safely outside in the street, carved into the lines of her face.

'I'm so sorry, Mr Franklin. So sorry. Losing your wife so young – that was enough for any man – but now *this*. Was it your sister who...?' For a moment, I am unable to fathom her meaning. 'The girl's mother?'

'No, she was my brother's wife.' I reply, adding, 'He died a long time ago,' to parry her condolences before they appear. I've had enough of those to last a lifetime.

'Well, God bless you for taking her in. There's always been goodness in you. Always.'

I grunt a reply, then leave to join Aggie outside. If there were a God watching, I doubt a blessing is what he'd be bestowing upon me.

The rest of the day passes slowly. As much as I wish to make arrangements for her future as quickly as possible, making the trip to London for that alone seems a waste, so we pass the hours in my cottage. She appears as uncomfortable in my presence as I am in hers, so avoiding interaction proves easier than I thought it might. And yet, although I have work to occupy me for the remainder of the morning, her presence across the room is a constant distraction. She fidgets in her chair, intermittently mumbling to herself, before walking uncomfortably round, every so often twisting her toes into the floorboards like she is crushing something underfoot.

Luckily, the afternoon brings the first appearance of the sun in days, and Aggie jumps at the opportunity to go outside and explore. As she leaves the cottage, I feel as if a yoke has been lifted from my shoulders. How anyone can bear to live with a child, I have no idea. The damned things are relentlessly frustrating; bunches of nervous energy, constantly moving, twitching, making noise. With her gone, time passes more quickly, and the touching up of the prints is soon done. I pull some paper from a drawer, so I can compose my message to Kirk, instinctively reaching for a candle to supplement the fading light.

And I realise I haven't seen the girl in hours.

I suppress the urge to rush, walking calmly across the room, before opening the door to the outside. Darkness is still a good half hour off, but the light has taken on a grey tinge that seems to turn the whole world into silhouette. Aggie is nowhere. I step over the threshold and out onto the path that leads to our front gate. As I look from side to side, it strikes me how manicured the garden still is, its borders neat and ordered. And suddenly I have no idea why. Why I have bothered week in, week out to bud and prune, when I have let everything else in my life go? But I know the thought to be a distraction, and I cannot stop it gradually giving way to the panic I have been feeling since I realised I have no idea where Aggie is.

'Aggie!'

The world responds with a blank silence, the clouds that now coat the sky absorbing the sound in an instant. Suddenly I become aware of the sound of my own breathing; my heartbeat echoing dully in my ears, like a toy drum muffled under a blanket. My eye catches the front gate, and I notice it is ajar, and I recall the sound of the latch falling behind us as we returned from the bakery. I look off into the woodland that starts at the end of the small lane at the front of the cottage. Within the shelter of its trees, the light is already gone, and I am filled with visions of her deep within its darkness, a girl from a fairy tale who has strayed from the path, unable to find her way home. I shake the thoughts from my mind. The woodland doesn't stretch far, and this is England – the modern day – where words can be sent across continents, and steam trains travel underground – not some ancient German forest, alive with wolves and dark magics. She won't be far.

I walk around the cottage to the garden at the back, my pace deliberately measured, a reminder to myself that nothing is wrong, nothing amiss. The hidden sun now behind me, it is clear the light is dying faster than I thought. I scour the garden but Aggie is nowhere. I had convinced myself she would be here, looking out towards the fields beyond, innocently unaware of my presence and calls. My panic.

I shout her name again, the words dissipating into nothingness.

'Damn it.'

Marching back round to the front of the building, I dally over whether to fetch my coat or push straight out into the woodland beyond, my worry beginning to disorient me. I shouldn't waste time. The longer I hesitate, the worse the light will be, the further she will be from the edge...

'Sir?'

I turn to find Aggie behind me, emerging from behind the low wall that hides the chicken coop.

Scoldings and reprimands echo round my head, but the words there remain unuttered. Instead, I just stare at her, the silence between us a mumbled whisper; and rather than relief, all I feel is that familiar emptiness once more.

'Let's go inside.'

For dinner we eat the bread and butter we bought from the village. I cut us each a wedge of cheese from the wheel sitting on the sideboard, before re-covering it with a tea towel; then we sit at the table, the sound of chewing and occasional staccato snap of a knife against china the only things that punctuate the quiet.

Aggie eats bird-like, no longer burdened by hunger, pinching off fingerfuls of her bread, seemingly preferring the crumbs of cheese that dot her plate to the slices she deliberately cuts. I watch her as she finishes her food, framed by the wall of photographs behind her, the only living thing in a tableau of death, but my gaze is not returned with so much as an inquisitory glance. Instead, her eyes remain down, focusing on the faded blue pattern of her plate, and the bone-handled knife beside it. The composition triggers a pang of guilt within me.

'Would you like more?'

Aggie shakes her head but does not raise her eyes.

'I've an apple if you'd like one? They're from last year, but they're still good.'

'Yes, please.'

I go to the pantry to fetch her one and another for myself, standing there for a moment to compose myself as I unwrap them from the paper, before returning to the table.

I hand Aggie her russet and lean back in my chair, cutting a slice from my own. Aggie bites into her apple with an almighty crunch. I look up and our eyes meet for a moment, before she suddenly releases a giggle. For an instant the tension between us is broken. And then we both look away once more, descending back into our silence.

'Do you have a photograph of my mother?'

I look up, surprised to hear her speak, more so by my sudden urge to please her.

'No,' I reply. 'I would like to have one to show you, but I... I don't have it any more.' I hesitate, a thought occurring to me suddenly. 'I may have the plate.'

I go through to my lab, looking through the pile of crates where the plates are stored. It doesn't take me long to find the right one – my years of solitude having been characterised by an obsessive classification, order colonising the space that emotion once inhabited. A few seconds later, the plate is balanced delicately between my hands and I return to the parlour.

'It's a negative. The colours are backwards – I can print it for you, if you like.'

She reaches out to take it from me.

'Don't touch the picture – hold it by the edges.'

She does as instructed, holding up the plate to examine it more carefully.

'I recognise the shapes. Did you make this for her?' I nod. 'My mother had it next to her bed. She said it was very special to her, but the man in it made me feel creepy. I used to have nightmares that he was chasing me.'

'He was your father,' I reply.

She doesn't respond. I suddenly realise I don't know what she's been told, what she knows. Asking outright seems like it would be wrong, so I let it lie, and Aggie hands the picture back to me, turning to the others cramped into their spaces on the walls like prisoners on a ship.

'Who are the people up there?'

I start to answer, only to change my mind and parry the question. It is better that the truth of the photographs should be kept confined, hidden away where she cannot see.

'Just people I took pictures of.'

Aggie considers my response, and begins to walk around the perimeter of the room, so she can examine the photographs in more detail.

'They look strange.'

'They're sleeping.'

'Then why are their eyes open?'

I shift uncomfortably in my chair. 'I don't think we should be talking about this.'

'Couldn't you have just taken the pictures when they woke up?'

It is as if I can hear my secrets struggling below decks, shouting angrily for their freedom, pleading with a voice that aims to shame me into action.

'They weren't going to wake up.'

Aggie doesn't break my gaze, responding in a tone that suggests she knew all along; that all she was looking for was an admission.

'Then they're not sleeping.'

For the first time, I see an anger within her too. I hadn't noticed it before, but it's there. A righteous indignance at the lies that she has been told, at the shadows that the adults told her were alive, while they made shapes with their hands at the fireside.

'Someone told me my mother was sleeping, but she wasn't. She was dead. It's not the same.' There's a strength behind her words that shames me. 'Dead people don't come back. No matter how much you want them to, they don't come back.'

In an instant, her composure topples, like a body whose balance I have misjudged, and she struggles to hold back her tears, her expression contorting into angular shapes as it fractures for one moment after another before returning once again to a stasis of quiet desolation.

'She said she'll always look after me though,' she suddenly says in defiance, 'so I know she's watching me, even if she is dead. She's in heaven so it doesn't matter if her eyes are closed or open. People in heaven can just see you anyway.'

I manage to draw a smile upon my countenance in an attempt to reassure her; but it lasts no longer than the contortions she was experiencing a moment earlier, and is filled with hesitance and doubt.

'I hope so. I hope they judge us kindly.'

I imagine my wife looking down upon me, wondering whether, if she were here, she would still love me, having seen what I have done, who I have become? I change the subject, eager to avoid the answers that lurk beneath the surface of my mind.

'She was kind to you, your mother?'

Aggie nods, a slight smile playing on her lips.

'She was,' she replies. 'She was the kindest mother I could want.

She would take me out to the park and once we even had ice cream, which was really cold.' Her pace increases as she becomes intoxicated by the remembering. 'At Christmas she would let me decorate the tree, and we would put on sweets and fruits and decorations and candles, but we wouldn't light them for long in case they started a fire, and every night when I went to sleep she would sit by my bed and stroke my head and call me her beautiful darling, and...'

The cracks in her voice finally give way to her pain, and her tears come unabated.

'Please... Please don't cry...'

'Sorry, sir.'

'Don't be. Come here.'

I go over, hesitantly reaching out towards her and she comes in, burying her head in my shoulder.

'It's always hard when we lose someone. But you find a way to cope.'

I feel as if the words have been spoken to my younger self as much as to her. She doesn't look up, and I put my hand on her head, stroking it as tenderly as I know how. Her hair is soft, and the warmth of her head penetrates my waistcoat, the first feeling of human contact I have had in years. I can see how people learn to love children, their vulnerability, their need. It makes no sense, I have seen younger than her fend for themselves on the streets, and yet I feel a sudden urge to care for her, to protect her.

The intensity of the feeling disarms me, and suddenly her proximity seems cloying; her presence an imposition on my space. I edge away from her, holding her at arms length, before relinquishing contact entirely. When I speak, my voice has taken on the formality of a stranger.

'We'll go to town in the morning to try and contact your uncle,' I tell her, coldly. 'Then you can be with your family again.'

The words land heavier than I intended. Perhaps not to her, but to me.

In the morning, before she wakes, I make a print from the plate of her mother, masking the part of the negative that contains Orpha's husband, the man who pursued Aggie in her dreams. I superimpose Orpha's image upon the empty backdrop of my studio through a plate I keep to correct substandard pours.

And then it is as if he was never there. Erased from existence, as I was from her history, until the moment she arrived at my door.

CHAPTER XIX

Too many people

We arrive in London before lunch.

The War Office has little information on Kirk, except for the barracks in India where he is stationed. Whether he is still there or has been moved on, they cannot say; but it is all we have to go on. I know there is a telegraph office in Blackfriars, close to where I'm meeting Bates – so I determine to send a message from there.

We choose the discomfort of the omnibus over the dangers of a hackney carriage or hansom, a token nod to some hidden paternal instinct. The weather is good so there's little chance of the bus turning over, whereas a cab would not offer the same reassurance. The presence of the girl seems to preclude me from the roof, so we squeeze ourselves inside. Aggie passes through into the compartment with ease, whereas I am forced to crouch beneath the low ceiling.

A woman in her forties eyes us as we get on, and the only seats free are the ones next to her. Warily, we take them. I keep my eyes downward, but I can feel her gaze from my periphery, her head constantly pirouetting towards us, attempting to engage. For some reason, she reminds me of a pelican I once saw in the zoo, waking from its sleep and struggling to move its head with anything approaching grace.

'Your daughter's quite lovely,' she caws, attempting to break what passes for silence in the roar of a London thoroughfare.

I nod politely, fearing any denial will just prompt further enquiry, but she appears to have already committed to the endeavour.

'I saw you coming from the war office,' she notes. 'Are you a soldier?'

'No.'

'Well, that *is* a relief to hear! A relief indeed. I always feel it's such a shame when a child is denied their father's presence for such long periods. A mother's love is, of course, central, but a father's strength: irreplaceable!'

Her declaration has enough volume to make the other passengers turn and look at her. She accepts their stares as admiration, a picture of haughty pride and self-assurance. I feel my jaw tighten, and look back down to the dirty straw beneath my feet, only allowing myself to turn back to her for a moment to imagine her dead; her mouth hanging open, her face painted and rouged, strapped to a chair like a coach driver to the post behind his seat as he descends Holborn Hill, while I mould her into a picture of dignity – dead, gone, yet still more use than she ever was in life. My imagined cruelty shocks me, and although I wish to share a glance with Aggie, I am ashamed meet her gaze. The woman continues her 'chatter' as the wheels continue to turn noisily against the cobbled streets, and we travel onwards to our destination.

***

'I need to send a telegraph to Lieutenant Andrew Kirk. He's stationed in Calcutta.'

The clerk at the telegraph office seems to have the weight of the world pressing down upon him.

'We can try, sir, but arrangements aren't always the most reliable over there. The line's good of course, but once it leaves the office, what happens next is anyone's business.'

'Aren't they employees of the company?'

'Of course, sir, but, one must understand, *India.*'

I shrug, and hand him the note.

'Send it.' It's not as if I have a choice.

He takes the message from me, pawing its edges between finger and thumb.

'Is he expecting the communication, sir?'

'No.'

He considers my response with an expression of the utmost seriousness. 'Then, perhaps I might suggest you send a letter as well, sir…' His eyes glance down to the paper and he scans the message upon it. Tragic loss, a plea for assistance and the practicalities of locating me condensed down to twenty-one words. He looks back up at Aggie, his eyes full of compassion, drinking in her loss like a tourist taking in the Jura Mountains. '…if it's important.'

His eyes jump up to mine, and his mournful look is replaced with the smile of good customer service. 'Three pounds and ten shillings, sir.'

I balk at the price, but nod and hand over the money. 'How long will it take?'

'Twenty-eight minutes, sir,' he replies, as if it is a feat he has achieved single-handedly.

His specificity almost makes me smile, but my head is already calculating how long it will take for Kirk to come home and take the girl off my hands. If the message reaches him quickly, it will be a month or so at best – substantially longer if the telegraph fails and I have to rely on the letter. It's longer than I'd hoped for, but I am unable to see an alternative.

'Right – we're late.'

I usher Aggie back out into the street, feeling the clerk's doleful look of sympathy heavy on our backs. The studio is only a few streets away so we walk the remainder of the way. It surprises me how different the London streets feel with a child in tow. Aggie moves more slowly than I am used to, and her speed coupled with her diminutive stature, means she is constantly almost trampled by men of industry strutting between appointments. When then find they have to alter their trajectory to continue along their route, tuts follow as predictably as night follows day, as if the crowds should part for them like waves for Moses. As we stop to cross to the other side of the street, Aggie takes it as a cue to speak.

'Will it reach him, Mr Franklin?'

I don't want to lie to her, but she needs hope right now. A sense that things are under control.

'We'll send a letter to make sure, but, yes, I think it will.' I cannot read her reaction. 'Does that please you?'

'Of course, sir.'

'Please, call me Charles.'

'Sorry, sir… Charles.'

She looks back towards the road, and we take the opportunity to cross as a pair of cabs get into each other's way and stop the oncoming thrall.

But her hesitation has made me curious. 'What do you think of your uncle?'

'He's nice. Very nice. He's doing good work in India. Mother said so.' I struggle not to scoff, but instead prompt her to continue. 'My uncle showed me India on a map. It's a very long way away, so he must be nice if he will travel all that way to help.'

'So you've spent some time with him?'

'A little. He's visited us a few times. Mother said it was kind of him to send us money so she could look after us while he was away. I think he would have liked to have visited us more, but he was doing important work for Queen Victoria.'

'You know I'd have sent you money if I'd known?'

'What do you mean, sir?'

162

'If I'd known... There was you.'

I'm distracted from the conversation by a face I see walking towards us. It takes me a second to place her – Rowan I think was her name – and just as my memories of Percy have been absorbed by the photographs I have of her within our home, this woman's face is branded on my consciousness by the print upon my wall – I have not seen her since I took a picture of their weightless child all those years ago. She notices me too, the memory taking her a few seconds longer to access, but then she registers my presence with a look of horror and dismay. She stumbles a little and stops walking, the memory of her loss made flesh in my being. Without acknowledgement, she looks away, as if she has spotted something cursed, a medusa that might trap her in the stone of memory.

I watch on as she draws her hand unthinkingly to her stomach, reaching to comfort the child that once grew within, before suddenly turning to look behind, panicked and desperate. From the crowds emerges her husband, smiling, unaware of what has caused his wife her sudden distress. Holding his hand is a small boy. Their child. She rushes to him, and I see the relief on her face as she looks halfway back towards me, before thinking twice and turning back to the boy, then urging her husband down a side street, away from the man who once photographed their dead child.

'Do you know her?' Aggie asks me. 'The woman you were looking at?' I hadn't realised she'd noticed me staring.

'No,' I reply. 'She just looks like someone I met once. Come on – the studio's just down here.'

I spot the men carrying a body into the studio from halfway down the street, squatting down to distract Aggie from what is happening ahead of us.

'You're going to need to do exactly as I say when we're inside,' I explain. 'This is my work, I need you to behave.'

Aggies nods, and I glance over her shoulder to see the men returning to their carriage before clamouring off down the street. I get to my feet, and lead her the last few hundred yards to the studio entrance. I haven't worked at Bates's for six months at least, but a number of families have clubbed together following an industrial accident, and it will take two of us to arrange and photograph their late husbands together. Personally, I don't see the point in it – it won't save much time (or them much money) – but Bates has offered to take a cut in his share of the payment, so they can afford it. It's the same as always – as much as Bates professes to only care about pounds and shillings, he's a soft touch when it comes down to it.

'You're late,' Bates scowls as he sees me ascending the stairs, a moment later noticing Aggie mounting the steps behind me. 'Oh,' he says, surprised, 'Who 'ave we 'ere then?'

'Aggie, sir.'

'I'm not "sir", but he's *definitely* not,' I interject.

'Don't listen to 'im – you can call me what you want. "Sir", "Madam", I don't mind. Although if you call me "Mr Franklin" I'll take it as an egregious insult, so you better save that for them that deserves it.' Aggie smiles in reply. It's more than I've got out of her since we met.

'Where'd you pick up this little angel?' he asks, looking at me, suspicious. Perhaps he sees something of me in her features, perhaps he is merely intrigued by her sudden appearance. Either way, he chooses not to press the issue.

'We got five of 'em in there,' he says, standing.

'Five? *Christ.*'

'Don't worry – only three of 'em are mangled.' He regrets the utterance the moment it comes out of his mouth, trying to soften

164

his statement with a smile in case Aggie had any inkling of his meaning. 'You go and sit in the waiting room, darlin'. We'll call you when we're done. I can bring her out that doll we use in the back of the photos.'

The suggestion sends a shiver through me, but I realise his idea is a good one. 'If you'd like.'

He heads into the studio, and I follow behind, turning briefly to caution Aggie once more, while Bates fetches the doll.

'Stay out here. Do not come in. Do you understand?'

Aggie nods.

Bates appears with the toy, and we enter the room together. As I shut the door behind us, I feel relief wash over me. Relief to be free of her for a few moments, free of responsibilities, free of the need to *care*; free to be with the dead once more.

CHAPTER XX

Hide and Seek

The session is a slow one, the work laborious. Over the years, we've developed prosthetics for situations such as this, but only a single instance of each. Two of the men both have the same side of their faces crushed, forcing us to improvise. Bates's attempts to pose one of them leaning, his chin on his hand (also mangled), look ridiculous. The fingers of the glove the man wears look chunky and obviously stuffed when elevated to such a prominent position in the photograph. In the end, we're forced to angle him away from the camera, as if he has been distracted away from the gentlemen's club to which he seems to belong, by a passing stranger. Still, I'm sure at least four of the families will be pleased with the result, and I am optimistic for the other – his faraway gaze lends him a certain nonchalance that I find pleasing. His wife will no doubt imagine he is distracted from the conversation of the menfolk by thoughts of her. To me, he is musing on the joys and pleasures he never had in his life. A life of toil, sweat, and, ultimately, an unkind death. But who would wish to think on such things?

Even en masse, the bodies themselves have long since ceased to have an effect on me, and the challenge of the work feels welcome after the upsets of the last days. I soon find myself absorbed in the task at hand, its exertions almost a kind of rest. It's not until the arrangement of the corpses is complete that Bates decides to engage me in conversation.

'She yours?'

He continues to stare through the empty box of the camera as he asks, as if the question means as little to me as he is affecting it does to him. I hesitate before answering, but lying seems an unnecessary complication. Especially around Bates. Perhaps it will be good to unburden myself.

'How did you know?'

'She looks like you, Charlie,' he says, finally turning to face me with a smile. 'Plus, I know you 'ave a thing for red 'eads. Always turning to look when one goes by – seen your 'ead turn when we passed a bloody ginger cat. Only goes to follow, that if you made a mistake, it'd probably end up looking like that.'

'My wife had red hair.'

'I got that, Charlie – don't need the bloody Rosetta Stone to work out what's going on with you. You ain't the mystery you think, y'know.'

I don't respond. Not because of his language; I have become used to his manner of speaking after so long – his crudity and directness now seem almost comforting, reassuring – I simply don't know where to begin.

'So what's the story?'

I communicate the simple facts. I tell him about Orpha and her passing, her brother in India (he remembers the beating), about how she kept Aggie's existence from me, and left me with a child on my doorstep seven years after the fact. He pauses, considering what I have said – the man has a capacity for thoughtfulness when he's not constantly trying to shock.

'Do you really think you would 'ave done anything different if you'd known?'

I go to answer but stop myself. Bates has a habit of bringing out a kind of honesty in me. Not honesty so much as a lack of the opposite. We hardly talk about anything of importance when we're together, but it always feels as if he can see through me, and, when it comes down to it, he's the closest thing I have now to a friend.

167

'…I don't know.'

'You wanna know what I think?' he asks, continuing before I can respond. 'I don't think you would 'ave. Come on, Charlie – you've 'ardly been a pillar of the community since your missus died 'ave ya? I've known you nearly ten bloody years and 'ow many times you visited my lodgings? Once. 'Ow many times I visited yours? Face it – you don't want people around – you don't like 'em. I ain't 'olding it against you, Charlie – not the biggest fan myself – but that's the way you are.'

I can't deny what he's saying. Would I really have sent money? Risked the possibility of meeting her, of caring?

I nod. 'I've sent for her uncle. He can take her.' But Bates pulls me up short.

''Old your 'orses, Charlie. I didn't say you *shouldn't* 'ave, I just said you wouldn't,' he says. 'You can't give 'er to that fucker – he beat you 'alf to death. For all we know, he might be the bloody Cannon Street Murderer.'

'She can't stay with me; I can't look after a child.'

Bates pauses, rubbing at his face, nails dragging along his stubble.

'All I'm saying is – think about it. She's a sweet 'un – you can tell just by looking at her. Might be good for you. A new start.'

'I don't want a new start.'

Bates's nostrils flare briefly, bringing an end to his chin-stroking contemplation. And then he is back to the task at hand. 'Right then. You want to do the plate or shall I?'

We exit the studio just before dark. None of the plates are perfect, but the light was running out. I am sure the clients will be happy. As happy as they can be.

Aggie is still in the waiting room. The same as when we left her, except now she is asleep, lying next to a doll that has rested in the arms of a hundred dead children. I scoop her up, cradling her as moments before she held the porcelain figure, and carry her half-conscious to a waiting cab. The men will be here soon to take the bodies. I want her away from here before they arrive.

***

The next morning I collect eggs from the coop as Aggie watches on. It was after eleven when we arrived home late last night and she is still foggy and bleary-eyed despite it being hours since dawn.

'What time is it?' she asks, an overcoat wrapped round her nightdress.

'Ten, close enough,' I tell her.

She nods, then thinks for a moment. 'Why do none of the clocks here work?'

I stuff another couple of eggs into the already full pockets of my coat. They've laid well today – I should have used the basket.

'…I stopped them a long time ago. I never bothered to start them again. I have my pocket watch – it's enough.'

'It would be good for me to know the time though. Do you think you might be able to start them again?'

'You can tell the time?'

'Of course I can, I'm seven.'

'Then perhaps I'll have a look at them.'

The next two chickens have eggs beneath them as well – they're the first they've laid for the last few days. I call over to Aggie, 'Bring me that basket – the one by your feet.'

She picks it up and comes over, the cold and damp of the grass forcing her onto tiptoes. I hand her the two eggs which she puts into the punnet, before emptying the ones from my pocket in too.

'You must like eggs to have so many chickens,' she observes.

'They're for my work,' I tell her. 'You use the whites to make prints.' Aggie looks confused. 'The photographs.' My explanation leaves her none the wiser. 'Perhaps I can show you sometime.'

'Were you taking photographs yesterday?'

'I was.'

'Who were they of? More sleeping people?'

'Just some men.' I change the subject quickly to avoid any further questions. 'Do you like the chickens?'

She nods, a smile cracking through her lips. 'I do. What are their names?'

I find myself smiling in return, 'They're chickens – they don't have names,' but Aggie looks genuinely shocked.

'Why not? They should have names – it wouldn't be nice not to have a name.'

I shrug. 'They stop laying, they'll soon be on my table. I prefer not to exchange personal niceties with something that's going to end up…' I swallow the word 'dead' – the open wound of her mother's loss suddenly filling my awareness.

'Hello?'

I look towards the voice calling around the side of the house, happy for the interruption. A few moments later, Molly appears, her arm threaded through the handle of a basket. She has a neat little dress on beneath her shawl; more something you'd wear to church than the usual work-clothes she dons at the bakery, her face opening up as she sees us.

'You're here! I wasn't sure you were in!' she continues. 'You didn't come by the shop, so I thought I'd come by and see if you were home… I brought the toys.' She holds up the basket as evidence of the reason for her visit, and Aggie goes to her, forgetting her aversion to the wet grass as she skips across its moist surface.

Molly bends down to show Aggie what she has brought. 'We've got a wooden cow, some books, and here's a dolly. Do you like her dress?'

170

She has such ease with the child, it makes me think she should follow Mabel's advice and get married. She would make a good mother. But it just reconfirms my decision to give the girl to her uncle. My relationship with Aggie is awkward, stilted – this is no home for a child. She needs someone who can care for her – who knows *how* to care.

I almost feel jealous of Molly, watching her with my daughter, the warmth emanating from her, flowing like water unimpeded by obstacles, but as I watch them I find my gaze lingering upon her. Molly's face is still flushed from the walk, and it strikes me how her complexion is somehow completely without blemish, like a plate flowed to perfection. She has, of course, the prettiness of youth, but it's more than that – her lips are full and eyes open as if the generosity within her has somehow formed her features to reflect itself.

'She used to be mine, when I was little, but you could have her if you like.'

Aggie nods with genuine elation. 'What's her name?'

'Theodora. But you could call her something else if you liked?'

'No. I like that one. I don't think she'd be very happy if we changed it anyway. Hello Theodora. Did you know Charles hasn't even given his chickens names?'

Molly laughs. 'It doesn't surprise me. Mr Franklin isn't good at the little things. He used to be before…' She stops herself short, an echo of my earlier caution.

'Before what?'

A large smile erupts from Molly's face, an explosion of warmth, its intensity so vivid it almost makes me feel as if everything will be all right.

'A long time ago, that's all. I also brought…' She reveals what had been balanced upon the toys, a treat wrapped in a tea towel, '…a curd tart. It's probably too big for you to eat alone, but I thought Mr Franklin might like some too.' She looks over at me

171

quickly, the same warmth now projected in my direction. 'If you like I could make us all tea…'

'That won't be necessary.'

'Please, sir?' Aggie asks.

I glance down at her pleading expression, her eyes stretched to their limits, imploring me to reconsider.

'Fine. I can work on my…' Aggie's look makes me check myself. I should at least try to appear grateful. 'Thank you. That would be very good of you… Let's go inside.'

***

The freedom of paper makes me long for the limitations of the electric wire. The blank space waiting to be filled makes it feel like the letter is calling for explanations, justification for my actions, but I resist the urge, because I have none. Neither do I need them – my life is my own, I can do with it as I please. But, though arduous, the struggles of the written word provide a welcome distraction from the scene of domestic bliss unfolding across my cottage room. Aggie and Molly are playing together, Aggie serving the doll (Theodora – a ridiculous name for an actual living human let alone a toy) tea and tart, pseudo mother with inanimate daughter, daughter with pseudo mother.

Molly looks over and I flick my eyes to the tea perched on the side of my desk, taking a sip from the china cup as if this were my intention all along. When I glance back, Molly is once again absorbed in the tea-party, the wooden cow next in line to be served, its refreshment poured from an empty pot into an empty cup, a parody of sustenance. Then Aggie presents the cow with some milk. For some reason it makes me smile, the beast being offered the very thing that has been taken from it, its lack of reaction comical in its blankness.

'Right,' Molly announces, standing up from the rug by the fireside, 'Hide and seek. I'll be the finder.' Aggie jumps to her feet enthusiastically.

'You have to close your eyes while I find somewhere.'

'I know that,' Molly replies, her voice tinged with humour. 'I've played hide and seek before.' She puts her hands over her eyes and starts counting exaggeratedly. I turn my attention back to the paper while Aggie pounds across the room.

I don't know if it is Bates's suspicions of Kirk or the giggles undermining my concentration, but finishing the letter feels more difficult than the writing itself; and signing if seems wrong, transgressive, final. Nevertheless, it must be done, and I blot the ink, writing the address on the envelope as Molly calls, 'Coming! Ready or not!' from across the room.

'Come on – you have to help.'

I look up to find Molly standing over my desk.

'No, I don't think so.'

'You've finished – you're writing the envelope.'

'I... I...' The words emerge stumbling from my mouth, as I flail round for an excuse.

'I don't know my way around. If you don't help, I'll be here forever.'

Her expression reminds me of Aggie's, wide-eyed and innocent. Like a stray dog trying to steal your dinner.

'Alright – I'll come... I'll come.'

Molly grabs my sleeve in triumph and drags me up from my chair. She starts to look around the ground floor, while I hover in the background, my arms crossed.

'Come on – you said you'd help.'

'She's not in here – I heard her run across the room.'

Molly shakes her head, as if I am a child who hasn't the first idea what he's talking about. 'You've got to look in the wrong place as well – it's no fun if you just go straight to where they are. Check behind there.'

'Fine.' I walk towards the chaise, shaking my head, looking behind as instructed, knowing Aggie will not be there.

'Better,' Molly replies. 'Now try and look surprised.'

I make an unenthusiastic pantomime of amazement, and Molly rolls her eyes, but the performance somehow affects me, and I find a smile breaking out on my face. Molly smiles back, and we resume the search, our investigations taking on a new lightness.

Molly looks towards the staircase, eyebrows raised. It strikes me how, in another context, her expression could take on a far less appropriate meaning than it does now, but Molly seems naive to the implications. I nod and we creep up the steps like hunters stalking their prey.

It feels strange having her in my bedroom. The space that has been mine alone for almost a decade, now having not only been invaded by a child, but also by a woman I barely know, but Molly seems not to share my discomfort, and her ease begins to spread to me.

'You check the blanket box,' I tell her, 'I'll look behind the curtain.'

We search our respective areas, our eyes meeting after we find them both empty, then we look towards the bed. I go round to the far side, while Molly approaches the other and we stand in our respective positions, imagining Aggie beneath, seeing our legs, trying to hold in her giggles as we somehow fail to find her.

Molly counts down with her fingers, and on one we drop down to the floor, looking underneath the frame, only to come face to face with one another once more, the amusement on our faces replaced by confusion at where Aggie might actually be. We come back to standing and Molly's eyes dart to the wardrobe, the door slightly open. She takes my hand, leading me over, her finger on

174

her lips calling for silence. We open the doors together, finally triumphant…

To nothing but my suits, and Percy's old dresses.

It changes everything. Suddenly, I can feel Molly's hand in mine, the warmth of her touch, the sound of her breathing. Without Aggie here, we are a man and woman alone in my bedroom. We look at each other, and it seems even Molly is no longer naive to the implications. She smiles at me, softly, and hesitantly we let go of one another's hands, as if to rush might imply something was amiss, our fingers lingering upon each other for a second more.

'We should look downstairs again,' I stumble.

'Yes…'

I close the wardrobe doors, and Molly leads the way out of the room, turning back for a final look before heading down the stairs. I follow, and as we descend the steps our conversation turns back to the game, protestations of our surprise in not having found her there uttered with a stilted formality, admiration for her skill in hiding wrapped around our discomfort like a bandage over a wound. But the room downstairs seems as empty as when we left it – the front and back doors both closed, as if Aggie were never there in the first place, the entrance to the back room…

I stop, seeing the door ajar, and rush forward to the room I use as my lab, hoping, praying she is not there.

I had thought the door locked, but the key is still in it – I must have left it there when I put the plates in this morning. I wrench it open, letting the light from the parlour flood into the space, and there she is, sitting amidst the bottles of chemicals, her arms wrapped round her knees, grinning with triumph.

'I fooled you running halfway up the stairs, didn't—'

'What the hell do you think you're doing?'

Aggie's face drops, a picture of hurt and confusion.

'Get out of here – and be careful for God's sake – these chemicals are dangerous.'

She gets to her feet, almost knocking over a bottle. There's a stopper on the top, but it's glass and could easily shatter, flooding the place with collodion. The bloody stuff can kill you or send the whole place up in flames, not to mention the ethers, the pyrogallol, the potassium cyanide. I grab her by the arm and pull her up, forcing her out of the room.

'You never go in there again – do you hear me? *Never*.'

Aggie just stares at me, forlorn, and Molly comforts her with a hand on her shoulder.

'She was just playing, Charles.'

'Quiet,' I snap. Molly's expression takes on the same hangdog look as Aggie's. 'If you ever go in there again, you won't be able to stay here – do you understand?'

She doesn't answer.

'Do you understand?!'

'Yes, sir,' Aggie stutters.

'Good. The door stays shut. There are things behind it that can hurt you. It stays shut.'

CHAPTER XXI

Behind closed doors

Shut doors become the backdrop of Aggie's existence over the next few weeks.

The passing of a number of society figures means I am constantly engaged in house calls, to which Aggie must accompany me. We take the train up to London, then a cab to the studio to fetch my equipment before going onwards to our destination, where I work and Aggie sits outside; on a landing chair, in the sitting room down the hall, in the parlour downstairs, browsing the same few books, the ones that Molly brought. It's no life for a child, but that is of no matter. It is temporary.

Still, when I am called to photograph the body of a child, it makes me uncomfortable, knowing that she is sitting on the landing outside. I can hear her singing to herself as I work, a whispered refrain that floats melancholically through the cracks around the door. At moments it feels that the dead girl in my chair is serenading me from beyond the grave, a call from the other world to treat her with delicacy, for she could have been mine.

Her family has requested that she be standing. It's not something I would normally acquiesce to, but the girl is slight and the family has obscene amounts of money. We brace the body with a T-frame up to the shoulders, which will carry the majority of the weight. Her head flops forward as would the rest of her, were we to release our hold on her corpse. My new assistant, Arthur, arranges a counterweight, which he attaches to the frame while I bear the weight. He works slowly, and my back starts to ache, bent over holding the girl – it's something I should have done myself while he held the body, but I'm trying to train him up to be more useful. He's not bright, but neither is he squeamish, and, although I fear his resilience may be due more to a lack of imagination than anything else, it's a rare enough quality to make him worth keeping on.

This is the situation I am in when I hear the voices from the corridor outside.

'My darling!'

It takes me a few moments to realise that what is happening may be a cause for concern, as the woman's tone seems so joyful and light. It fails to strike me how at odds it is with the mood that extends throughout the house, my focus on the pain in my body, my need to prevent the corpse from falling on its face, leaving it unrecognisable for the pictures.

'You're here. I knew it wasn't true! I knew you weren't gone! My darling. My wonderful darling.'

It's only when I hear Aggie's noises of confusion that I begin to understand the scene that is taking place outside.

'Arthur – take the body off me,' I command him.

'I had the most awful dream that you'd died,' comes the woman's voice once more, this time skirting the edge of hysteria. *'But you're here, and you're alive! My darling Joanna, you're alive!'*

'Ma'am, I think you've made a mistake,' Aggie replies.

'Arthur!'

'Almost done, sir—'

'Take the body off me NOW.'

'My name's Aggie, ma'am.' I can hear the panic rising in her voice.

'Don't be silly, Joanna, you know your own name. Hold your mother.'

Arthur's bovine intellect finally registers the urgency in my

178

voice, and he rises to take the body from me. I dart to the door, swinging it open to reveal the events unfolding on the landing.

The dead girl's mother is pawing at Aggie, trying to put her arms round her and kiss her, while Aggie attempts to push her away. Aggie's noises of distress have already drawn the woman's brother from an upstairs room, and he is trying to pull his sister away from the girl, while she grabs desperately at her clothing. The woman's husband stomps down the corridor to help, while I run in and try to put myself between Aggie and her, feeling her nails dig into my neck and face as the men try to drag her away.

'What are you doing? Let me see my child. Let me see my child!'

I hear her protestations fade away behind me as her family lead her into a bedroom to calm her down, but my attention is on Aggie, her gaze darting from side to side, her eyes wide in a mixture of shock and surprise.

'Who ... who was that woman?' she gabbles.

'No one. She was just confused,' I whisper, attempting to soothe her. 'She lost someone, and she wants to find them, that's all. But she doesn't know what's happening. It's nothing to worry about. You're all right.'

Little by little, Aggie's breathing begins to slow, and I feel her grip on my arms start to loosen. I draw her into me, holding her close, and she rests her head on my shoulder, wrapping her arms round me like a drowning man grabbing onto the remains of their ship. And then something strange happens. As the panic subsides, I feel an affection growing within me. Towards this child. Unusually, it doesn't horrify or repulse me, and I feel, for the first time in many years, real, useful. Needed. As if somehow I can be rescued from my exile. But not by my own efforts, by the achievements of my art. But by her.

The spell is broken with a gasp.

I turn to follow Aggie's stare, thinking the woman has returned, only to come face to face with what she has seen: the open door, left agape as I ran onto the landing to help, now revealing the tableau I left behind a few moments before, my assistant propping up the body of the girl, her head lolling forward, a flower wilted.

I feel Aggie edge away from me.

'Aggie – it's my work – there's nothing to worry about,' I reason. 'It's just my work.'

But her face has the same look of horror towards me that it had towards the woman a few moments ago.

'Aggie, please…'

I reach out to her, but she steps backwards, recoiling from my touch. Each attempt I make to comfort her pushes her further and further away, like two magnets whose poles are at odds; further and further towards the top of the stairs.

'Aggie, no!'

Her heel hits the top step and she stumbles backwards, losing her footing for a moment, starting to topple.

I hear the sound of a body crashing downwards, as Arthur, drawn by my shout, runs out of the room, abandoning the dead girl to the floor.

Aggie screams; and my hand shoots out towards her, and hers towards mine in blind panic, our fingers stretched longing to connect, hers searching for safety, mine for protection.

I feel the gentlest contact, like butterfly wings on paper, her hand floundering desperately from side to side, missing its target.

And then, with one last strain, I push myself over the precipice of balance, starting to fall myself, feeling the pull of gravity downwards as my other hand reaches out to the banister behind.

And I make contact.

The fingers of my left hand wrap around her frail wrist, those of my right folding around the newel post, and we pause there for a instant, suspended in mid-air, before I pull her and myself back to vertical, and up onto the landing.

Now it is my turn to wrap my arms around her, pulling her close, as she does to me, clinging desperately to my form, her revulsion towards me momentarily forgotten in the shock of the moment.

'It's all right,' I whisper. 'You're safe now.'

***

It pains me to have to finish the job rather than simply leave, but the girl's body will not wait. Aggie sits in the drawing room below, with the maid for company, under strict instruction not to leave her alone, with the understanding that if the woman engages with her again I will walk out, there and then.

Upstairs, I finish with the girl as quickly as I can, now having to fix the results of the fall. Her bent nose I crack back into place. It still has a kink in it that I cannot fix, not to mention her crushed cheekbone, but I do what I can, shading parts of her face with powders to sculpt her back to her previous appearance. As I work, a sense of distaste comes over me, as if somehow I am seeing the scene through Aggie's eyes. What, before, was clay ready for the moulding, is now once again a cadaver, empty and grotesque, fixed into a parody of life by a creature parading in the clothes of a gentleman, performing a task akin to that of a grave-digger, fulfilling the twisted needs of his society, a whore to the pound and shilling.

I shake the thoughts from my head, trying to focus on the light, the composition of the frame, but the task is an onerous one. Within an hour, the photograph is taken. It won't be anything I'm proud of, but perhaps nothing would be. Not today.

I fix the plate and leave, telling Arthur to pack the equipment and deal with the family. The cameras will be fine but he'll make a hash of talking to the client – I knew social niceties were not part of his skill set when I took him on – but it can't be helped. I need to get Aggie home; to get her away from here.

We ride to the station in silence, Aggie staring out of the carriage window to avoid my attempts at conversation, the incessant humming she often fills the gaps in our conversation with replaced by a brittle nothingness.

The train journey follows the same pattern, and we walk to our cottage down the woodland path accompanied by nothing but the sound of footsteps, the birdsong itself absent in the fading light. Her silence feels like a reprimand, a chastisement for my transgressions, an accusation unuttered, and thus impossible to refute.

It is almost dark when we reach the cottage. There is a cutting chill in the air unusual for this late in May, so I light the fire I set in the grate before we left. A few minutes later, it is roaring with the warmth of home, and I turn to Aggie with a smile. She doesn't see me; her thoughts are elsewhere.

'I can make us tea if you like.'

Aggie turns to me, 'No, thank you.'

'Perhaps you'd like something to eat?'

'I'd like to go to bed if I may.'

'Of course…'

The warmth will take a while to spread to the upstairs room, so, no ashes yet forthcoming, I fumble a half-burning log from the fire into the bed-warmer, blowing it out as I do so. I stand up, and carry it towards her room, along with a candle for her bedside. She follows me silently upstairs, and sits on the bed, while I slot the pan in between the sheets.

'You'll have to wait a few minutes for it to warm up.'

'I'd rather just go to sleep, sir.'

'Oh. Of course.'

I put the candle on the table at her bedside, and remove the bed-warmer, leaving with it still in hand, and she shuts the door behind me. I descend the stairs, and return the logs back to the fire – propping the pan up on the hearth. I stand there for a few moments, looking into the flames, their heat failing to penetrate the cold I feel within. Perhaps if she knew … if she knew…

I cut a wedge of pie to distract myself, then look towards my desk, the letter I wrote to Kirk still propped up against a stack of books. I had convinced myself sending it was unnecessary, that the telegram would suffice, but now I know that for what it was – weakness, an unwillingness to say goodbye…

I go back up the stairs, knocking on the door, opening it gently when I receive no response. Aggie is sitting on the edge of the bed, her candle sending shadows dancing around the room.

'Aggie, do you know who I am? Why you were brought here?'

She stares ahead as if she has not heard me.

'Your mother and I met just before you were born,' I explain. 'She was a very nice woman. I think you know that.'

Once again, she doesn't respond, and I continue talking, an awkward courtier hoping not to be spurned.

'I just don't know if she told you who I was.' I pause, a moment to reconsider before I reveal the truth. 'You see – I'm… I'm your father.'

Aggie looks at me, as if hearing me for the first time.

'Yes,' she replies, her voice without emotion, 'I know.'

I nod as she turns her gaze back to the wall, feeling the strange blankness that I didn't know I'd lost return once more. I stand there in the flickering light for a moment, then leave, closing the door behind me. Some doors should stay shut. Some doors have danger on both sides.

I slump into the chair by the fire downstairs, pushing away the

183

slice of pie I had placed on the table by its arm, my hunger gone. What was I thinking? That I could start again? Build a new life with this child? My face twists into anger as I consider my foolishness, my immaturity, my hope.

I make a decision, getting up and walking to my desk. Standing there looking down at the envelope, I feel that I have found a rare moment of clarity in the confusion I have been feeling of late; that I am finally lucid, rational. I reach down and pick up the letter, inserting it into my bag, ready for my next trip into town. It will take some time to reach its destination, but at least it is a guarantee. A guarantee that this period of my life will soon come to and end.

CHAPTER XXII

A good day

'I was wondering if you might be able to take her for the day? I have to work.'

Molly smiles at me from behind the counter. She seems pleased I've asked. Not knowing the context, it's understandable – an acceptance of the olive branch she has offered, a bridge laid between myself and the wider world; but this is no cause for celebration. The girl hasn't spoken to me in two days – I'd be dragging her into town by her collar, pulling her down the Strand like a tugboat going against the tide. As far as she's concerned our relationship is over. She's seen me – her father – for who I am. And I cannot disagree with her appraisal.

Molly turns to her mother, standing in the doorway to the kitchen, her sleeves rolled up, her apron caked in pastry. 'Mum?'

Mabel nods, and Molly turns back wearing the same wide smile on her face. 'It would be a pleasure.'

Mabel rubs her hands together, warming them up before she goes back to work. 'You gonna help us with the baking today then, are you?'

I turn to Aggie. She has raised her eyes from the floor for the first time since we entered the shop. She nods, a flicker of excitement in her eyes.

'Come on then,' Mabel says, beckoning, and Aggie skips after her into the kitchen.

The relief I thought I'd feel at being rid of her fails to materialise, in its place a creeping annoyance; a jealousy that her smiles, her excitement, can be so easily won. By anyone, it seems, but me.

I brush the thoughts away, and nod a thank you to Molly before heading out of the shop. If I move quickly, I can get the steamer – the sun is out, and it will be a welcome change from the bustle of a second-class carriage.

'Is everything all right?' Molly asks as I reach the threshold. I turn to see her previous expression replaced by a look of concern. 'You don't seem yourself.'

'I'm completely myself – everything's fine,' I grunt, turning away, only to be pulled back once again.

'Only you've been different recently,' she continues, 'more like you used to be.'

I sigh. These women and their interminable wishful thinking.

'I can't look after her,' I explain. 'It doesn't work.'

'You don't have to do it alone. We can help.'

I shake my head. I don't want this – I don't want their help, their charity.

'It's always good to have an extra set of hands round here – she's a good girl – it'd be a blessing.' She sees the look of scepticism on my face. 'Charles – it's all right to ask for help – we want to. And it needn't just be us. She could go to the school as well. Get an education.'

She takes my hesitation as a sign that I might acquiesce, that I might suddenly embrace the monotony of the life these people lead.

'There's a community here. You can be part of it.'

Despite myself, I feel my resistance soften. Not towards her offer, but towards these people. How is my life better? At least theirs bring them joy, some moments of happiness. Not that I'd want it – but perhaps I should not dismiss it; dismiss them.

'It's not for me, Molly.'

She looks at me as if I am fool, as if she too is finally seeing me for what I am.

'It doesn't matter if it's for you,' she scolds. 'It's for her.' The compassion that underscores her usual speech has gone, in its place the tone you use when dealing with a spoilt selfish ten-year-old.

'You're looking after a child now. I don't know how long she's with you, but while she is, she's your responsibility.' She breaks off for a moment, unsure as to whether to continue, but steels herself, summoning up a hardness that I was unaware was hidden within her. 'We all know you miss your wife, Charles. And no one's judging that. But she's gone. And she ain't comin' back. I'm sorry to say it, but it's true… Maybe it's time you started thinking about them that's still alive.'

***

I hear her words repeating in my head as the steamer takes me into town. Despite the morning sun, it's cold on deck, the openness of the Thames exposing us to the winds that dance above. I bury myself in the shelter of my overcoat, my raised collar proving scant protection from the elements. Around me, my fellow passengers do the same, submerging their frames into scarves and shawls, their empty eyes staring off into the middle distance – each one of them lost, motionless, as if held in position by stands and fixings, trapped in their place in the grand photograph.

And for the first time I realise I am one of them. Not the ascetic who sees through their illusions, standing alone in their midst, bravely facing the meaninglessness of the existence that surrounds us. I am the same. Another empty vessel, my character moulded into shape by the events that have made up a life, a leaf that floats in the wind; and, rather than facing those events head on, I have sought escape in a living death.

The thought shames me: the realisation that, through it all, I have been somehow … proud; attached to what I have become. To my pain; my distance… Oh Percy, if you could see me now. How disappointed you would be. At how I have sullied your memory, at the callousness with which I have treated the man you once loved; suffocating him, depriving him of the air of warmth, emotion, until he became nothing but a shell, as lifeless as his subjects, his very form manhandled and abused by the creature that has taken his place.

The sound of the steamer's horn jolts me from my funk. I rub my face, and stretch my neck upwards, exposing my skin to the breeze that arches up from the water, reviving me like a tonic. A new-found determination accompanies the chill that flows through my body.

It is too late for me. I know that now. I cannot be saved, but perhaps Aggie … perhaps things can be different for her. I cannot infect her with my malaise, with the cancer that grows within me. The joy I once had I treasure to this day; and I must allow her at least as much. Even if it does not last, is extinguished before its time, it must still be brought into this world; not quashed and disfigured, wrapped in a dirty rag, stillborn.

For her I will be better, stronger. It cannot be more than a few weeks until her uncle comes. After that it does not matter – but until then … I must try. I must at least try.

For her. For my daughter.

***

'Come on! Are you dressed yet?'

I shout the words up the stairs, desperately looking for the inlaid cufflinks that Percy gave me on our second anniversary. I rifle through the dresser drawer, eventually finding them lodged in a corner at the back, behind stacks of photographs and receipts. I feel a pang of guilt as I take them out; a token of affection so long neglected buried underneath the paraphernalia of the last decade of my life. I roll them over in my fingers by the gentle light from the window, the moment Percy gave them to me appearing vivid in my mind, as detailed as a photograph, but moving and colourful, as if one of the bodies that have filled my frames for so many years has been jolted back to life.

My thoughts are interrupted by the sound of Aggie skittering down the stairs, her pinafore dress buttoned to the top, neat and pristine, her hair clean and freshly brushed. She looks like the subject of a Millais painting. She stands stiffly at the bottom of the steps as if she is awaiting inspection.

I smile at her, and she looks up at me, unsure.

'You look nice.' The compliment draws a response from her, and she smiles back, then blushes shyly. I grab her shawl from the side and crouch down before her, wrapping it round her shoulders.

'But, we can't stand around here all day admiring you,' I explain. 'It won't look good if we're late.' Aggie glances over at the clock, my having finally restarted its machinery, and nods, heading towards the front door.

It's the first morning this year where spring has seemed like summer; the halcyon summer of our imaginations rather than the oppressive heat that seems to characterise August these days. That day in May where the light radiates downwards and warmth penetrates your bones, and you look around to see that greenery has coated the world while your back was turned. I struggle with my right cufflink as we walk through the woods, remembering how I would complain to Percy about the same thing.

'Can I help?' Aggie asks.

I look down at her, and stop, presenting her with my wrist.

189

Aggie's delicate fingers make difficult work of the task, but it brings me pleasure to watch her try. Eventually she gets it half through, its toggle still hidden under the fold of the double cuff, but I can hear the church bells in the distance announcing the upcoming service, so I thank her and we carry on.

I can feel the eyes upon us as we enter the village, sideways glances from the inhabitants as we walk alongside them to the church at the far end of the street. I can sense their stares, hesitant, unsure, looking at me as if I am lost, a traveller walking the wrong road, torn between their duty to inform me of my mistake and their wariness of a stranger.

And yet I recognise them all. The faces I have seen looking back at me from doorways, alleys and across train carriages, now confused to find me facing in the same direction. We file into the churchyard together, the silence that surrounds me encompassing them too, their jolly Sunday morning chatter quieted to a whisper as we take our place in the pews.

The service is as dull as I remember. The vicar's platitudes as uninspiring as they ever were, and yet, despite my discomfort, both within my overly starched shirt and the presence of these people, I feel something; a lightness, a lifting. Despite the lingering presence of incense and dust cloying the atmosphere, I feel I can breathe more easily, as if the air itself were of a different quality, no longer weighed upon as heavily by the smog that hails from my consciousness.

It is not until after the service that I notice Molly across the aisle. Mabel and her father are next to her, all of them tucked into the far end of a pew on the right side of the church. It is Aggie that Molly notices first, Molly's face blossoming into a smile at the sight of her, only for it to be instantly supplanted by a look of surprise as she suddenly realises Aggie's presence implies my own, and looks up to meet my gaze. The smile she gives me is smaller, but no less warm, a subtle blend of disbelief and satisfaction rising from deep within her, a smile of triumph, but not over me – over the adversities of the world. It stirs something in me, and I nod a greeting, in an attempt to contain it. She nods back.

As we file out, a few of the villagers brave their wariness, greeting me with understated tilts of the head, and utterances of 'God's blessing be upon you'. I return their words, reminding myself that I am doing this for Aggie, not myself, and yet feeling a tenderness towards them nonetheless, at their attempts to include me, despite my extended absence from their world.

'Charles! So glad to see you!'

Arnett, the vicar, reaches out enthusiastically to shake my hand as we exit the church, the fervour of his greeting only mildly curtailed by the fact that he noticed me earlier from the pulpit.

'And this must be little Agnes – I've heard so much about you!' He holds out his hand to her, and she takes it, performing a little curtsey.

'Charming. Absolutely charming! I'm so pleased you came. We're glad to have you.' He takes my hand again as if his delight cannot not be expressed with a single handshake. 'You know, it's the fair in a few weeks. You should come along and take some of your photographs. I'm sure a lot of people round here would be most excited to have their picture taken by a London professional.'

'I don't think so.'

'Ah. Of course not. Forget I even mentioned it. Business with pleasure, eh? Business with pleasure!' He suddenly stops himself, afraid his request may have deterred me from attending the fair itself. 'But you will come?'

My hesitation prompts a noise of disappointment from Aggie. I look over and she stares up at me pleadingly. Although I fail to supress a sigh, I realise I cannot deny her. 'Yes, we'll come.'

191

Aggie reaches up and squeezes my hand, and we continue our journey down the path of the churchyard, the graves that line its borders masked by dawdling locals, exchanging greetings and gossip. As we pause to pass a group of elderly men clogging up the thoroughfare, Aggie finds her other arm grabbed by a boy of about her age, who looks more uncomfortable in his suit than I was in the church. A moment later his mother appears from behind.

'Oh, Mr Franklin, sir…' she says, struggling to regain her breath after the exertions of a three-yard dash. 'Tom was… Tom was wonderin' … was wonderin' … if Aggie could come… 'n' play … with him?'

I laugh, despite myself, but the woman is too breathless to notice. 'Would you like to?' I ask.

Aggie nods enthusiastically. 'Tom's my friend. He comes into the bakery every day.'

'Very well then.'

Aggie and Tom let out a little whoop of celebration.

'I'll take them over to the green if that's all right?' she says, reaching down for Tom's sleeve a moment too late – Aggie and the boy are already running out of the churchyard hand in hand. Tom's mother looks down with an expression of shock at the space where the children were a moment ago, then galvanises herself into a run that is reminiscent of a duck that has forgotten it can fly. I smile and follow, stealing a glance over my shoulder to see if Molly has emerged from the church yet. She is talking to the vicar, but sees me almost instantly and beckons for me to wait. As soon as she finishes, she bounces down the path in my direction.

'I'm really glad that you came,' she says, the smile she gave me in the church seemingly having not faded in the interim.

'I think it was good for Aggie,' I reply. 'Although I've already lost her to a ne'er do well boy that I'm not sure I want her interacting with. As long as he doesn't get any ideas…'

She laughs. 'That's Tom – he's all right. Just got more energy than he knows what to do with, that's all. They're a right pair when he comes into the shop.'

I turn to look over at them in the distance – Tom and Aggie running across the road onto the green, his mother waddling breathlessly after them.

'I should probably go over. I'm not sure she'll be able to cope if she actually needs to help at some point.' I turn back to Molly. 'It's nice to see you.'

'Well … we was actually planning to have a picnic there … if you'd like to join us? Mum's just popping home to fetch some stuff. Be a shame not to enjoy the weather.'

I look up at the sky, as if it attempting to judge its qualities.

'I'd like that. If it's not too much trouble.'

'No, not at all… Well, that's that then – I'll go and tell Mum.'

She darts off in the direction of her mother, glancing back with a smile, which I return with no small measure of enthusiasm. It would be a shame not to enjoy the weather.

***

We return home in the late afternoon, tired but happy. Aggie helps me with the chickens we neglected this morning, and for supper we dine on hard-boiled eggs and the remains of the picnic that Molly packed up for us. We eat on chairs outside until the evening cold starts to set in, when we move inside, sitting with the door still open, grasping onto the remains of the day's light. Aggie tells me stories about her mother – but her tears are fewer and further between, and at times it feels like she is with her once again, embraced in the arms of memory. It makes me wish I had known her better – her mother – but, as with every child, there is something of her in Aggie I am sure. Perhaps one day there will be something of me.

193

I tuck her into bed just after eight, and listen at the doorway as her breathing takes on the slow subtle rhythms of sleep. It has been a good day. The idea almost hurts me to accept, but it is true. A good day.

I sit down on the chaise, smiling as I think on it. The sun has nearly gone outside, and I get up to light a candle, nearly tripping over a box of Aggie's toys in the process. The annoyance I normally feel has gone, and in its place is a mellow acceptance, amusement almost. I find myself going through the box, looking at the items that will one day becomes objects of nostalgia. For her... For me... If she even remembers.

A copy of *Through the Looking-Glass* is wedged about halfway down. It's new – the date in the front only last year. So much for Molly just bringing over her old toys... I browse through the first few pages. It makes me wonder: have I been through a looking-glass of my own? Trapped in another world, where all is backward, a perverse reflection of its true self? But then something else catches my eye.

In the hollow revealed under the book are a couple of coconut halves. I take them out, holding them in my hands, their rough exterior coarse beneath my fingers. I have not seen Aggie play with them; I'm sure I would have noticed – the unmistakable click-clack of a horse's hooves recreated through their hard shells as she skipped around the parlour – no doubt I would have told her to stop. The thought brings a smile to my face; but beneath it I can feel the tears welling in my eyes. This must be the one, 'the most expensive coconut in England', hollowed of its flesh and water, but still here, a shadow of a day long past. Of happiness.

I put the coconut down, and go to a drawer I haven't opened for years, pulling out a handful of prints. The top one has faded slightly but the rest look as good as they did when I took them. I sit back down, filing through them one by one. I have limited

194

myself to looking at the plates themselves for my work, but in these Percy looks so young, so happy; the life in her eyes even more intense now it is no longer looking out from the faces of the dead. For a moment I feel regret that the prints had been hidden in my drawers, but I think I had almost ... feared them ... as if somehow they might reveal her as someone else, someone different from the woman who stalks my memory. And thus I made do with the few I have mounted on my desk, my wall. But those have become stale with familiarity, and here she is as she once was – vital, alive, a sculpture seen from every angle, somehow becoming more than each of them put together. Oh Percy, how I love you. How I always will. And now I will honour you; by being the man I once was. The man you loved.

The final picture jerks me to a halt. Rather than Percy staring back at me, I see my own face; bruised and beaten, deformed by the blows of Aggie's uncle. Although the memory has haunted me for year after year in my weaker moments, I am shocked by the brutality of the image. His anger painted onto me by the crude brush of his fists. And I realise it is not myself I am looking at, but him; his 'art'. The ugliness inside him made flesh.

And I realise I cannot give her to him.

Although I am sure he would not harm her, beat her if she displeased him, I am just as sure he could not give her the love that she needs to fill the void left by her mother's absence. Not that I am sure that I could myself, but I know I would be better. I know I would try.

Suddenly, the unposted letter still buried deep within my bag takes on an unbearable weight. I curse myself for even considering sending it. I must have known all along. Why else would it still be lingering within, if part of me had not been aware of who he was, of how I could not give her to him.

I withdraw it from my bag and walk to the fireplace, a candle

195

in my left hand. The flame takes the letter's corner with ease, and I hold the envelope between my thumb and finger as the fire spreads up its body, throwing it into the fireplace moments before it reaches my fingers. I watch as the last of it is consumed in the grate, its retreating edges becoming lined with black before crumbling into dust. And a moment later, it is gone. As he is, I hope, from her life.

My mind thinks upon the telegram. If it had reached him … but I think not. If it had got through, he would be here by now or at least have sent a letter. He is gone. And she is mine.

And we can start again.

CHAPTER XXII

The world in negative

'Where are all the pictures?'

Aggie looks confused as she scans the bare walls of the cottage room. The shapes where the photographs once were are now marked in white, revealing the wall that surrounds them to be not the pure alabaster I had thought, but coated with a light dusting of soot that puts the shapes of the frames into sharp relief. It looks like a picture in negative; the plate that the previous room was printed from; but now, here we are, on the other side of the looking glass.

'I didn't think you liked them?'

'I didn't but…' Her eyes search from side to side, trying to make sense of her discomfort with the new décor, 'it looks a little strange.'

'Well, that's because it's not finished yet. I was thinking we might take some new ones,' I tell her. 'I was wondering if you'd like to help me?'

A wide grin spreads across Aggie's face, and she nods her assent.

We head out into the woods a few minutes later, turning off the main track before we reach the village to go deeper into the forest. I've arranged for the small mobile darkroom I built to be left by Elwood's pond. I loaded it with chemicals before they collected it, so all I need carry is the camera and tripod. Aggie is tasked with bringing our lunch, and she walks, struggling with the half-full basket, dragging it along on her hip at an angle that constantly threatens to leave a trail of bread and cheese in our wake.

'Couldn't we ask Molly to come?'

'Why? Do you want her to carry your basket?'

'No – I thought she'd like it.'

'I thought it would be nice if it were just the two of us. Besides, we're seeing her at the fair tomorrow – you can wait till then can't you?'

'I suppose,' she shrugs.

'You also seem to be forgetting you're here to help me with my work. It'd be good for you to learn a trade where you don't end up covered in flour.' She looks at me, slightly unsure as to whether I'm joking or not.

'I'm learning lots of things at school: numbers, arithmetic...'

'Well, a hobby then. You can always help me with the books instead if you like.'

She seems satisfied with that, and we walk on for a while in silence, enjoying the freshness of the morning before her curiosity gets the better of her.

'What are we going to take photographs of?'

'Whatever we can find.'

'A squirrel maybe? The sky?'

'Well, I doubt a squirrel would stay still for long enough. And the way the camera works you can't really take pictures of things that are blue, but I'm sure we'll find something. Here we are.'

We emerge into a clearing by the ponds. The darkroom has been left where I instructed, and Aggie seems to find its presence almost miraculous.

'Did you know that was going to be here?'

'I did. When you're as old and jaded as I am, you develop a nose for these things.'

She looks at me, unsure as to whether I am joking once more, then heads to paddle in a stream while I unpack the camera equipment. The day already has a balmy warmth, and I pause for a moment, watching as she pads around barefoot, kicking up rivulets of water that surround her foot like an aura. If only the camera could capture that – the split second where the drops hover there in mid-air, frozen in time. I smile at the absurdity of my imaginings, but a second later I am back to looking at her – better than any picture could ever be.

'Watch you don't get washed away in the current!' I call.

She laughs, and then continues to kick about in the shallow waters, the sound of her giggling blending with the birdsong around us – nature's music in ensemble.

The camera unpacked, I begin to look for a subject. I spot a wild rose that has come into blossom away from the path, and tread down the weeds and nettles that lead to it to examine the flower more closely. The light plays beautifully on its leaves, smaller and more delicate than those of its cultivated cousin, and I judge it to be a suitable start. However, walking back towards the path, I see something in the mud below my feet – a frog, dead but not flattened by a boot – and an idea comes to me. Perhaps I could arrange it by the riverside, within the rushes it could easily be propped to create the illusion of sitting, nature transferred to a plate without the fear of it jumping from the frame.

I stop myself immediately. That's not what I wanted for today. I have had enough of death. Today was meant to be a fresh start, a new beginning. That was the point our expedition: life. Today, I want life.

***

'Right – lick your finger.'

Aggie does so, the rose shifting gracefully before us, bowing and swaying to the wind, as if constantly yielding to its will, a subject desperate to accommodate the whims of its master.

'Now hold it up. Which side is coldest?'

199

Aggie's face takes on a look of seriousness as she considers the question. 'I'm not sure… This one I think.'

'Good – then that's where the wind's coming from – which means we have to set up a barrier over here.'

She nods enthusiastically, but is off again before I can ask her to help, so I hammer the stakes into the ground while she attempts to climb a tree. I watch Aggie while I work, struggling to walk up the trunk while she hangs from a branch at head height; eventually she manages to loop her legs over another bough, pushing herself up to it in a manner so inelegant it would embarrass a circus contortionist.

Once the windshield is up, I go into the cramped space of my darkroom, and flow the plate, bent over double. The process is too difficult to involve Aggie, but I plan to let her help with the prints later, using the sodium thiosulphate fixer that I bought to teach Arthur, rather than the potassium cyanide I usually use. I've never been as happy with the results – the prints being less vivid (as well as taking five times as long) – but sometimes it's necessary to take the safer option. Especially with someone like Arthur. Or with someone who's too precious to risk losing.

A few minutes later, the plate is finally loaded into the camera, and I emerge from the darkroom. 'We're ready!' I call over. 'Do you want to come and help?' Aggie seems to not hear my words, being too engrossed with her simian antics, so I abandon myself to working alone, determining the final composition of the frame now the light has shifted slightly. I reach up my hand to remove the lens cap.

Only for Aggie to come in and pick the flower.

'Aggie! For God's sake!'

'We can take it home and put it in a vase!'

'I was photographing it.'

'Well, why don't you photograph me instead?'

200

She twirls around, lost in a whirl of childhood. I feel my irritation fade, charmed by her energy, her delight.

'Would you like me to?'

'Yes please. I was only little when I had the other one done.' I recall the carte de visite she brought in her things. She can't have been older than five when it was taken. 'And I'd definitely be interested in seeing what I look like the right way round,' she continues. 'Mrs Kettle says mirrors make everything backward.'

'I suppose that's true. It'll have to be now though as the plate's drying out.' I haul the camera onto my shoulder and carry it back to the clearing, Aggie following, her excitement visceral.

'All right – when I say "now" you have to stay still – do you understand?'

She nods, posing before the camera with the rose held between her hands.

'Here we go then. Three, two, one...'

I take off the lens cap, and Aggie holds her pose; innocent, angelic.

Until she moves. Five seconds in.

'Aggie, *still!*'

'Sorry, it's just so hard.' She takes her position once more. I haven't the heart to tell her the photograph's probably already ruined, and, even if it hasn't been, it definitely is a moment later when a bird chirps from the branches above and she decides to look up and locate it.

'*Aggie.*'

'I'm trying, but I keep forgetting,' she protests, smelling the flower in her hand without even thinking.

'You have to be still.'

'I don't want to be still – it's not fun.' She launches herself out of the frame, dancing round, twirling once more – a wood spirit in a forest glade, consumed by her impulses.

'Aggie, these chemicals aren't cheap,' I say, an impotent attempt at a scolding.

But it's too late, I've already lost her. She continues to pirouette, absorbed in her movement. To begin with all I feel is annoyance, but gradually it retreats, leaving wonder in its place. That I have somehow helped create this – life itself, rather than a squalid imitation of it. Life itself.

I notice my pocket watch in my left hand. The exposure time is done. I replace the lens cap, more through force of habit than any hope in the results, a small chuckle that becomes a smile emerging from within me.

And I watch her. Watch her in the dance.

***

We sit by the pond, eating our lunch of eggs, bread and cheese. Across the water we watch a heron, perched on a makeshift jetty that someone has inexplicably built. The bird is as still as a statue, the only indication that it is not one the occasional flicker of its pupil as it scans the water for potential victims.

The mud on Aggie's feet has dried in the sun, and she grins at them, pleased with the result, as if she is slowly becoming the golem of the East – a transformation, it seems, she revels in more than she perhaps should. I'll make her wash it off in the stream before we return – she won't cope well with a walk back to the cottage barefoot – but for now I let it stand, the pleasure it gives her more important than anything else, and I am beginning to realise that is something that should be truly protected.

But I cannot totally relax. I have something to ask her, something weighing on my mind, so I soften her up with a few early strawberries that I had hidden in the bottom of the hamper. Though they are slightly under-ripe we both bite into them with relish.

'Can I ask you a question?'

'As long as it's not about taking photographs,' she replies. 'I don't think I'm very good at that.'

'It's not about taking photographs,' I smile.

'All right then.'

I gather my thoughts, wary of how to proceed. Although the conversation has been on my mind constantly for the last few hours, now I have to actually utter the words, every approach I had conceived seems contrived and awkward. I decide it is better to just be direct.

'Aggie… Do you think you'd like to stay with me?'

I continue before she can answer, damming up the possibility of rejection with justifications and explanations. 'I know I haven't been a very good father to you, but I think I can be. And, well… I'd like you to stay with me, to live with me – permanently that is – if you want to.'

She doesn't waste a moment and nods, her smile the full width of her face.

'Good,' I reply, the word holding back the tidal wave of emotion underneath. 'Good.'

***

We walk back in the late afternoon, our few attempts to photograph the heron having met with failure, the bird relocating to a different part of the pond every time we got within fifteen feet, but our endeavours proved their own end, Aggie providing a whispered commentary of our treks through the African jungles as we stalked closer, only for us to burst into laughter when it took flight the moment I put the camera down.

We sing as we walk, Aggie leading us in a chorus of 'Mother, mother, I feel sick'. For the first time in years I feel satiated, as if for a few hours the grief and worry that has characterised so much of my life has been washed away like mud in a stream, and I realise I am happy. It is something I thought I would never feel again, its simplistic charms having no place in the maze of my psyche, and yet, here it is. Happiness once more.

As we walk down the path that leads to the cottage, I see a figure at the gate. Aggie is the first to spot that it is Molly. Abandoning her empty basket, she runs to greet her. I pick up the handle and follow along.

By the time I get there, Aggie and Molly are embracing, Aggie regaling her with stories of our trip and our aborted attempts at photography, but when Molly tilts her face up to me, it is painted with concern.

'I need to talk to you about something.'

Her tone puts me on edge, and I feel a sense of worry shooting through me.

'All right.'

I turn to Aggie and smile. 'Why don't you go in the house and get those drawings you did yesterday? I'm sure Molly would like to see them.' She runs off enthusiastically towards the front door, blind to what has passed between Molly and me, but as soon as she is out of earshot I press for more.

'What's happened? Is everything all right?'

'I don't know. A man came to the village today. He was asking after you.'

The implications are clear immediately, as my hopes of a few months ago are transformed into my worst fears.

'I'm sure it's nothing,' I say, attempting to reassure her.

'He didn't seem nice, Charles. He was from the army.'

I feel something in me drop, all possibilities of denial now gone. Kirk is here, in the village.

'What did you tell him?'

'We didn't tell him anything. But someone else might have. He was asking where your cottage was.'

I nod, taking the information in, before pasting on an insouciant smile.

'I see. Thank you for telling me,' I reply, but it does little to put her mind at ease.

'Is it trouble, Charles? If you want, you can come and stay at the bakery for a bit. Just till it passes over. I'm sure Mum won't mind.'

'Thank you, Molly. But it's nothing I can't deal with.'

Aggie comes out of the house, waving her drawing like a flag of surrender.

'Who is he?' Molly asks quietly.

'Her uncle,' I reply in a whisper, 'her mother's brother. I'll talk to him. We'll straighten things out.'

Aggie reaches us, and I raise my voice back to its normal level, attempting to project reassurance with a smile. 'Everything will be all right. I'll see you at the fair tomorrow. Aggie – why don't you show Molly your pictures? I need to go inside to think about something.'

I walk down the path to our door, the sound of Aggie's giggles behind me seeming to withdraw into the distance faster than their proximity might suggest, the peace I thought I might find diminishing just the same, a dream dissipating, as I awaken once more.

***

I put Aggie to bed early, kissing her head tenderly as she starts to drift off into sleep. As I sit by her bedside, I find my musings always lead me to the same place. Kirk's reaction to my decision to keep my daughter will not be one of warm-hearted acceptance.

He will want to take her from me. Not because of some avuncular affection for the girl, not because he wishes the best for her, but because he wants to hurt me, to finish what he started all those years ago. And if she should also suffer in the process, so be it.

As Aggie finally succumbs to sleep, I head to the kitchen and search through the drawers. The doors are already bolted, the windows shut tight despite the need for a summer breeze, and there, at the back, I find what I am looking for – a policeman's truncheon that I bought when we first moved here. I felt paranoid that we were too isolated out here in the cottage, and got it under the counter from a stallholder in Houndsditch. It hasn't left the drawer since. Not until tonight.

I move my chair to the middle of the room, turning it to face the front door and take my place, turning the truncheon over in my fingers, trying to find reassurance in the smooth mahogany of its form, in the cord at its base looped around my wrist. But neither provides it. So instead I sit. Sit and wait.

CHAPTER XXIII

A weapon strikes true

I wake with a start, grabbing for the truncheon, which has fallen to the floor. I leap to my feet, a blow at the ready, only to find the room is empty. It takes a few seconds for me to orient myself, the reality of my dream bleeding into this world like stigmata. I had seen him take her, the giant from a fairy tale, pushing me aside with a hand that spanned my whole body. But he is not here. He did not come.

I walk to the washstand, laying the truncheon on the wood of its surface, pouring cold water from a jug into the bowl to splash my face. The water brings me fully to my senses, and suddenly I feel a rush of panic. Aggie. I run up the stairs, wiping my face dry with my sleeve as I leap up the steps. But she is still there. In the bed, sleeping.

'Daddy?' comes a half-conscious whisper. The word wipes my panic away in an instant, touching something deep inside.

'Did you sleep well?'

'I had a dream.'

I go over and sit by her bedside. 'Was it a nice dream?'

She nods. 'We went out to take more photographs. Only this time some of them worked.'

I laugh. 'Perhaps some of the real ones did too. We can try printing them today. I'll go and make breakfast.'

I head towards the stairs to warm some kippers. I'd been saving them for fair day – to try to make the whole thing into a celebration. Now it seems more like they might be a last meal.

'I'm glad I can stay here,' she says as I reach the doorway. The words break my heart.

'I am too, my love. I am too.'

I find myself too preoccupied for us to make the prints from yesterday's plates, so, instead, we sit outside the front of the house. She plays, running around after the chickens, while I pretend to read a battered copy of *The Hunchback of Notre-Dame,* all the time scanning the path that approaches the cottage, and the woods beyond for any sign of movement.

At my side the truncheon has been replaced by a less conspicuous gooseberry knife; but its curved blade reminds me of a meat hook and when I imagine it cutting through flesh, I begin to doubt I would have the heart to use it, so I ask Aggie to join me inside for a moment, distracting her with talk of the chickens, while I exchange it for my previous weapon.

But after that, the day passes without incident, and by the time the evening comes I begin to relax. The feeling scares me, and I cannot help but think of Jackson at Chancellorsville. I remember reading about it with Percy, and us imagining how his men must have felt exactly this way, reclining by their cooking fires, imagining the threats of the day done, only to see tens of thousands of soldiers running out from the undergrowth ready to spear them with bayonets. The man's a soldier. I have to remain alert, to stay vigilant at all times.

We take the long way round to our destination that evening, skirting farmers' fields and navigating kissing gates, just as I did with Percy so many years ago. I keep an ear out for movement around us as Aggie talks. That Kirk should know my route does not seem possible. It's a path I've only walked a few times since Percy died, when I have wished to summon her memory once more, her gentle teasing on the way to the fair, another recollection I have attempted to leave untouched, lest repeated use might diminish its brightness.

Aggie is excited, constantly barraging me with questions about what will be there.

'Will there be horses? Trick horses?'

'I don't think so.'

'I went to the circus once, and there were men standing on the back of them.'

'It's a fair, not a circus.'

'What about monkeys? Will they have monkeys?'

I tell her they won't, becoming aware of the sounds of life a few hundred yards in front of us, stopping and squatting down to talk to her, trying to impress upon her the import of what I am about to say.

'Aggie. There are going to be lots of people when we get there. You have to promise you'll stay around me all the time. Even if you see one of your friends. Do you understand? I need to be able to see you. Can you do that?'

She nods.

'I need you to promise me.'

She smiles, as if now she is the one needing to provide protection.

'I promise.'

***

As we walk around the stalls, Aggie's eyes are alight with wonder.

'Can we go in here?' She doesn't even give me time to answer. 'No, we should do this one. Or perhaps we should go and watch the music first? Oh, no – look! Look at this!'

I can't help but laugh as she whirs around in a flurry of hyperactivity, spinning from side to side like a top that can't make its mind up. Her eyes finally land on a confectioner's stall, packed top to bottom with candies and sweetmeats, so much so that it seems as if its very frame is edible. She runs over, looking back at me hopefully as she reaches its threshold. I smile and begin to

209

follow, and she turns back to the Aladdin's cave of sugar, sensing acquiescence in my approach.

'This is the most sweets I've ever seen in my life!' she pants.

'What would you like?'

'What am I allowed?'

'Anything.'

'Anything?'

'Anything. It's the fair. Sweets are obligatory.'

Her look of disbelief becomes one of utter concentration, as she turns and focuses her attention on the jars of boiled sweets, liquorice and preserved fruits. With Aggie distracted, I turn my gaze to our surroundings, my eyes flitting from stall to stall, analysing each face and checking it against the vagaries of memory, looking for any sign of him hiding within every passer-by, projecting his features onto the faces of strangers, hoping that he is not come.

A few minutes later, we are sitting eating Turkish delight from a bag, on the well-trodden grass of a small bank. Aggie is on her third piece; I can feel the sugar rushing through my veins one bite into my second.

'What do you think?'

'Mmm,' she replies, unwilling to pause between mouthfuls of stickiness. 'Delicious.' She chews some more. 'Not quite as nice as ice cream, but nearly. What about you? What do you think?'

'I think… I think I'm glad we came here.'

I make her put the confects away after her fourth, telling her she should save some for tomorrow. But, as I say the word, I feel a rush of fear run through me. Tomorrow. We walk onwards, talking pleasantly, as if calm and carefree, but I continue to scan the crowd, looking, hoping that he is not here. We should be safe. There are people around – he wouldn't dare attack me; because that is what it will take. If he wishes to steal her from me.

As we walk towards the merry sounds of music, we pass some stalls and sideshows I remember, each of them scarred by the passage of time. In one, Cerberus has now become a Great Dane, his additional heads the same as before, but now looking small and malformed in comparison with the new dog's form. His master's fake grey beard has been replaced with the genuine article, but his staff and crown have a fresh coat of colour, advertising their newness despite the flaked texture of the old paint visible underneath. At another stall, the 'fat child' has become 'the world's fattest man'.

When we reach the dance floor, there is still no sign of Kirk.

'Molly!'

Aggie shoots off ahead of me, having spotted Molly and her parents sitting at a table with drinks in front of them. Molly stands and hugs her, letting Aggie try a sip of her ginger beer as I catch up, which makes Aggie wince in horror. Molly's father nods me a greeting, and then says something to Aggie which I don't quite hear, before Molly starts over in my direction.

'Was everything all right?'

'It was,' I reply. 'It is. So far.'

There are too many people to be sure he is not present, lurking somewhere in the shadows, hiding amidst the multitude of faces, and my eyes dart towards Aggie once more, checking she is there.

'You two youngsters should be on the dance floor!' exclaims Mabel, interrupting my thoughts.

'I'd hardly call myself a youngster,' I retort.

'When you get to my age, everyone's a youngster!' she replies.

I smile, but make my excuses. 'I'm sorry – I can't leave Aggie.'

'You're not going to – she'll be up there too.' She turns to the girl. 'You're dancin' with me if that's all right, darlin'?' Aggie nods, and I realise I have no alternative. 'Sorry, husband dearest.' He waves her off, glad to be left alone with his bottle of ale, and doing nothing to disguise the fact.

211

I turn to Molly. 'Would you do me the honour of dancing with me?'

'I would,' she replies, holding out her hand, as if we were on the edge of a grand ballroom, rather than beneath an open sky listening to the melodies of five men who look like they haven't bathed in as many months. But the music they make is beautiful. And so is she.

I take her hand and we follow Aggie and Mabel to the dance floor, paying the man at the entrance as we pass. The women go free as before, and we take our place on the wooden boards. Each moment seems like an echo of past times, my memories of Percy intermingling with the present; everything the same, and yet different.

Another song starts, and I look over to see Aggie standing on Mabel's feet. They start to sway from side to side with the music, Aggie laughing at the charade. I look back at Molly, who is smiling at the scene as well, and she turns to me, our faces closer than they have ever been before, her pupils large in the oncoming darkness. Suddenly I feel a nervousness that I had not expected, and I break her gaze. Hesitantly I put my other hand on the small of her back, and we begin to dance.

The tune is a slow one, and although our bodies are at the distance respectability requires, I feel a thrill course through me at the intimacy. We step backwards and forwards in time to the rhythm, and the music begins to work its hypnotic charms, luring us into relaxation, the hesitation in our touch disappearing, our bodies moving closer.

I feel the past receding, falling away like snow melting from a tree's branches, until all that is left is *this*. We look back up at one another, and everything feels right. I see a promise of happiness. Of a future. Not just with Aggie, but with a woman by my side. A woman I could love.

And then I see him.

Across the dance floor, buried in a crowd of people watching the merrymakers is Kirk. He is staring directly at me, his eyes aggressive and hateful.

'Oh, God.' I am unsure as to whether I have said the words out loud or merely thought them. 'Molly – I have to go. I need you to watch Aggie while I attend to something.'

Molly looks confused as if she has somehow done something wrong. 'She's with Mum – she's fine.'

'This is important. I need you to watch her and keep her safe while I do this – do you understand?'

Molly nods, apprehensive at my sudden change of mood, but comprehending the seriousness of my request. She goes to her mother, and I walk across the dance floor to the exit at the side, leaving its frivolities behind, skirting its perimeter towards the place where I saw Kirk.

I weave through the seats and tables where people sit and drink, the bustle of their conversations flitting in and out as I pass, all of it underscored by the backdrop of the band. Seconds later, I have reached the main thoroughfare, fairgoers milling past me in all directions, an artery feeding the fair with its customers. I push through the crowds, making my way to where Kirk stood, the going slower as the throng intensifies near the ropes that mark the edge of the floor.

But Kirk is gone. For a moment, I wonder whether it was all in my mind, that he was never there at all, then a sudden moment of panic draws my eyes to the dance floor, seeing visions of him climbing over the barrier and forcing his way through to my child. Finally, I spot Aggie; still laughing and dancing with Mabel. Molly is standing next to them looking around. She spots me and gives me a wave of reassurance, and I find I can breathe again.

'Got yourself a new whore, have you?'

213

I turn to see him standing behind me: Kirk; a small clearing forming around him, as if people have somehow sensed the danger that he represents.

'Does she know what you are?' he asks. 'I assume you haven't fucked her yet if you're still here.'

People around him glance in his direction; men take their wives by the arms and lead them away, mothers do the same with their children; not only wary of the words he's uttered but of the tone that pervades them.

'I don't want any trouble,' I tell him, attempting to hide my fear beneath a calmness of voice, wary that I am doing anything but.

'Then you won't get any. I'll take my niece and be going.'

'You got my telegram.'

'I did. You were the last person I expected to hear from when my sister died. Yet hear from you I did. Remember what I told you last time we met?'

I ignore the question. 'I'd rather we weren't meeting either.'

'Then let's keep this brief. Bring me the girl.'

I hesitate, attempting to summon the strength to deny him in a way that will make him think twice. Make him think I might have the power to stop him.

'She... She's not coming. She wants to stay with me.'

He laughs in my face.

'Is that right? She wants to stay with you?' he drawls. 'She's eight. She doesn't know what she wants. Bring her to me.'

'No.' This time my speech is more forceful, but it only serves to anger him. He lowers his voice to what is almost a whisper.

'I don't think you understand,' he explains. 'You bring her to me now; or I beat you till you're unconscious, then I take her anyway. This isn't a choice, Franklin. This is what's happening.'

'She's not going with you.'

'Well,' he chuckles, prompted to a smile. 'Someone's grown some balls since the last time we met…'

'She's my daughter, Kirk. She needs me. She's staying.'

'Your daughter?' he laughs. 'You think your name's on the birth certificate? Her father died before she was born. You took pictures of him from what I remember. How he managed to get my sister pregnant in the state he was in before he died I have no idea. But that's the way it was.'

'I'm her father and you know it.'

'Just because you chose to dishonour my sister with your unholy advances doesn't make you the girl's bloody father. Bring her to me now.' A finger shoots in my direction.

'She's mine and she's staying,' I say through gritted teeth, watching the anger rise within him.

'She's not yours,' he spits. 'What did you ever do for her? When did you ever care for her? Did you feed her when she was hungry? Did you pay for the clothes on her back? Did you make sure there was wood on the fire when most of England was freezing?'

'I didn't even know she existed!'

'And you never should have. My sister wore that child like a badge of shame around her neck. Wasn't it enough that she'd lost her husband?! You had to bring this on her as well?'

'You're not taking my daughter.' My voice comes out as loud as his, and I notice the crowd has backed away, and their eyes are watching us intently – a large circle having been cut out from their midst with us at its centre. And there, on its edge is Aggie, tucked into Molly's side, an arm wrapped round her, as she tries to find comfort. But I can see the fear in her eyes.

Kirk follows my gaze towards her.

'Aggie – it's me, your uncle. Come with me, we need to go.'

Aggie does not move. He grunts in frustration, her resistance prompting him to action.

'I've had enough of this. What's he been telling you? What have you said to her?' He starts in her direction, and I step into his path. Kirk bats me away with a single blow, the force knocking me to the floor.

My head spinning, I get up, blocking his path once more. He goes to strike me, but this time I am ready, managing to raise my arm to block his fist, the pain reverberating through my body; but the surprise throws him, allowing me to strike a blow of my own, and I hit him full fist in the face. He looks at me, curious, unphased, like a dog, whose master's stick has merely angered, not tamed it. And he hits me again. This time his punch is more focused. The offhand show of irritation of his first attack, replaced by the technique of a trained fighter. I try to raise my hands in defence, but I am too slow, and, as he makes contact with my jaw, I feel myself lose consciousness for a second, finding myself opening my eyes on the ground a moment later.

I reach out grabbing desperately towards his leg, managing to get a handful of trouser by his ankle, pulling him backwards to knock him off balance. But he remains on his feet. He turns to me, his mood beginning to move beyond mere irritation, and he looks down at me, his expression filled with disdain.

'Get your fucking hands off me.'

He kicks me hard in the face, sending me backwards into the coarse jaggedness of the dry soil. In the background, I hear Aggie screaming. Even as the world feels like it is falling apart, I hear it, and I know I must protect her.

Pushing myself up again, I feel the warmth of blood dripping down my face. My thoughts fade in and out of focus, and I can sense the strength seeping from me, his violence beginning to take its toll, but I push forward, as he gets closer to my daughter, ready to take her away forever.

The band has stopped now and the crowd is silent, the only

216

sound that remains, the clomp of Kirk's footsteps as he marches towards Aggie over the well-trodden ground. She edges back further into Molly's embrace, and I see Mabel step forward to block his way.

I stumble onwards, regretting my decision not to stash the truncheon inside a bag. I know I cannot stop him – I can barely stand – but everything in me propels my frame towards him. The shame of my powerlessness runs through my body as I move, the shame of not being able to protect her. What is the use of my existence if I cannot save her, cannot stop him from taking my daughter? What use is my love? How impotent it now seems. Mabel's attempts to intervene are as futile as my own. It would take an army to stop him.

An army.

I stop, raising my body to full height.

And I start to speak.

'My friends…' My voice cuts through the silence with ease, and I feel the crowd's eyes upon me. Kirk pauses, the words stopping him in a way my fists could not, turning round to look in my direction.

'This man is trying to take my child,' I continue. 'Many of you know her; her name is Aggie. She goes to school with your children, she serves you in the bakery, she greets you as you pass her in the street.

'I know I haven't been part of life here for a long time. But I am now. And so is she. So I'm asking you to help me. I don't care about my dignity; I don't care about my pride. I will give my life trying to stop this man, but I fear I will not be able to. If you have it in your hearts to help me, please, *please* do it now. I beg you – for the sake of my daughter.'

No one moves, but I feel a mutter ripple through the crowd at my admission of her illegitimacy and my final sliver of hope drops away. Kirk looks around at the faces of the farm workers and shop owners who surround him, and laughs, his eyes filled with a mix of superiority and scorn.

'Good try,' he scoffs, before turning back to Aggie and advancing upon her.

Until a woman steps into his path.

She's a friend of Mabel's – fifty years old if she's a day – her hair in a bun, wearing what I'm sure is her nicest dress, a shawl round her shoulders. But she's there, in front of him, fearless.

'Get out of my way,' Kirk spits, but the woman does not move. 'I said get out of my way!'

He raises his arm, ready to backhand her across the face. I start to move forward – I cannot let him strike her for me. But her husband steps forward as well.

'You hit my wife, and you'll be sorry.' The man is frail and drawn, far weaker than I am, but still, he stands there, strong.

Kirk pauses for a moment.

'Then I'll go through you as well.'

'Then you'll go through me too.' A new voice. Another man steps into Kirk's path.

'And me,' says his friend, the butcher's boy – tall and well fed, with a strong arm.

'Through all of us.' A woman this time, handsome despite her ruddy complexion.

I see doubt start to creep into Kirk's stance, a subtle change of balance that says he is no longer in control. He turns to me, a look of bewilderment on his face, a smile of amusement almost, but it fails to form, and he turns back to the ragtag assemblage that has gathered before him. He spits on the ground in front of them, but they do not move. He could probably kill them all without breaking a sweat, but he remains on the spot, the Englishman of his birth struggling to hold back the savage he has unleashed elsewhere.

218

As I feel an acorn of victory begin to grow within me, he spins back in my direction, his forefinger jabbing at the air as if trying to make a point for which he has no words. His confusion is gone now, replaced by hatred, his mind searching for a solution and finding none, his voice taking on a tone of mockery laced with arsenic.

'So this is how you protect your child, is it? Hiding her behind women? Behind men who look like they'd break if you so much as touched them?'

But the words bounce off me. All I care about is Aggie.

'I'll do what I must to protect her.'

He snorts with derision. 'You should be ashamed. Call yourself a man?' He stops to look me up and down, a wolf's grin on his face. 'Seems like she still has a mother after all.'

I feel a strange calm come over me, despite the fact he is still here; still a threat. 'I think it's time you left.'

But he is not quite done. He turns back towards Aggie, looking for an opening, but the villagers close their ranks. He steps to the side, and the crowd moves with him, subtly shifting its mass to block his approach. He steps backwards and turns to me, all attempts at humour gone.

'I'll be back, you know. And I'll bring people,' he threatens. 'Friends of mine – and you can imagine what kind of friends I have.'

He lowers his voice to address me directly. 'You won't always have them to protect you. So you'd better watch out. I'll be back. *Soon.* And I'll be taking her with me,' he whispers. 'You haven't won, Charles. You're on reprieve.'

He storms past, knocking into my shoulder as he goes, and I stumble, barely managing to stay upright. I watch as he walks away from us – making sure he is really going, making sure that it is not a trick. The crowd parts as he moves through them, peeling back like they are in the presence of a wild animal.

I turn back to those who have helped me, and they break their ranks, revealing Molly and my daughter. As I fall to my knees, Aggie looks over at me, and smiles.

'Thank you,' I say, addressing the people who have saved us, the people I have so misjudged. 'Thank you so much.'

A few heads nod in acknowledgement, trying to pretend it was nothing beyond the expected, but the gratitude I feel towards them almost matches the love I have for the little girl they protected. Gradually they go back to their business, static still crackling through the air from the threat of conflict. I walk over to Aggie, the band starting up again behind. I am too broken to feel anything approaching relief, but as I hold her in my arms once more, I thank heaven that she is still with me.

CHAPTER XXIV

Back to where the danger lies

'Ow!' Molly cleans the cut above my eye, as I sit before her on a hard stool in the room above the bakery, the liquid sharp in the open wound. 'It stings.'

'It's vinegar. It's better for burns, but it'll do in a pinch.'

She continues to dab up the dried blood from my temple, her face close to mine so she can work in the candlelight. Her voice low, she begins to speak.

'We thought she might be yours. She looks like you.'

I break her gaze, shame overtaking the pain that fills my body.

'It's all right, Charles,' she says. 'It's good that she's here. In the world. There're some things more important than custom. No one's judging you.'

I look back up at her, astounded by the wisdom within this woman, her capacity for understanding, forgiveness. She presses the cloth to the cut once more, the acerbic liquid squeezing out from the fabric into the wound, and I flinch once again.

'If it didn't sting, it wouldn't be working,' she says, raising her voice to normal volume. 'You men. Always talking tough, but as soon as there's a bit of pain, you're babies.' She winks at Aggie, who's sitting on a chair across the room, swinging her legs backwards and forwards beneath her. Aggie gives her a conspiratorial smile in return. 'Done.'

I get up, and look at my face in the mirror. The cuts and bruises that pepper my face seem slight in comparison to the unrecognisable mess his last beating left me with. I can't help but feel I got off lightly. I turn back to Molly. 'Thank you.'

221

Molly nods an acknowledgement, and I walk over to Aggie, crouching next to her chair to talk. I know she won't like what I've got to say, but its better that I'm upfront about it, that I'm honest with her.

'I've been thinking,' I explain, 'We have to go away from here. To leave.' I see the look on her face, her hesitance to leave these people who have become her friends, her family. 'It's not what I want either, Aggie, but I don't think we have a choice. We won't be safe here. Not while he knows where we are.'

Aggie's lower lip folds back under her teeth as she considers what I've said, until resistance gives way to acceptance. She pushes back her sadness and speaks. 'All right, we'll find somewhere else then.' I feel a pride rise within me, that she can be strong when she needs to be. As if she is setting an example for me to follow.

I stand back up, turning to Molly. She pastes on a smile, trying to display her understanding, but underneath it, her reaction to my words is plain to see. Mabel's eyes dart towards her, full of concern, and Molly turns away, busying herself with tidying the bowl she's been using to clean my wound.

'Molly. If you'd like … you could come with us.' She looks round, her face a mixture of confusion and curiosity. 'I know you have your family here,' I continue, 'but Aggie and I would love to have you. If you'd be willing.'

The suggestion seems to have blindsided Molly. She stands there, no response making it as far as her lips. Her mother is not so reticent in her reaction.

'Is that a proposal, Mr Franklin?'

'Not yet,' I reply. 'But it will be… When I have a ring, and a face that doesn't look like a piece of bruised meat.'

A smile breaks out across Molly's face; a beautiful, beautiful smile. 'Then yes, I'll come.'

I nod, my own smile more cautious; a thousand problems

brewing underneath, and yet the possibility of happiness taking form in my mind's eye. 'I'll make arrangements. Can you keep Aggie here? I'll be back tomorrow.'

Mabel nods, and I grab my coat to go, turning to look at Molly one last time before I leave, unable this time to hold back my delight at the potential future before us, my hope finally overcoming my fear. And I head out into the night.

***

I pack late into the evening, finally abandoning the task as my mind fogs with tiredness. The trunks half-full, I retire to my bedroom, drifting into unconsciousness on top of the sheets, the truncheon in my hand. Surprisingly, I sleep well, Aggie's safety and my return to a proper bed bringing me a depth of rest I am unused to, but, when the rooster crows outside, I wake with a start. Thoughts of Kirk's return fill my head – I have no idea how quickly he could rally people in London, and besides, how can I be sure he really left? Suddenly, a fear for my own safety comes over me. Aggie needs a father – I am no longer expendable – I cannot let her lose me.

I finish the packing of our clothes and sundries, and start to fill another trunk with photographs. The drawers I have that are brimming with the images of the dead I leave untouched, but the pictures of Percy I cannot abandon. I lay the framed prints in the lined trunk, screwing up handfuls of newspaper between the layers to protect them in transit. Each one of them makes me smile once more as I place it in the crate, my newfound hope allowing me to enjoy her once again with an unguarded wonder. Gone is the feeling of loss that has accompanied each viewing over the last ten years, and instead each one is a memory made solid, a celebration of the wonder that was Percy.

A banging at the door knocks me out of my reverie. I put the photograph into the trunk, and reach for the weapon on the table. Stalking to the window, I lean to check it is not Kirk, but the angles are not in my favour, so I cannot be sure. I make my way over to the door, ready for whatever may come.

'Who is it?'

'It's me, you bloody idiot,' comes the response from the other side of the wooden barrier. I open the door to reveal Bates, an eyebrow raised ironically.

'You're not going to use that on me, are ya? I thought I was doin' ya a favour?'

I smile and forego our usual handshake, embracing him warmly. I am glad to see him – and not just for the cart he has parked on the other side of the garden wall. His very presence seems to make things better – and I finally recognise him for what he really is – a friend. My friend. 'Thank you.'

'Don't start that,' he says, pulling himself away from my hug. 'I thought you were a bloody old woman cowering behind that door – now I know you bloody are.'

I laugh and he flashes me his usual haphazard grin as he comes inside, surveying the multitude of crates and boxes that litter my parlour.

'Jesus – you're really going, ain't ya? Never thought you'd leave this place. Your little hermit hole.' He overenunciates the words, with an expression intended to goad me. 'Nice to be invited finally though. I feel honoured.'

'Stop talking and help me pack.'

He smiles, pleased to have a bit of pushback at last, and takes off his jacket, rolling up his sleeves ready to work. It's a routine I've seen a hundred times before, but the lack of corpses lends it a different flavour, a wholesomeness. 'Thought it'd be a bit more homely,' he comments as he works, his eyes scanning over the

224

shapes of the frames still cut out of soot on the wall. 'You packed your pictures?'

'Some. And it's been a while since it's had a woman's touch.'

'That it has,' he says, his voice touched with a rare note of empathy. 'Though if I'm getting a woman's touch, I'd prefer it not to be on me 'ouse.'

His joke draws a cackle from deep within him, and the laughter affects me too, lifting us out of our momentary melancholy. 'Right,' he continues, 'let's get to work.'

We finish the remainder of the packing by the early afternoon as I tell him about Molly, Kirk's return, and everything else I had been unwilling to entrust to the messenger. 'Never thought you'd end up a family man,' he drawls. 'Suppose it comes to us all eventually.'

'Not to you.'

'Nah, not to me,' he replies. 'I've got you misfits to take care of as it is.'

***

We dine on a cold game pie that Bates picked up in London and then begin to load the cart. The trunks are heavy, but with the two of us, we make quick work of it. We are halfway done when I notice Mabel shuffling down the path in the distance. By the time she reaches us, she's breathless, but when I see the expression on her face, what she has to impart is as good as spoken.

'He's here, Mr Franklin,' she pants. 'The solider – he's come back.'

'Damn it,' I curse, unable to keep the words within. 'Tell me what's happening.'

'He's got men with him. Three of 'em.' She stops to catch a breath, but continues almost immediately, judging her recovery less important than the matter's urgency. 'Aggie's still in the bakery, but it's only a matter of time before he finds her. They're pushin' people about something proper, and someone's bound to talk. They don't know where she is, but I wouldn't put it past someone to hazard a guess.'

'I'll go and get her.' I turn to Bates, 'Can you finish with this?' He nods his assent. 'I'll be back in an hour. They might send one of them here – be careful, they're probably army men.'

'It'll take more than some fuckin' soldiers to scare me. You've seen the cunts I 'ave to deal with.'

I start towards the wood. Within yards, I'm running.

Hoping that I am not too late.

***

It takes me less than ten minutes to get to the edge of the village. My shirt is soaked in sweat, and I struggle to get my breath, my left knee twisted from the impact of running on the dry ground. I take a few moments to compose myself on the edge of the wood, pushing my hair back into the semblance of a style and pulling my jacket on atop my sodden shirt. Kirk knows me but the others don't – I need to blend in. That way, if they spot me I'm just another scared man from the village – not one of the very people they're looking for.

Looking out through the greenery, I can see the men in the distance going from door to door – one of them drags a middle-aged farmhand from his house and starts to rough him up, his wife watching from the doorway. They slap him hard around the face, and she runs out to stop them, only to be pushed to the ground herself – scrambling back to the threshold of her home as she spots her children emerge to see what's going on, all thoughts of her husband gone as she ushers them to the supposed safety of their home. I realise it won't be long until they start on the children, and then someone will talk. The whole scene shames me – to think that I am its cause. But I realise I do not have time for recriminations, and I suppress my desire to hurt the people who are doing this, to take revenge, focusing instead on how to get Aggie away from here.

I stalk along the boundary of the woodland, cutting myself on bramble bushes as I push through the thicket. When I am level with the buildings that make up one side of the street, I stamp down the branches and nettles to make a way through to the dirt path beyond, and run to the house at the end of the row, nestling against its wall. I remember there's an alley down the back of the shops and houses and move to the rear of the building, only to find the owners have put up a wall to claim its entrance as their garden. The only way to reach it is around the front of the house.

Edging around to the front once more, I look again at the men terrorising the population. Kirk has joined them now, and is holding a woman by the face as he screams obscenities at her. If it were just me, I would have no choice to present myself to him and suffer the consequences; but I know what the consequences of my nobility would mean for Aggie.

Kirk backhands the woman hard, and three men rush him, only for him to punch the first, knocking him to the ground, making the others think twice about their attack. I take advantage of the commotion, and walk out into the street, my head bowed (both in disguise and ignominy) and skirt around the front of the house. The distraction proves sufficient and I slip down the gap between the dwelling and the butcher's next door, hoping that none of the other buildings have taken it upon themselves to lay claim to the alley as well.

I reach the rear of the butcher's to find there is no wall, but turning the corner, I come face to face with a carcass split end to end. Its bloody form makes me recoil. Hanging from the bracket, it is inhuman and raw, but somehow flesh enough for me to fail to identify it as a dead lamb, rather than a man. Almost immediately, my perceptions right themselves, but the mistake is still enough to put me even more on edge. But ahead of me the alley is clear.

I stumble onwards down its funnelled path, the intense sunlight making me feel exposed, the brittle dirt beneath my feet advertising my approach to anyone within hearing. Ahead of me I hear voices as I near the door I am heading towards, the door with Aggie on the other side of it. They are close, but as far as I can tell, unaware of my presence.

Reaching the bakery, I bang on the wood, sensing movement upstairs, followed by whispering within. The voices of the men in the side alley increase in volume as I wait, their proximity so threatening that I do not dare to knock again.

Suddenly, the door opens to reveal Molly's father. He pulls me inside briskly, closing the door behind us. A moment later, I hear the men's voices on the other side of the door.

'It's clear!'

I hold my head in my hands, the anxiety of my journey finally catching up with me, and listen as the voices fade away once more.

'She's still here?' I ask, in a whisper.

He nods, and beckons for me to follow into the sitting room. The curtain is drawn but Aggie is on the floor playing with Molly, unaffected by the drama outside. On seeing me, she jumps up and runs toward me, wrapping her arms around my neck as I bend down to hold her.

'Daddy!'

I shush her, worried that her voice is too loud. 'You have to whisper. There are men outside who aren't very nice. You can't let them hear you.'

She nods. 'Molly told me. I just forgot.'

'That's all right. We'll be all right.'

I stand up and go to Molly, taking her hands in mine.

'You can't come with us. We have to avoid being seen.' Molly's face drops, misinterpreting my meaning, but I continue, 'You can meet us in Leaford in the morning. They won't hurt Aggie, but anyone they catch with her…' I leave the rest unsaid.

'Will you definitely be there?'

'I hope so.'

She nods, presenting me with a smile that immediately starts to wobble, tears forming in her eyes.

'I'm being silly,' I say, correcting myself. 'We'll be there. Definitely.'

'Then I'll see you in Leaford,' she replies. Both of us know the truth, but it feels better to speak the words out loud, to pretend that the night is without risk, that in the morning we will be doubtless reunited. We look at each other for a moment before our lips meet, the tenderness of their touching sending electricity through my body, hope blooming from the chaos like a rose in the dirt. As we part from each other, I can feel her breath on mine, warm and sweet. She smiles. This time as if she truly believes in what we have said.

'I shall see you in Leaford,' she repeats, more confidently; as if happiness truly can conquer all. She bends down to Aggie and bids her farewell. 'Really quiet, my little one – make sure you do as your father says.'

Aggie hugs her and we go to the front door. Molly's father checks the alley from the upstairs window and gives us the all clear, and we go back out into the narrow passageway behind the houses, Molly's whisper of 'be safe' cut short by the closing door.

We skitter along the alleyway hand in hand, as light on our feet as the heaviness within me will allow. The hanging carcass marks

229

the junction we must take back to the road, and I see Aggie hesitate, then give it a wide berth when I signal her to move on. We reach the road a few seconds later, my arm dropping to block her path like a turnpike gate. The men are closer now – too close to avoid. I curse under my breath, heading back the way we came to examine the possibility of getting over the wall that blocks the direct route to the woods. It is too tall to scale and the owners have set broken glass into the mortar at its top. I had hoped I might be able to vault Aggie over, but she'd probably end up bleeding to death on the other side. Damn it.

I join her back by the exit to the road.

'Aggie – we may have to go back inside the house. I don't know for how long.'

The plan is compromised almost instantly. Three buildings down I hear the thugs hammering on a door, then what I can only assume is a kick – the sound of the wood splintering accompanied by screams from the tenants as the men push their way inside. I risk a glimpse round, hoping the break-in might provide sufficient distraction for our escape, but three of them, including Kirk, are still out in the street, working out their next move. Then Aggie says something that makes my heart sink.

'Tom!'

I look across the way to see her school friend standing in a doorway. He is staring directly at us, his gaze a finger pointing at our hiding place.

'No, no!' I gesture for him to turn his eyes away, but he keeps staring in our direction. I grab Aggie by the hand, and start leading her back down the alley.

And then, behind us, he speaks.

'I know where she is! Oi, you lot! I know where she is!'

I turn back in disbelief. I never liked the boy, but that he would give her up like this? I tell myself he is only a child – a boy who has watched men strike his elders, threaten those who make up his life, that he cannot truly know the consequences of his actions – but it doesn't make me hate him any the less.

I watch as the men approach him, my stillness mirroring his own.

'You ain't findin' her though. I'll warn 'er before you even get close!'

He darts off in the opposite direction, piquing the men's anger, and they give chase, accompanied by screams of violence and retribution.

It is all the distraction we need. We sprint out into the road towards the edge of the wood, the shouts in the background heading in the other direction, and I find myself blessing the little boy who I was cursing a few moments before. Aggie is clearly a better judge of character than I.

We move through the woods in silence, the boughs strangely absent of their usual chattering – the birds, the crickets, even the wind has lost its voice, as if nature itself is in hiding today from the evils that humanity can wreak upon one another. Aggie begins to tire before we reach the cottage, and I pick her up as we continue on. She grabs on hard like a monkey on a barrel organ.

'Do you think they caught Tom?' she asks, her voice laced with worry.

'He'll be all right,' I tell her, 'Tom can look after himself.' My words are a paean to hope rather than victory, but I swear to myself if Kirk harms a hair on that boy's head, I'll come back and kill the bastard.

The first sight that greets me at the cottage is Mabel's smile. It sends a shot of relief through my body; even though there was no way the men could have beaten us here, in imaginings the rules of dreams take precedence over those of logic, and it is only her unguarded greeting that reassures me the laws of nature still apply.

'Is everything all right?' she asks.

'I think so. They're knocking people about, but I don't think they'll go any further.' I hope they won't. 'Molly's meeting us tomorrow – will you ask her to check on Tom – make sure he's all right?'

I see the look of fear in her face. She'll be sad to see us go, but she's also losing her daughter. 'Mabel, we'll be back to see you when all this blows over. We're not going forever.'

She nods, but cannot keep herself from crying. 'Come here, my little one,' she says, wiping away her tears and bending down, opening her arms to Aggie. Aggie leaps forward to hug her, but my mind is on other things. I glance back to the woodland, expecting the men to appear at any moment, their forms shrouded in darkness against the diffuse light of dusk, as if the remnants of the day's sun have not seen fit to touch them.

'You should get yourself back to the village,' I tell Mabel. 'I don't want them finding you if they make it this far.' Mabel breaks off the hug, and stands up, modelling the decorum of a butler at a grand country house.

'Then I shall see you on your return,' she replies. She goes to continue, then stops herself, knowing that the front she has presented will only last a moment, a trick of the light that will disappear if stared at too long, and she turns towards the village, not looking back as she walks.

'We've got to go,' I say turning to Bates in the doorway.

'There's still a few more things.'

'It has to be now,' I tell him, Kirk's presence looming behind me, as if I can feel him in the ether.

Bates senses the seriousness in my voice, grabbing his coat and coming up the path towards us, while I lift Aggie to the cart's front seat. Aggie glances over at Mabel, wondering why she does not turn around and smile, before turning back to look at me

232

confused, the ways of adults a mystery to her. The girl is too young to understand, and thus she must be batted about by our whims and machinations. It breaks my heart to see her subject to our foolishness, but there are more important things at play here.

I climb up next to Aggie, and Bates trots round to the driver's seat, sandwiching her between us. He flicks the reins and the horse starts to move, and soon the cottage and the woodland are far behind us, and we start on our way towards the distant hills.

***

We make good progress over the next few hours, the subtle roll of the countryside that surrounds the village gradually giving way to the steeper inclines beyond. Our ascent into the hills slows our pace, but the horses are strong and, although the journey will not be remembered for its comforts (the wooden bench channelling every jolt in the road directly into our bodies) the going is good.

The sun now far below the horizon, a subtle chill begins to permeate the air, and I notice Aggie is starting to tense up.

'Are you cold?'

She nods.

'Take my jacket.' I wrap my coat around her, the padded angles of its shoulders dwarfing her form. It fits her as badly as the role of father does me, but perhaps one day we shall both grow into that which we inhabit. She smiles up at me, and I put an arm around her, squeezing her close to my body. 'Would you like a blanket as well?'

'If there is one.'

I turn to the trunks and boxes piled behind us, looking for the sack I stuffed with bedding and cushions.

And that is when I see there is something missing.

'Where's the trunk?'

233

'Which one?' Bates replies.

'The one with the photographs of my wife.' Bates looks at me as if he doesn't know what I'm talking about. 'It was by the chest of drawers – leather handle, the corners beaten up.'

'Should be there. I got most of the stuff.'

'Stop. Stop the cart. Just for a minute.'

I jump down, and work my way round the cart, searching for the missing trunk. It's difficult to see in the moonlight so I get Bates to pass me the lantern next to him, as I desperately search through the shantytown of boxes.

'I said we 'adn't got everything. There were still a few more things,' he mutters.

'Damn it.'

The trunk isn't there. The only thing that mattered, and it isn't there. The clothes, the knick-knacks – they can all be replaced – but those photographs… 'I need to go back.'

Bates looks at me incredulously. 'Christ's sake, Charlie. It's not safe – course you can't go back.'

'They're all I have left of her. I can't lose them. I need them,' I stutter, feeling my voice breaking as I speak.

'For fuck's sake, Charlie – you can send for them tomorrow. We've got to get away from 'ere. Think about Aggie.'

She looks round at me, her face a picture of concern. 'Is everything all right, Daddy?'

I feel my breathing slow, as I try to focus on what's important, thoughts of the photographs pulling like a child on the hem of my jacket, begging me to return. But I can hear Percy's voice behind me, telling me to carry on, that I must have faith, faith that I cannot lose her. I just need to keep going forward.

'Everything's all right,' I tell her. 'We'll carry on.'

We stop an hour later, high up the bank of a hill. There is good cover in the trees, and with the moon high in the sky we have a clear view of the route via which we came. If they're following us, we'll have enough of a head start to stay in front of them, but even so we can't risk stopping for more than a few minutes. Still, it seems as good a place as any to stretch out the compressions of the hard road from our bodies.

Aggie is asleep on my shoulder, and I lower her gently to the seat of the cart as I get out – propping a cushion from behind under her head. We walk to the side of the road, Bates handing me his hip flask. I take a drink while he relieves himself, and then take my turn. The thought of the photographs is still looming over me – and I am no longer sure that the voice behind me is Percy's. Instead, it takes on a different tone – evil, malevolent, making its play to take her away from me. I grab another swig from Bates's flask, the gin bringing me to my senses – its harshness cutting through the exhaustion that is attempting to smother rational thought.

'We should move on.'

Bates nods in response, and we walk back to the cart. I hoick myself up onto the seat, Bates doing the same on the other side, and stand tall for a moment, a final stretch before I attempt to insert myself beside Aggie without waking her. I look down below us, far in the distance to where I imagine my cottage might be, at the life we have left behind.

Then something catches my eye. Just to the right of where I had expected the cottage to be is a light. A subtle glow behind the trees that makes me think of a thousand fireflies, lost in their dance to draw in a mate. I think I read once that their light was a warning – telling predators to stay away, advertising their bitter taste, a caution to those who might dine upon them to stay away from the fire.

Fire.

My dreary brain suddenly makes the connections, putting the wooden pieces of the puzzle together to form the picture that has been waiting all along.

'No! NO!'

'What? What is it?' Bates asks.

'He's set the cottage on fire.'

'You sure? I can't see nothing.'

'There.'

He searches the horizon, and spots what I have seen.

'Oh God, Charlie. Fucking bastard. I'm sorry.'

I start to shake my head, as if I can deny reality, deny that this is really happening, but the truth is there before my eyes, and nothing can take that away. 'I have to go back.'

Bates hesitates, unsure if he has heard me right. 'We talked about this, Charlie: you can't.'

'I don't have a choice.'

'Listen, you bloody idiot,' Bates urges. 'Why do you think he did it? You goin' back's exactly what the fucker wants. You think he won't be there waiting for you? Sittin' on your doorstep with a bloody gun pointing at your head?'

I know he's right, but I can feel the pictures calling to me – and for a moment it seems it is Percy that is calling, not the photographs – her that is trapped in the trunk, flames licking the sides as the heat rises, her body being singed by the heat, her limbs scorched and burnt as the fire reaches her.

'I don't care. They're all I have. If they burn, that's it. She's gone.'

'Think about Aggie, for God's sake!'

'I'm sorry – I have to go.'

I bend over to kiss the girl's head. Somehow she is still asleep – unconscious through the commotion as only a child can be, trusting that she will be safe, looked after, that her protector will not abandon her.

'Take her to Leaford. If I don't catch up with you in a few hours, I'll be there in the morning,' I tell him. 'I promise.'

Bates's head falls into his hands, his voice taking on a tone of resignation, 'Fine, Charlie. We'll see you when you catch up with us.' It's clear he doesn't believe a word of it.

'Tell her I love her.'

'No need,' he says, his voice laced with sarcasm. 'You can tell her yourself when you're back.'

CHAPTER XXV

A flame dying

It takes me nearly two hours to make it back to the cottage. The going is quicker downhill, but no easier, and I stumble down the hard incline of the banks, trying to find footing on the brush as I go. As the hill begins to flatten, I return to the path; cutting across it no longer makes sense, the winding road having straightened out. My energies are already spent, the pain in my knee having returned from the hammering of my feet against the hard ground. The shin splints make it feel like the bone itself is shattering within my leg, but I push on towards what remains of my home.

As I reach familiar territory, I slow my pace to a fast walk. To arrive unable to act seems like a suicide attempt. As much as I need the photographs, they will do me little good if he kills me. I need my wits about me.

I circle around to the back of the cottage – if he's inside the building, he'll see me anyway when I enter, but going in through the front door feels wrong, as if I am offering myself up for sacrifice. The cottage itself is in bad shape. The roof is gone, but, the thatch having burnt out, the flames are dying, and now the frame of the walls is decorated with small wicks of straw at its apex. The walls themselves are dappled with black – a child's painting lacking rhyme or reason, the destructive force that has ravaged the place acting from nothing but instinct.

The sight takes me aback. For many years, its walls may have seemed more like a prison than a home to me, but, seeing it like this, those years are erased from existence, and I find myself mourning the cottage I once shared with Percy. Burnt away is the place I once heard laughter, felt joy, suffered the discomfort of hot summer evenings, the isolation of a snow that left us trapped inside for days on end. And now all that is gone. In its place a facsimile in black and white of the home that once was.

But even with the moon lower in the sky, I can see the ground floor is relatively unscathed, the flames having risen quickly to the top of the building. It gives me hope that the photographs have escaped the fire. I stalk forward through the garden, hunched over past the vegetables and roses. It strikes me that the peas will need to be picked soon, and I almost laugh. The triviality of my thoughts lending a sort of gallows humour to my approach. As if, should I survive the night, I'll come back to the carcass of this place in a few days and harvest the bloody vegetables. Or perhaps my body will supply sustenance to next year's crop.

I reach the house without too much noise, and press myself flat against the wall next to the doorframe, ready to enter. A piece of falling timber makes me flinch as it passes close by me, landing on the ground with a soft pad, as if its weight has been halved by the flames that still lick its sides. I watch it as it burns in the grass a few inches from my foot, then finally summon the strength to try the latch.

The door is unlocked, and I lift the catch gently. It grates in a whisper as I press down with my thumb on the handle. The sound is no louder than the subtle crackle of the flames that still burn around me, and yet I feel as if I have had my presence announced to the waiting throng at a society party. The hinge echoes its call, but I step quietly into the back room, regardless. The room is empty, and scanning it for signs that Kirk and his men have been here, I find none.

Ahead of me, the door to the parlour is closed, and I take the opportunity to grab a hammer left on the side, unaware of what lies in the room beyond. I raise the weapon as I enter, mindful that it will be no match for a man with a gun, but the room too is clear. The fire has taken its leave of the parlour, as have its occupants. The chaise is gone too, along with most of the staircase, and, when I look upwards through the remains of the ceiling, I can see the stars themselves staring back at me. Chemicals from the lab are piled up in the corner – by the look of it, they tried to drench the place with alcohol, repurposing the ethanol with which I make the collodion. It would appear the silver nitrate gave them faster results than they were looking for, forcing them out before they were done. The fools clearly knew more about intimidation than chemistry. I survey the room for the trunk, but it is conspicuously absent. It doesn't make sense – they couldn't know its value. The photographs are virtually worthless to anyone but me. But then I spot something, hidden underneath a sheet of fallen ceiling.

I step forwards, and, placing the hammer down on the floor, push the charred plaster to the side, revealing the trunk beneath, blackened but intact. I almost cannot believe it is still in one piece. I pat out the glowing embers of the few inches of ceiling timber that sits upon it, before opening the lid. Except for a dusting of black where some charred leather has fallen through a hole in its top, the contents are safe. I thank the heavens (so clearly viewable above me) for their mercy.

But I am sensible of my vulnerability. Closing the trunk, I start to drag it out the way I came. There's no way I can get it anywhere without the cart, but stashing it in the tool shed will mean I can send for it in a few days.

I stumble backwards, pulling the trunk with both hands, the weight almost too much to manage, barely managing to react in time as a crunch of ceiling beam above me warns of its impending descent. I raise my arm to my head just in time, and the timber glances off my forearm, rather than cracking my skull in two. Luckily the blow is a glancing one, and, although the pain is intense, I can still move my fingers. I reach down to take hold of the trunk once more so I can drag it the final few feet to the back room.

And that is when I hear the voice behind me.

'Hello, Franklin.'

I turn round to come face to face with Kirk, standing in the front doorway, his chiselled frame silhouetted in the moonlight from outside. 'Going somewhere?'

He steps forward into the room, and I glance toward the hammer on the floor next to where the trunk used to be.

'You won't reach it in time,' he drawls. He's right. He'd be on me before I was halfway there. But then I remember the truncheon in the drawer of the sideboard. If I can get that I might have a chance. I dart to the drawer, ripping it open.

But it is empty, the discovery accompanied by a laugh from behind me.

'Looking for this?'

I turn to see Kirk holding up the truncheon, a malevolent grin haunting his face. He starts to pace round the room, beating his own palm gently with the weapon, the blunt sound aping the rhythm of a ticking clock.

'You'd never survive a war,' he says, taking a break from his tapping to point the truncheon towards me. 'You're too easy to lead. Even a bloody Indian isn't stupid enough to go back to a burning house.'

Suddenly, the madness of my return comes into focus. I've abandoned Aggie, and for what? A few photographs, a memory. I put myself into this situation, and because of it I may never see her again.

'Where is she?' The perverse playfulness of his earlier words is gone.

241

I edge backwards, my thoughts turning to the door behind. If I can just find a moment, I can run. The semi-darkness outside might give me an advantage. I know the territory. He doesn't.

'I'll never tell you.'

Without warning, Kirk brings the truncheon down on a table, sending shattered glass in all directions. The bowl that was sat there is now gone, and in its place is nothing but a glinting pile of shards reflecting back the firelight that still fringes the room.

'You might,' he replies. 'It's amazing how quickly your friends in the village talked when I started threatening their children. That little Tom's a keeper though. Very loyal.' His eyes are alive with mockery and I can feel the rage building inside me as he continues to speak, all thoughts of escape momentarily forgotten. 'Kept his mouth shut even after we gave him a couple of black eyes. His mother, however, was a little more forthcoming.'

I lunge towards him and he swings the baton in my direction. I stop myself barely in time and the truncheon misses my face by less than an inch. I back up, aware that I have no chance against him without a weapon. He points the truncheon towards me again, a finger of accusation.

'Do you *want* me to hurt you, Franklin? Because that's what happens here if you don't cooperate. I know you think you won't talk – but you will. I've seen it a million times. People who can't speak a word of English pointing at the place their wives and children are hiding, begging me to stop hitting them and start on their bloody family. All I have to do is make it hurt enough.'

He stalks forward, and I edge backwards another step. Another step closer to the door. All I need is a distraction.

But then, suddenly, Kirk stops. For a moment, I don't understand why. And then he squats down next to the trunk at his feet.

'I should probably have a look at what's in here. At what was worth you coming back for.'

He opens the lid, and I realise this is my chance. My chance to get out into the night, to escape. But instead I just stand there, transfixed, as he takes a photograph from the trunk.

'Pretty,' he purrs. 'Another one of your sluts?' He bares his teeth in a smile once more. 'Must be special for you to have come back for her. I thought you normally just fucked them and left?'

'Put it back.'

'This?' he says, his voice thickly buttered with irony. He stretches his fingers out beneath the paper, and, a second later the photograph becomes a ball of angles in his hand.

'No!'

He tosses it aside, and continues without missing a beat.

'Let's have a look at the next one, shall we?' He pulls out another photograph, showing it to me briefly once again before scrunching it up into rubbish, a sheet of newspaper ready to start the kindling.

The effect that it has on me is written all over my face, and an air of calm comes over him. 'Tell me where she is.'

'No!' I can feel the tears falling down my cheeks as I speak, watching him take away my memories one by one, but I won't tell him. There's nothing he could do that would make me tell him.

He reaches deeper into the trunk and pulls out a piece of glass wrapped delicately in tissue paper. He unwraps it to reveal a plate from the day Percy discovered she was with child, examining it curiously. 'I like this one,' he drawls, unable to understand the image in negative. 'Makes your little ladybird look like she's gone native. Fancied a bit of the forbidden fruit did you?' He holds it up like an auctioneer's gavel, pausing for a moment to see if someone will stop him with an offer…

Before bringing it down on the corner of the trunk with a percussive crash. 'TELL ME!'

'Never!' I shout, choking on my tears. 'I won't let her be raised by a man like you.'

He sighs, then gently lays the truncheon down on the floor next to him. He stands, rolling up his sleeves, a workman on a factory floor about to start his shift.

'My dear Mr Franklin,' he drolls. 'I'm going to find her. That's what's happening here. All your little hero act means is that you'll be dead when I do.' He smiles. 'Perhaps we can get someone to take a picture of your corpse for her to remember you by. Wouldn't that be nice?'

I realise this is my last chance, and I launch myself towards the door. I have the handle in my hand when I feel his grip my shoulder, and he tugs me round, landing a fist hard on my face. I feel my legs collapse from under me, but he keeps hold of my collar to stop me from falling, and punches me again. I hear the bones in my nose crack as he makes contact, then he drops me to the ground, where I collapse into myself like the folds of an accordion.

Grabbing for breath, I push myself to my knees and lunge forward to hit him. He steps backwards laughing, as if I am nothing, before pushing me back to the ground with his foot. Standing over me, he looks like an ogre from the stories, towering above, backlit from the flames. And I realise his face will be the last one I ever see.

'Still want to die, Franklin?'

I spit at him in defiance, cursing his very being.

'Good,' he says. 'Otherwise this wouldn't feel right.'

He walks towards me, raising his fist to hit me one last time. There is a look of triumph in his eyes, as if searching for Aggie was merely an excuse; taking revenge all he ever truly wanted, an end in itself. All he needed was a reason.

'Stop!'

A man's voice echoes around the room. Kirk turns to reveal Bates standing behind him, a knife in his hand. I hear Kirk exhale, as if he is almost bored by the tedium of having to deal with another of us.

'For God's sake,' he complains. 'Do you think I've got all night?'

Bates points the knife in towards him, and Kirk puts up his hands in light-hearted surrender, as if this is all a joke to him. As if the stakes were not *everything*. But even through a haze of delirium, I can tell something is wrong – not only that Kirk is waiting to attack, but something else… And then the implications of Bates's presence become clear – if he's here, so is Aggie.

'Be careful…' I mumble, '… he's dangerous.'

'I can 'andle 'im, Charlie. Fuckers like this're ten a penny in London.'

'Please. *Go*,' I beg him. 'You shouldn't have come.'

'She ain't with me, Charlie, if that's what you're worried about. Stashed 'er a long way from 'ere…'

'Then I need you safe.'

'I ain't leavin' without you, Charlie. Girl's already lost her mother, can't 'ave 'er losin' you as well.' He raises the knife higher. 'This bastard's going to put 'is 'ands out, and you're gonna tie 'em.'

Kirk pastes on a look of displeasure, and presents his supine palms to me. But I can see laughter in his eyes; as if he is merely going through the motions, a player in a parlour game.

'So you're going to tie me up, are you? Allow me to help.'

He drops to the floor, and a moment later, the truncheon is in his hand, swinging with full force towards Bates's jaw. The knife hasn't moved by the time it makes contact, and next thing I know Kirk is standing over Bates's prone body. He prods him with his boot a few times, before throwing the truncheon to the floor. Then he turns to me.

245

'You,' he growls, 'I'm going to do with my bare hands.'

He bends over me and wraps his hands round my neck. 'One last time – where is she?'

'Weren't you even listening?' There is almost laughter in *my* voice this time. 'You just knocked out the only person who knew.'

He pauses for a moment, 'Which means you're no use to me any more,' then he starts to squeeze. His thumbs force my Adam's apple deep into my throat, cutting off any vestige of breath, 'You *know*, Franklin. So *tell me:* Where is she?!?'

I try to respond, but nothing comes out.

'This is your last chance.'

He bangs my head against the floor, again and again, each time harder than the last, his pressure on my windpipe unrelenting, 'Where… is … she?' Every impact sends pain shooting through my body. I can feel the life draining out of me as I fight to stay conscious. But my vision starts to blur…

'I'm here.'

This time the voice is a child's.

Kirk relaxes his grip, and drops me to the floor. Fighting for breath, I push myself up on my arms, edging myself forward to see who is behind him, already fearing, already knowing, and there, standing in the doorway, is my daughter. Offering herself up to him.

'Aggie, no!'

The words in my head come forth formless, steel scraped upon stone. But Kirk has already forgotten me.

'Hello, Aggie,' he says. His voice is gentle now; as if he were not a man who had just been choking the life out of her father. 'You did the right thing to come to me – we can go away now. To somewhere safe. Do you understand?'

'As long as you don't hurt him any more,' she replies. Aggie's crying, but fighting to hide it. The sight stabs at my heart, more than anything Kirk could ever have done to me. The child I am meant to be protecting, sacrificing herself to protect *me*.

'You can't,' I strain, my voice barely rising above a whisper, but this time the words take on a shape in the darkness.

'Don't listen to him, Aggie,' Kirk continues, softly, 'I won't hurt him. But he's not your family. I am. You're going to come and live with me in India. You'll be safe there. We'll have a happy life together. I can promise you that.'

He reaches out his hand, and I struggle to my feet, watching on. Drinking in the last few moments before he takes her away forever.

There is a hesitation in her eyes. I can see she doesn't want to go, to leave, but what does it matter? I have no power here – physical, legal – nothing I can do will stop him taking her, the oceans in my heart cannot change a thing.

She stretches her hand out towards him.

'Good girl, Aggie.'

And as their hands meet, I feel my heart break.

Then suddenly there is a flurry of movement.

In the half-light the details are difficult to discern, but Kirk's scream of pain is not. Aggie steps backwards, revealing a shard of glass protruding from her uncle's palm. He looks down at it, his expression almost confused, as if he is considering where the translucent wedge could have come from, his breathing heavy with pain. He clenches his teeth, and pulls it out, tossing the bloodstained shard to the floor, anger building up within him like the pressure on a steam valve.

'You ungrateful bitch.'

He explodes, slapping her hard across the face, the blow sending her flying into the bottles of chemicals on the other side of the room. A burst of rage propels me forward, and I grab the truncheon from the floor, unnoticed by Kirk. He is consumed by a rage of his own, and he steps towards Aggie, the girl curled up in a ball on the floor for protection.

'You've got your mother's bloody stupidity – that's for sure,' he shouts. 'When you're living with me, you'll learn some manners, you little shit. Some respect for your elders. I'll beat it into you if I have to.'

He pulls out his belt, ready to whip her, but I am already on him.

He turns as I reach him, but it is too late. I bring the truncheon down hard on his skull, hearing a crack as it hits him. He stumbles, but does not fall, and I bring it down again.

'You don't hit my daughter!'

The third blow knocks him to the floor. I see blood pouring from his skull, and it suddenly strikes me that I've killed him. I squat down, putting my fingers to his neck, only to find a pulse as strong as an unborn baby's kick. As much as I want him gone, I don't want his murder on my conscience. Besides, what good would I be to Aggie on the inside of a prison cell? I look over; she is sitting up amidst the bottles of chemicals, dazed but conscious. And I realise that somehow, inexplicably, we have won.

'Are you all right?'

'I think so.'

She smiles at me, and I smile back, relief dulling my pain like an anaesthetic. Before my mind suddenly turns to Bates.

I rush over to his body, sprawled on the floor, again checking for a pulse. It is weaker than Kirk's, but still present, and I let out a sigh of reprieve, moving back across the room to Aggie, and sitting by her side, I examine her for injuries.

'Did you hit your head?'

She nods. 'It doesn't hurt too much. I think I cut myself though.'

Aggie holds up her hand to reveal a deep gash across the palm. Its nothing serious, but I want to stop the blood loss so I pull out my handkerchief and press it against the wound, spotting the broken glass of a chemical bottle on the floor by her side, no doubt the culprit.

Seeing her like this reignites the fire inside me, and I think for a second that perhaps it would be better if Kirk were dead. I could take Aggie outside, then come back and suffocate him, as he tried to me. All fear of his return would be gone; and would not the world be better off without him? The body they would find would be a victim of the fire, choked by the fumes, his head crushed by a falling beam, his botched attempts at arson having backfired more than he could have imagined. My eyes stray towards him, the notion no longer an idle fancy, but a potential course of action, understandable, rational.

'I don't feel right.'

Aggie's words draw my attention back to the present. Her breath is catching – shock perhaps – but she seems pale, her pupils shrunken. I put my hand to her face, and she is cold. I've seen shock before, and it's never as extreme as this. And then I see what is beside her.

On the floor is a small pile of crystalline white powder. It looks pure, unsullied, reminding me of fresh snow. I have used it every day for as long as I can remember, each print kept in place by its almost magical qualities. Potassium cyanide.

I feel a coldness pass through me as if part of my soul has drained from my body.

'Did you put your hand in this?'

She can hear the urgency in my voice, my panic making her stumble over her words, 'I don't know. I think so, just a little bit.'

'Tell me you didn't, please tell me you didn't.'

'I don't know – I'm not sure.'

I grab her wrist, examining her palm, the subtle dusting of white telling me everything I need to know.

'I'm sorry – did I do something wrong?' she asks, questioningly; her eyes full of innocence, a fear that she might have displeased me, but they are also glassy and faraway, as if she is speaking from elsewhere.

'No, no … you didn't do anything wrong,' I reply, trying to reassure her.

I drag her to her feet, pulling her around the room behind me as I search for something to wash the wound. The jug on the side is empty, but I find a bottle of purified water from my lab, overturned a few feet away, still corked. I bite the stopper from its neck, and soak the cut with water.

'I don't understand…' she protests.

'I need to wash the powder off. It's bad for you.'

'Why do I feel so strange? I don't understand.' Her breathing is shallow, a rasping sound accompanying each inhalation. 'Am I all right?'

'I don't know. I'm worried you might have…' The rest of the words don't come, but I feel a dull ache beneath my eyes as they begin to moisten, the truth of the situation flooding my mind. Like the poison beginning to flow through her veins.

'I feel dizzy, everything's spinning.'

'No, no … try to…' The strength goes from her legs, and she collapses into my arms. 'Please… We need to get you to a doctor.'

'I just want to lie down.'

'Not again, please no, not again.' I find myself looking to the heavens for mercy, for assistance, but all that stares back at me is an empty heartless sky, the stars now covered by clouds, their message of hope extinguished.

'Can I lie down? Just for a moment?'

I lower her to the floor, tucking a cushion from the side under her head, my mind desperately searching for a solution. But nothing comes. Bates is still unconscious on the floor, and there is no one here to help. And so it is just me and my daughter. Alone in a room. In the middle of nowhere. The life falling away from her.

'I'm sorry… I'm so sorry…' My words trickle out, unwilled.

'Why? I can stay with you now. He can't take me any more. Can he?'

'No, my love. He can't. No one will ever take you away again.'

She smiles. 'Did I do well coming back?'

'You saved my life.' The tears are already pouring down my face. 'You'd already saved it.' I bend over, holding her as hard as I can; but I can feel her slipping away.

'Why… Why are you crying?'

'No reason. I'm just happy, that's all. Happy that you're here. Happy about all the things we're going to do together. We can print some photographs tomorrow if you'd like.' My voice breaks more with each utterance, crumbling away what was left of my soul.

'I'd like that.'

For I know there shall be no more tomorrows.

I press my lips against the cold of her forehead, telling myself I did everything I could to keep her safe, but I know it is nothing but deception. I did this. I brought this fate upon her. My selfishness, my obsession… But, as all hope is exhausted, I remember…

It comes in flashes. An old photographer's trick, a remedy that has skirted my awareness over the years in snatches of half-heard conversations. For a moment, the specifics elude me, but then the words begin to appear on the plate of my consciousness: sodium thiosulphate. The fixer I bought to use with Abel, with Aggie. I hadn't possessed any for years. But I do now.

Leaping to my feet, I rush to the lab, praying the bottle was not part of the soldiers' pyrotechnic outbursts. I push through the vials and bottles on the desk, unable to locate it, until my recall is stirred by a vision of moving it to a higher shelf across the room. I dart towards its location, only to find it gone, a space where it should have been.

My heart sinks, my eyes drifting to the floor... And it is there I see hope in the form of another broken bottle, its shards curving upwards in points like the blade of a scythe. I scramble over, raising it in consecration, scanning the hand-written label still attached to its side, my heart swelling when I see its contents are still present. There is still a chance.

I race back to Aggie. Her eyes are glazing over, but I shake her back to consciousness.

'Father?' she murmurs.

It is enough. I pour the oversized crystals of the thiosulphate into my hand, letting them cascade down the palmist's lifeline into the thin neck of the water bottle, replacing the cork and shaking its contents as vigorously as I can. Time is of the essence. If I am not too late already.

'Drink,' I say, pouring the solution down her throat, unsure how much to give her. In desperation I splash the liquid over her wound, ignorant as to the best way to administer it, hoping that it can work, that I am not mistaken. Hoping I am not too late.

I hold her to me as I wait, the words tumbling from my tongue, 'I love you, Aggie; I love you so much.'

'I love you t—'

But her voice trails away before she is finished, and I am left there, kneeling on the cold stone floor, sobbing.

Alone.

***

The photograph is similar to so many I have taken before; a body, a camera, a miscellany of stands hidden from view.

Yet today everything is different. Today I take a photograph of someone for whom I care.

I try not to think about the fact she is gone, attempting to distract myself with the task at hand, but its motions provide scant solace, so full as they are with a tragedy of their own. And I find myself letting out a silent curse, that if there is a God somewhere in this cold, cold universe, he has heard the malediction within me. And he feels shame.

I approach the body, propped on the studio chaise across the room, its back straight, head raised and upright, the emptiness within disguised by the mimicry of form. Crouching down, I add the counterweight to the stand behind the chaise, then, moving to the front, arrange the collar to disguise the presence of the grip protruding around the front of the neck.

Stepping back to check my work, for a moment I feel that I have succeeded in my task, my subject merely resting his eyes in a moment's repose, a short break between exposures. But, then, the man before me is a body once more; meat, a corpse, the appearance of life only emphasising that its owner is gone, never to return.

I nod to Abel, who withdraws to the dark room to prepare a plate. In his absence, I walk to the window, unable to bear being alone with Bates's body.

Staring into the world beyond, the corpse's presence looms behind me, as if its shape has been cut out of the world, like a paper doll from its surroundings. At least Aggie is alive. On a ship to India with the man who killed my friend, but alive. Her departure feels like a punishment for my doubt, my hesitation in claiming her as my own. But I know it is not the case. The laws that rule this world are not those of justice. Its punishments fall as readily on the innocent as the guilty.

Beyond the glass, a rare summer rain has shrouded the season in greyness, the fine mist that fills the air muffling the world into silence, its blankness reminding me of the instant before a print begins to appear, the paper primed and ready. But in it I see no potential, no hope; just a reminder of what is. Of what could have been.

'It's ready, sir.'

I turn to find Abel next to me, looking like he has been there for some time. I glance over to the camera; the plate is loaded, the box closed and ready. I turn to him and nod, then lower myself onto the seat next to the empty shell that was my friend. The photograph was his final request, a token to be bequeathed upon the world. I suppose he thought it humorous, requesting my presence as tomfoolery, requesting my handiwork as an assurance that it should be done right, all of it, his sick joke, that his dead body will look down upon the unsuspecting from the wall it adorns in Warwick's shop. Or perhaps it shall be a monument to his pride in what, together, we have achieved.

A stroke they said, brought on by Kirk's blow to the head. He held onto life for weeks, neither speaking nor stirring from his sickbed, a corpse in all but name, and yet, beneath it, I believe he was fighting. Fighting not to abandon this world, the few he called friends, the woman who took his shillings in place of a vow. But perhaps that is mere fancy, my own struggle bleeding into that of my dying friend, while he merely waited for the inevitable.

I neglected him in his final days, my hours consumed with the fight to keep my daughter, but I am sure he would not have wished it otherwise. I went without food, without sleep, spending that money which I had and more that I did not. And yet, each petition I made was rejected, each door I approached closed. Kirk was right. I had no claim on her, not in the eyes of the law. What was blood to them, compared to the marks of ink on paper? What was love, but a shadow of the favours they afforded their own?

'Are you ready, sir?'

I raise my hand in response to Abel's question, in need of pause, my strength giving way to the tears building within me, Bates's death and Aggie's departure conflated into an amalgam of loss and pain. 'Give me a moment,' I stumble, attempting to regain the composure the photograph will require. 'Another second if you will.'

'The plate, sir...' Abel persists.

I nod, thinking of how many times have I reminded my sitters of the very same thing. But now the ticking clock of necessity bears down upon *me*, and for the first time, I truly feel its stifling oppression, its unrelenting progress.

What a small a window we have in which to capture life. A few moments, after which the opportunity is lost; that strange concoction of chemicals that creates magic left empty of its powers, soon to be nothing but dust. But if we act quickly; and with purpose, we can create something permanent.

Something that will last forever.

I raise my eyes to Abel, my jaw set.

And I tell him I am ready.

EPILOGUE

Over the next few months, I supervise the rebuilding of the cottage. The structure is still sound, but the roof must be rethatched, the beams replaced, the internal walls reconstructed. The building's resurrection gives me a sense of hope as I imagine its future. It shall be a future without me, but perhaps its next occupants will live a life more fortunate than mine, and, though all belief has been wiped from my soul, I find myself offering up a prayer that they shall find happiness here. This place has seen enough pain for many lifetimes.

I rent a room in the village while the work is done, then move into the bakery with Molly after our marriage. The ceremony is a bittersweet affair, mired in loss, but alive with promise, and though I cannot deny the wish that the circumstances had been different, I am grateful to have found her.

It is October by the time the work is done. Our cart is packed, our plans made, and Molly and I stand outside the cottage, bidding our farewells to her mother and father.

'You're sure we can't persuade you to stay?' asks Mabel.

I shake my head. 'You know we will be back to visit…' I reply, an attempt to reassure her she shall not suffer a loss of her own. 'And you're welcome to come and stay with us, whenever you wish.'

'If it weren't for the bakery, I'd be comin' with you now.'

'Well, when the baby is born then.'

'Couldn't keep me away,' she replies, smiling through her tears.

Molly's belly is already swollen. We felt our first kick a few weeks ago; the subtle tap on my palm as it rested upon her stomach bringing back a thousand memories, but the pain that had accompanied them for so many years was gone. Instead, I felt the same joy that the first kick within Percy's womb had originally granted me. I felt the hope.

'I've one more bag,' I say, making my excuses so they can say their final farewells. Molly thanks me with a smile as I walk to retrieve the last case from the cottage.

Inside, I say my own goodbyes. Perched atop the upright form of my portmanteau is a picture of Aggie, the only one I have – the small carte de visite taken in the years before I knew her, mounted in a frame too large for its size, like the girl herself sitting on the seat of our cart, swamped by my greatcoat. It is the only photograph that will accompany me to this new life, but, as I look down at the picture before me, I find I cannot locate my daughter within. It is just paper, a chemical sheen wearing her form.

It will not do.

I open the trunk in the corner, the one I shall leave behind, and search through the photographs; those of my wife, of strangers, of our aborted attempts to capture the heron … until finally I find what I am looking for.

Picking up the frame once more, I prise open the back and take out the carte de visite, returning it to the trunk. I lay it gently upon Percy's dress, which is tucked neatly beside the photographs, allowing myself one last touch of the fabric, before shutting the lid on it, and so much that came before.

Carefully, I place the print I have retrieved in the frame, finding satisfaction at how snugly it fits in its wooden surround. I replace the back, then turn it over to examine the result.

And, suddenly, she is there.

A blur, a wood sprite dancing in nature. My daughter. My Aggie. *Life*: irrepressible, uncapturable.

'I love you,' I whisper, the words inaudible to anyone but me, but for a moment I almost feel she replies. That somewhere a thousand miles away she has heard.

And though I feel anger, hatred, helplessness, beneath it all, I feel thankful: thankful that she came into my life; thankful that she taught me to love once more; that she taught me to *live*. And, though the pain of her loss will never leave me, my actions that night haunt me forever, this time I will honour her. Not her memory, but her *spirit*. I will honour her with life. And perhaps one day, when she is grown, I will see her again, and she will forgive me. And I will learn to forgive myself.

The picture in hand, I pick up my portmanteau, willing my feet to move, but unable to truly depart from all that has transpired here, annoyed when a knock at the door attempts to dislodge me from my furrow.

'Charles.'

It is Molly's voice that calls me, the same word I have heard from her lips a thousand times, but something in her tone sparks my curiosity.

'Molly?'

I open the door to find her crying.

'What's the matter, my love?'

She tilts her eyes up to mine, and I see that beneath her tears is a smile, a beaming joyous smile, as if everything is right with the universe once again.

I look behind her, confused and there, beside the cart, stands Warwick, talking to Mabel. His unexpected presence seems a mystery to me, as if he has been added to the scene by a photographer's trick.

'What are you doing here?'

Wordlessly, he steps aside with a smile, and then the source of Molly's joy becomes clear. There, standing behind him, is my daughter.

'Aggie?' I stumble, hesitant.

I look from face to face, unsure as to whether what I am seeing